LONE BRITISH SNIPER TAKES ON US MARINES

OUR WILFUL ASSASSIN

BASED ON TRUE EVENTS

THE LONG-AWAITED PREQUEL TO THE LONDON SNIPER

LONE BRITISH SNIPER TAKES ON US MARINES

OUR WILFUL ASSASSIN

BASED ON TRUE EVENTS

THE LONG-AWAITED PREQUEL TO THE LONDON SNIPER

Daniel Pascoe

First published in 2021 by Daniel Pascoe

ISBN 979-8-594624-07-8

© Daniel Pascoe 2021
danielpascoeauthor.com

Daniel Pascoe asserts the moral right to be identified as the author of this work in accordance with the Copyright, Design and Patents Act 1988.

All rights reserved. No part of this publication may be reproduced, stored in a retrieval system or transmitted, in any form or by any means, electronic, mechanical, photocopying, recording and/or otherwise be circulated in any form of binding or cover other than that in which it is published and without the prior written permission of the publishers.

This is a work of fiction. Names, characters, businesses, places, events and incidents are either the products of the author's imagination or used entirely in a fictitious manner. Any resemblance to actual persons (even those with identifiable names), living or dead, or actual events and places is mostly coincidental.

Daniel Pascoe was brought up on smog and boiled cabbage in London many years ago. Sent away to boarding school at 13, he dreamed of life in the army and became a medic. He worked as a cancer specialist in the north-east of England for thirty years.

He now spends much of his time writing, far from the hubbub of city life, enjoying peaceful periods of contemplation. The world is waiting, weird and wonderful. Writing fiction is a form of exploration and discovery, exposing truths and falsehoods in equal measure.

He lives with his wife and family on Teesside, thinking of ways to counteract youth disappointment that seems to have blighted an entire generation. He has four children whose refreshing and entrepreneurial spirits always manage to shine brightly in the gloom.

January 2021

OTHER NOVELS BY DANIEL PASCOE

THE LONDON SNIPER *(new unexpurgated edition)*

DEAD END *(new revised edition)*

deadline

FAIR GAME FOUL PLAY

The US marines were taught that civilian deaths
were just the cost of doing business, and that they were
in Iraq to get the job done, no matter what it took.

**"The intentional killing of non-combatants is prohibited
by modern laws of war derived from the UN Charter,
the Hague Conventions and the Geneva Conventions,
and constitutes a war crime."**

Contents

Prologue
Haditha, Iraq, November 19, 2005 1

Four Years Later (Part 1)
London, November 6-9, 2009 7

Midlogue
Iraq, November 19, 2005 101

Four Years Later (Part 2)
London, November 10-12, 2009 121

Epilogue
London, January 13, 2012 205

Prologue

**Haditha, Iraq
November 19, 2005**

Saturday morning

The roadside explosion was as thunderous and devastating as it was unexpected. They usually were.

Streaks of cadmium and orange vapour have crept over the eastern horizon, sharply silhouetting rows of spiky date palms along the embankment of the Euphrates. The colours were beginning to harden before they would melt into a wispy white haze. A few distant early morning calls to prayer could be heard warbling across the city.

A little after seven and at the makeshift US checkpoint on the western approach road, a collection of traffic had gathered in a ragged queue. Casual labourers in trucks dangling their legs over the tailgates, farm workers with their fresh produce, a few taxis and cyclists, some people on foot: all heading into the city for another day's graft. They took their turn being ordered out into the middle of the road, to stand obediently with legs apart, arms reaching upwards, while armed soldiers patted them down, the women too. Last week, two troopers had been wounded when an insurgent hidden in the back of a truck broke free with a pistol and opened fire, but he was gunned down, quickly disposed of, and the daily routine had soon resumed. The vehicles were looked over, rifle barrels poking into bulging sacks and under rugs, lifting the lids off boxes. They were hassled through under the single wooden barrier.

Two Red Cross tankers with a fresh water supply for the thirsty city were waved on. With supplies to deliver up at the Dam, four desert yellow Humvees, boxy beetle-like utilities that were often seen roaring across the desert sands without apology, rock and roll music pumping at high volume, rumbled through in a stretched-out line along Route West. On the roof of the lead truck, a padded figure hunched attentively over his .50 calibre swivel machine gun.

Keeping a regulation twenty-five yards apart, the Humvees turned one by one into Route Chestnut that swept through the Subhami slum neighbourhood. A dusty pock-marked avenue, it was wide enough to have a central reservation dotted at intervals with telephone poles and stunted date palms. Set well back on either side were muddled rows of cheap breeze block and dried stone-walled housing, scarred and battle damaged, with their spiky aerials and satellite dishes. A good way down, a bedraggled dog was snapping at the dead carcass of a buffalo calf straddled over the kerb. Watched by a clutch of black crows, a family of squawking vultures hovered anxiously as they took their turns with the rotting carrion. Further on, a herd of goats roamed among the street life, hopping across the road, emerging from the gaps between houses, looking for something to chew. Some of the potholes that lined the road contained puddles of water that attracted their attention. A man in flowing white thawbs and matching headgear wandered among them.

Dozens of minarets poked up above the skyline of dense flat rooftops, as the warm glow of early morning wavered across the huge desert landscape. A mile away, the attractive blue and gold dome of Rifai mosque, the largest in Haditha, popped up like a buoy floating calmly amidst the sea of urban sprawl.

The Humvees rumbled on in the glaring light. A white Opel sedan taxiing four men half asleep inside was caught between the first and second. At a nearby area of waste ground, water in a stagnant pool polluted with petrol attracted a couple more dogs and a few kids to play and urinate. There was a charred mattress dumped nearby, close to the burnt-out remains of a truck twisted on its side that had been there so long nobody noticed anymore.

The hideous vultures shrugged their crooked wings and stretched their claws over the carrion on the carriageway opposite to the approaching Humvees. With their feeble bleating and bell-jangling, a few goats trampled down the far embankment towards the road. The dog persisted with its futile efforts to grab a decent meal and yapped at the crows. The first Humvee slowed down and for a second its brake lights flashed red. The marines had probably spotted the carcass across the roadside up ahead which had aroused their suspicions. Insurgents frequently hid explosive inside dead animals by the roadside, booby-trapped for the unsuspecting.

The front Humvee was soon to pass by the carcass on the far side, the white Opel hesitating close behind it. Sunlight glinted off the shiny dome of the distant mosque with eye-piercing sharpness, momentarily blinding the first Humvee driver - and it was then that the explosion happened.

An artillery shell and several cans of propane liquid burst into a massive conflagration under the trailing Humvee, which was bisected and thrown aside by the force, like so much discarded rubbish. A deep boom reverberated between the houses, as a mass of fiery incandescence erupted, pouring out clouds of black smoke that engulfed the scene. And then a second booming eruption spluttered from the backend as the diesel tank exploded. Chunks of flaming debris swirled in the air, sparks and hot dust spraying over the road.

The birds and the dog scattered to safety, abandoning their messy carcass that remained a sort of decoy, sixty yards further on from the buried bomb site. The other three trucks had one by one come to a halt, their occupants shocked. They would all have felt the crump and thrust of the explosions. Through the dense smoke, the third Humvee could be seen standing alone, its orientation knocked off kilter, but intact thirty yards ahead of a smouldering hole in the side of the road, three or four yards wide.

The remaining Humvees bumped off the road onto the dirt verge, parking up in a semi-circle. Armed troopers in their standard cammies and rounded steel helmets jumped out and crouched in defensive positions around their vehicles, watching, looking for more trouble, not knowing what to expect. The front gunner swivelled his sights from one side to the other, as confused as the rest. The white Opel remained alone in the road, a little way beyond the smoking crater.

The two halves of the original vehicle, blackened steel chunks of twisted bodywork, split asunder, hard to recognize, lay on each side of the road, rubber tyres burning. The front section with its engine was roaring in bright orange flames, black smoke billowing into the air. Everything else beyond the fire and the smoke seemed frozen in a bizarre stillness; even the goats had stopped moving.

The fourth Humvee had had a driver and two marines on board. A stricken soldier was spotted on his back twenty yards from the cratered road on the dusty sidewalk, painfully trying to lift his head, his arms folding across his chest. One limb had been ripped off at the knee, a splintered stump flailing in the air.

Another body was face down in the dirt under the back section of the broken truck, trapped under a wheel, barely moving.

There was the impression of a third body, felled on its back, and as some of the smoke swirled away, of a face turned upwards, restful in its repose, the eyes open. There was only half a torso, both upper limbs ripped off. The lower half was probably in the front of what remained of the truck trapped under the steering, his hands still gripping the wheel. A trail of strawberry charred entrails hung out across the dirt beside him.

Death would have been instantaneous. For the two wounded marines who were still alive, at least for the moment, their agony had only just begun.

Four Years Later (Part 1)
London
November 6 to November 9, 2009

Chapter 1
Friday November 6

There is a knocking at the front door, someone using the flap of the letter box. When was Jarvis going to get the bell fixed, she had asked him often enough? A uniformed courier, on a motorbike by the look of his leathers. Pamela, all a fluster, her hair unbrushed, in her old jeans and a loose top, pulls the door inwards a little way to peer out into the chilly morning air. A brown envelope, needs signing for, the helmeted man says, Asian, wide smile, white teeth. For a Mister Jarvis Collingwood.

Pamela shuffles back into the kitchen, a bemused expression on her tired face, uncertain as to why British Army Headquarters, Aldershot Garrison, was writing to Jarvis. Over one year retired now. Standard A4, BA logo top left, printed white label, their Baring Street address, privately delivered, no postmark or stamp. She wanted to ask the chap where he had come from, who he was working for, but by the time she had formed the questions in her mind, he had roared off.

They had been out late last night, a group of her workmates, women mostly, a party for one of the girls who was getting married, and Jarvis had come along, not like him. They had had a few as well, so they had both slept late and it is now nearly ten o'clock. Jarvis is still upstairs in bed.

A few minutes later he drifts in and takes a carton of orange juice from the fridge. Slumping into a chair at the table, he moans about his head. 'What did they have in those drinks, those shots, tequila or something, doubles?' He drinks straight from the carton, which annoys Pamela every time. 'God, they were lethal.'

'Vodka, tequila and amaretto. You didn't have to drink them all, I stuck to wine, me.' At 24, Pamela is pretty, without being beautiful, with a clear complexion and reddish-brown eyes. Her auburn hair is thick and wavy, with a natural gleam even in the low-lying winter gloom. Always quick to praise and quick to criticise, invariably spouting out the first thing that comes to mind, she generally means well.

Jarvis stares at the stiff envelope leaning against a tomato ketchup bottle in front of him, trying to focus on the address label.

'When did this come?'

'Just now, didn't you here the knocking. The bell still doesn't work.'

'It's only the battery.' They were renting and had not long been in the house, so there were all sorts of little things that needed the landlord's attention, like the slate that came off the roof last week. Jarvis reaches for the package and turns it over a few times, wondering vaguely whether it's a bomb. But it's perfectly flat, no suspicious ridges, so he slides a knife under the flap, ripping outwards. Fiddling inside, he extracts another envelope between his long fingers. White this one with a printed label, his name in upper case: CORPORAL J COLLINGWOOD. British Army. No address. The graphic on the outside, Navy-Marine Corps Court of Criminal Appeals, Washington, USA. Inside, a single sheet of cream paper, unfolded.

His face remains expressionless, his blue eyes giving nothing away, but inside a little niggle of anxiety plays in his belly. The letter is not unexpected, he has been waiting four years for it, but it is a surprise all the same, coming out of the blue. He thought at least his battalion chief would have contacted him, but all Malone had said weeks ago was that the investigation was continuing and that certain witnesses were being sought, so expect to hear from them. Jarvis assumed that they had sought his address from Aldershot HQ and the bloody Army, his army, had complied within their special relationship.

He slides the envelopes and letter across the table, creaking back into the wooden chair.

'What is it?' Pamela is spreading butter on a piece of toast, still standing on the side. 'Want some?'

'Thanks. It's erm …' and he hesitates, chewing on the inside of his cheek. 'A subpoena, to appear at the Navy-Marine Corps Court, Criminal Appeals in Washington DC. Navy Yard.'

'Who are they, when they're at home?'

'The most powerful US Armed Services Court for criminal activity.'

'Why are you involved?'

'I was witness to the event.'

'What event?'

Jarvis takes a deep breath and then sighs heavily. He has never told Pamela the details. Resigned, but not entirely sure what he will do, as yet, he needs more time to think it through. His thin white tee shirt stretches tightly across his chest, around bulging upper arms, with one solitary tattoo of a topless girl and Pamela is at least pleased he's not covered with the damn things, like all his mates.

'In the case of US Department of Defence versus Kilo Company, 3rd marine battalion,' he recites, 'for the deaths of twenty-four Iraqi civilians in Haditha on November 19, in the year 2005.' The exact details with all their sharp and painful edges are forever etched in his memory.

Pamela pauses on her munching, trying to recognise something of what Jarvis is telling her. She senses he is reluctant to speak of it. 'But that was ages ago?'

'These things take time, especially when you reach the appeals stages. Can go on for years.'

'When is it?'

'Six weeks, December 14.'

'And you've got to attend in the States, in Washington?' She squares up to him, leaning against the sideboard and licks the stickiness off her fingertips. 'Or what? Do you have to go?'

'Served in the British Army, worked in close cooperation with our closest ally - difficult to refuse. Malone or Shawcross should be in touch, any day soon. They'll expect me to do my duty. They might be involved, as well.'

'And who pays for it, your travel and stay et cetera?' Ever the practical girl, Pamela.

Jarvis shrugs a little without taking his eyes off the sheet of paper on the table. 'The Army'll pick up the bill. I expect.'

'It says "US Naval Criminal Investigative Services" here,' leaning over the table and bumbling close to his side.

'Yes, well, they get everywhere. The primary law enforcement agency of the US Navy: officers in all the major countries of the world. A lot of leeway, how they conduct themselves - usually get what they want, go where they want to go.'

'And the Navy covers the marine corps?'

'Right. They've been conducting this investigation, been told several different versions of events, I gather. Revealed a massive cover-up, all the way up the line. Desperate for some eyewitnesses. The local Iraqi witnesses, if there ever were any, all suddenly disappeared or refused to say what they saw.'

'And you. You got to witness what happened?'

'Yeah, front row seat, magnified twenty times. Me and Joe.'

On Saturday, November 19, 2005, in the Iraqi farming city of Haditha, it was just after seven in the morning, another routine day in store, and they were at their observation post, an open flat roof over a garage. Jarvis Collingwood worked through his routine prep with care. Watching the stunning colour changes of sunrise across the vast skies, he was expecting another cloudless and irritatingly hot day. He smeared sun cream over his face, along the narrow ridge of his nose, around the back of his neck and over his forearms. Wearing an army tee shirt and fatigues, helmet on, boots laced. He checked the usual set up: precision rifle fixed on its front bipod, balanced on a makeshift platform of wooden boxes, set back so as not to poke through the parapet. A thin muslin screen hung on the inside of the brickwork to cover the gaps and help with camouflage. Chewing an oat biscuit and sucking cold water from his freshly filled camelbak, he settled prone on a low metal bedframe and discarded mattress. A stack of 5-round box magazines was placed in the shade under him, his head comfortably positioned behind telescopic sights. Beside him was a bar of dry chocolate wrapped in silver paper.

Private Joe Street was in his position too, British Army sniper and spotter working together. Jarvis lowered his shades into position and looked out eastwards, over the crumbling city towards the river.

Everything had already begun to chafe against Jarvis's skin. Bloody flies were buzzing around his face. A bleached cloth erected like an awning above them offered only primitive shade. He nudged Joe with a booted foot to get himself together: they had a US convoy to watch over.

Four US Humvees passed within a hundred yards of their position, turning one by one into Route Chestnut and keeping a regular interval of twenty-five yards between them. A white Opel had come between the first two trucks. Magnified in his sights, Jarvis watched a group of ugly vultures and crows arguing over a decaying carcass way down the Route by the side of the road. Even further down, a disorganised flock of sheep was wandering around over the carriageway. His attention wavered from the first Humvee to the yapping dog to the moving sheep and back to the white Opel. He focused on the scavengers and the dead animal. He was acutely aware that if it were booby-trapped, he could do nothing to warn the convoy. He could see no wires trailing across the gravel, but he would not be able to make out a mobile phone aerial exposed enough to pick up a signal at the road surface.

Apparently, bomb-making equipment with al-Qaeda connections had been found in the area, although he had not yet seen any untoward signs. He had not had a hit for several weeks. Violent activity had been oddly quiet of late, but he was sure it was only a temporary pause. He constantly warned Joe to be alert at all times, even when he was asleep.

'You have to catch your sleep when you can, Joe, but always have your eyes open. You'll soon get the hang of it.'

He scratched at the patches of blond stubble over his jaw. Joe had managed only a wispy growth along his upper lip, and with his sticky-out ears, he looked so young, barely out of school. Joe looked tired, taking on a hurt expression. 'I need a good ten hours a night, my Mum says so.'

Jarvis ignored him, concentrating. A flint of sunlight reflected from the glittering dome of Rifai mosque and caught Jarvis's sights at that moment. He blinked slowly and waited for the blinding brightness at the back of his eye to dissipate. And in that blink, that was when the explosion happened.

'I didn't actually see the precise instant that the bomb went off, but I heard the boom and felt the vibration through the flimsy walls of our hideaway building. I saw the fire and the plumes of smoke and the two halves of the broken Humvee crash back to the ground. It was a real eye-opener. Joe was all agog. He crouched below the parapet next to me. His eyes were wide in surprise. He scanned the area through his Mil-Tec binoculars, murmuring expletives to himself: bugger me, what the hell. He was seeking the means of the blast or any signs of the perpetrators, hiding in nearby buildings, watching through gaps or windows. For sudden movement, figures turning away, heads bobbing from behind a wall, anything. But nothing caught his eye. I was scanning the area as well, through the dense smoke, looking for bodies.'

Pamela sits gently in the chair opposite, listening to her husband, her soldier hero, with her soft brown eyes fixed on his handsome face, willing him to spill the details of that morning from his flashing memory. It is all news to her. She has never heard him speak before at such length and knows that he may clam up at any moment, when he thinks he has said too much or might have upset her in some way.

Jarvis had seen this sort of thing before. 'Even at that distance I could hear the screaming. All the marines had broken cover from their vehicles and were dispersing to find other protected spots, against a clump of bush or behind a brick wall. They had no idea who had set off the bomb or whether there might be an armed attack to come. They didn't know what they were looking for or what they were protecting themselves from. But they were shouting. Some of the marines ran to their stricken comrades, tried to help. One dead driver, two injured soldiers. I mean they were incensed. In the chaos of the billowing smoke and roaring of the fires, sounds were confusing. Was that automatic gun fire? Were they under attack from insurgents hidden among the surrounding buildings?'

Jarvis's pale unblinking eyes reflect a sense of dismay.

Another dog was barking at one of the twisted wreckages. The soldiers were shouting at each other, orders and responses as they dispersed along the road, looking around them, nervy, on edge. Flames were roaring from the broken truck, thick smoke swirling around. A couple of men were trying to help the trooper under the wreckage, shouldering the fuming structure onto its side to haul the body out. They bent over him, inspected the damage, handled him, patted his face to get a response. Another marine was helping the poor fellow with his leg ripped off, trying to wrap the horrible thing with some bandaging he had frantically fetched from a first-aid kit. He was calling out on his radio. A couple of others were looking for something to cover the remains of their dead colleague. The watching vultures adjusted their perches from atop the nearby trees and telephone poles.

The wounded soldier had fainted or at least his screaming had stopped.

There was one soldier who stood out, belligerent and loud, with three green stripes on both his upper sleeves. Like all US marines, in his desert camouflage uniform, pot helmet, body armour, back pack and big laced-up boots, he was kitted out for battle: tinted visor, black gloves, with radio strapped to his chest, carrying the ubiquitous semi-automatic assault rifle, with hand gun, splicing knife, baton and tons of ammo in his munition pouch, and a hand grenade or two for good measure. He stood close to the steaming crater in the road, taking charge.

Sergeant Robert Wosniak was gesticulating and barking orders, pushing his men to find protective positions facing the nearest houses, to recover their wounded. Jarvis could hear his angry voice, rasping into his radio, as he crouched against a palm tree, probably reporting in to his superior: IED attack, needing back-up, one man down, two wounded, air rescue wanted. He listened and shouted some more after receiving instructions. He stood up and ran over towards the stationary white Opel saloon, screaming at the occupants to get out, pointing his rifle at them and waving his arms. Some marines were standing around the car, also gesticulating and shouting profanities at the occupants. The Arab driver was manhandled out of his seat. He had cropped hair, a stubbly face; he looked overweight in his shapeless white robe and sandals. His four confused passengers clambered out. They looked like teenagers, boys with clean chins in tee shirts and shapeless trousers, trainers, students probably. The marines were pointing their rifles at them from a distance. The Sergeant stamped nearer, shouting and swearing; he seemed to be demanding to know who set off the bomb. 'You explode the Humvee, you fucking idiots?' seemed to be the gist.

A couple of the others looked into the car but found nothing and then Wosniak, in his fury, still shouting obscenities into the faces of the driver and his frightened passengers, pushed them in the chest one by one with his fist. The driver did not respond, just looked innocent and shrugged. Wosniak fired off his rifle at him point blank and the startled man tumbled dramatically backwards off his feet. The four terrified teenagers turned away horrified, one of them moving as if to make a dash for it. The sergeant shot him in the head and then walked over to him on the ground and shot him again through the chest and stomach. The boy lay still in the dirt, crimson stains of blood spreading across the front of his ripped white shirt. The sergeant shouted at the other three who were rooted to the ground sinking at their knees, their hands up in the air, their faces pleading for mercy. He shot them, one after the other, through their chests, blood splattering as their bodies jerked backwards.

And then he fired more rounds into them, extra bullets for each of them to be sure. And a couple more for the driver. Dark puddles gathered under them in the dust, quickly drying in the heat.

In disbelief, Jarvis stared transfixed by the senselessness and cruelty of what they were witnessing. His mouth opened, but he was lost for words. It had all happened so quickly, all over in a few seconds. He was completely stunned.

'What the hell?' asked Joe, his wide eyes fixed on the scene.

'I had him in my sights and recognised the face, Bob Wosniak, a sergeant I had already come across at US base camp. Not a very nice bloke, a bit thick, to be honest. Full of himself, his own importance.'

Jarvis looks dazed at the memory, far away, but his mind is vividly alive to the recall of these details. Pamela hangs onto his every word. 'Five innocent men, with blood-staining clothes and leaking head wounds, scattered by the side of the road, the taxi doors wide open. The other marines have not protested; they did not try to intervene. The sergeant shouted at them furiously, to make their positions secure, to watch the nearby houses. He seemed to think that's where the danger had come from.'

Sergeant Wosniak called for three troopers to head to the first house he pointed to, set back thirty yards from the road, to clear it out; three more to head for the second and clear that out. They shot the doors down and threw in fragmentation grenades, while crouching either side of the frames. Jarvis heard the small explosions, like firecrackers, the inside of the ground floors lighting up. The marines stormed through the broken entrances, their weapons poised. He heard intermittent bursts of gunfire. Wozniak's anger knew no bounds. He stormed up behind the first group and followed them into the house. Smoke poured out of a side window and someone was trying to push open the frame and clamber out but was gunned down from inside. The body of a boy was flung across the dirt outside, two bare feet left sticking out from under a bundle of Arab robes.

Jarvis followed the sergeant with intense concern, as he marched towards the next house, shouting at his troops, his anger like a desperate hunger. From the two-storey building two figures were dragged out into the glaring daylight, young men with black beards in loose garments and sandals. They were unarmed, their hands half-raised, trying to keep their balance as they were roughly manhandled. Wosniak pointed down at the burning halves of his Humvee shouting at them, demanding to know who was responsible. It sounded like: 'Who did this, you fuckers?'

The sergeant unbuckled his revolver from its holster, still gripping his assault rifle. He cocked it, pushed the gun into one of the men's chests, berating him as a useless piece of shit, shouting into his face, pushing him backwards all the while. Obviously not getting the answers he wanted, he pointed his pistol at the head of the second Arab, without actually looking at him. He towered over the first man, bumping into him, knocking him backwards and shouting continuously at him. He fires his pistol with the most cursory glance at his companion, blowing a hole through the man's forehead. The head jerked horribly backwards, spouting wet globs from the back and the body dropped in a heap. Wosniak, still shouting, kicked it sideways and fired twice more. The first man stared horrified and started crying for mercy, shrugging and shaking his head, but none of it did him any good. A bullet lashed into his forehead, punching him backwards and more bullets from point-blank ripped his shirt to shreds.

Some of the other marines rushed into the next house and threw grenades around the door into small rooms that lit up. Jarvis picked up the crackling explosions like it was a fireworks party. Puffs of smoke emitted from the open windows and doors. A woman in a black burqa staggered out with her child from a side door, almost overcome, bleeding from a leg wound. A marine without hesitation gunned her down with a spray of automatic gunshot that threw her back against the whitewashed outer wall, where she left fresh crimson smears behind her as she slid down to the ground, an agonised grimace of pain etched across her young face. The child was shot in the chest and spun out of sight across the dirt yard.

Wosniak shouted his satisfaction and egged his troops on to clear the next house.

Pamela looks genuinely shocked. 'My God, how awful. What was he playing at, was it just revenge?'

'He was crazy.' There is loathing in Jarvis's expression, his lips pulled tight.

Pamela gets up to go round the table to comfort him, puts her arm gently around his neck, looks at him with admiration. 'And you had to watch all that? So now they want you to testify, as a witness against these marines?'

'Well, there has been an inquiry going on but no real urgency to get to the truth, no witnesses have ever come forward or they backed off at the last moment. The official investigation drifted along, no one admitting to anything, then the lawyers moved into criminal mode, prosecutions started to fly. Then the appeals started and the whole thing has been bogged down in legal niceties.'

'No charges? No one found guilty? No compensation for those poor people? And four years later.' Pamela feels equally disturbed and disgusted.

Jarvis swallows another mouthful of orange juice from the carton. 'What I saw was a symptom of everything bad the US military are ever involved in, same sort of thing in Afghanistan. A force of a hundred thousand strong Yanks descend on the Middle East, armed and trigger-happy men and women speaking only English, with no training in the local customs of the Iraqi or Afghan people. Unable to verbally communicate with either the civilians or the enemy, and they wonder why nobody trusted them or treated them with credibility or respect.' He lets out a puff of indignation. A rare moment for him, letting his feelings come to the fore, showing his anger over a professional incident. Deep down, Jarvis would welcome the chance to stick the truth of what happened back in the Americans' faces, rub their noses in it.

Pamela has seldom asked Jarvis about details of his army activities, she knows he does not like to talk about them, pride, modesty and all that. She had heard it several times from his mates and superior officers that he was an excellent sniper, highly valued among the top knobs, especially that Mike Malone chap, who always spoke really nicely about her husband. Jarvis had been decorated; she recognised him as a man of principle. But she also saw the coldness of it all, the blank emotional backdrop, the way it had changed him. It worries her sometimes and she is grateful that he took his discharge last year, returning home for good, unscathed, at least outwardly, no nasty wounds, no limbs blown off. His handsome face as good-looking as when she had first set eyes on him. But his mind is something that seems often adrift, lost in some memories of awful events. She knows how many friends and colleagues he has lost, seen killed in action. She often thinks about his poor brother Ed, and how Stella is barely managing without him.

Thinking of Stella reminds her that they will be meeting up at the weekend, the family gathering, time to catch up. And Jarvis's mother would of course want an up-to-date explanation as to why Pamela had not delivered her any grandchildren like Brenda and would once again relate all the positives about having your children young, getting them out of the way quickly, as it were.

'You're not wearing a bra, girl,' Jarvis observes, grateful to be able to switch to a totally different subject. His headache quickly forgotten, he narrows his eyes lasciviously on the impression her nipples are making on her cotton top, as she turns towards him. She is relieved that he has released the tension and presses a hard thigh against his muscular shoulder. He reaches up for her, enjoying her abundant perkiness that he loves so much. He stands up behind her, arms circling, loosely grasping her breasts and snuggling his mouth deep into the nape of her neck. 'And you answered the front door like this?' he mumbles.

Keen to contact Joe Street as soon as possible, without Pamela worrying, Jarvis dresses late, after she has changed and left for work. He phones the home number and it's the jolly, high-pitched voice of Joe's mother that answers.

'Oh, Mr Jarvis, sir, how are you?'

'Fine, fine, Doris.' He forces lightness into his voice. 'Listen, I'm looking for Joe.'

'Well, he's at work, dearest, out early these days.'

They chat on, Doris Street full of respect. She understands how her son worshipped Jarvis and how Jarvis had helped him on more than one occasion to get through his days in the army. Jarvis says he'll try again later.

Joe Street was from Royal Signals Corp. He found himself paired with newly promoted Corporal Jarvis Collingwood, the quiet para with a reputation. They had never actually met before, although Joe had heard all the stories about his endurance in harsh conditions, days spent away hidden and undiscovered, his relentlessness in chasing targets, his exceptional hit rate. Collingwood, halfway through his second Iraq tour, was the hero everyone admired, and Joe had been picked to pair with him in the notorious hothouse of Haditha. Nervous, yes, he was; but excited and proud, too. He could handle it.

'Pleased to meet you,' Jarvis had mumbled with a soft shake of his hand, when they met at the practice range a few days before flying out from Basra. Jarvis took life seriously. Tall, lithe and blond, he was a good-looking man, everyone's idea of cool: didn't say much, blue eyes almost arctic, expressionless, focussed on his work. Two L118 sniper rifles were lined up, on their front bipods, waiting for action. A magazine of five rounds lay beside each, on the groundsheet. They settled prostrate behind their weapons, elbows close, legs spaced apart, toes into the ground, relaxed. Through the telescope at low magnification Jarvis studied his flat target fifty yards away, a nasty-looking insurgent in thick black outline heading towards him with his automatic poised, with concentric circles emanating from its chest. They loaded their magazines in the understocks.

'In your own time, gentlemen,' called the Quartermaster.

Joe started nervously, firing off first, all too eagerly and managed to hit his man five times but scattered in the outer circle, every one. Jarvis was in no hurry, rhythmic in his approach, almost in slow motion, firing his five single shots at regular ten-second intervals, all five penetrating the enemy's heart.

Later they sat together outside the mess with their bottles of water and chewy bars. Joe felt a film of sweat over his body, as Jarvis quietly explained his technique and how he had taken out one insurgent enemy recently, from a distance of at least five hundred yards, by calculating the movement of the walking man and the likely angle of sag of the trajectory and deflection of his ordnance.

In awe of his new partner, young yet so mature, it was all experience for Joe, and he was soaking it up. They went off to the edge of the compound where, among the scrubby bush grass, they tried out their camouflage outfits, their ghillies, with their coloured hessian strips, sandy and brown, working with a couple of orderlies from Stores applying the finishing touches, attaching more twigs and leaves. The hoods came over the back of their heads, so they could lie flat face down and let the covers spread completely over them and out into the undergrowth, submerging them neatly into the ground.

'I once lay the ghillie down,' Jarvis explained, 'empty, in the position I wanted, distributed its folds and fixed the camouflage adding the foliage and stuff, throwing sand over it, so you really could hardly make it out even when standing next to it, right? And then I crawled into it from underneath, wriggled my way inside without disturbing the position (I was only wearing underpants), until I was right inside, my head at the top; so I knew I was perfectly hidden. Nobody found me for days.' A cheeky smile pouted his lips. He enjoyed sharing his stories with Joe, giving him his best tips. He showed him the stick of charcoal he kept in a trouser pocket wrapped in a bit of muslin, for smearing his face, back of hands, to darken the skin for nighttime. 'Most effective with a little damp cloth.'

Joe wanted to know what happened if you needed to go, you know, to wee and so on. 'Well, you go when you can, when you know you're safe but sometimes you have to hold it for hours; or even go where you are, lying still, no movement.'

'What, in your ... pants?'

Jarvis fixed his eye on Joe's innocent-looking face. 'It may be that or being found by an al-Qaeda rebel who will cut you up at will before hanging the pieces out to dry in the market square for all to see.'

Joe would never forget the intensity in Jarvis's expression that conveyed the truth of which he spoke.

Talking to Joe's mother has made him nostalgic for the old days. He has been missing the blokes he had shared a life with, had trusted. His reputation as a super marksman had earned him respect, which had given him a real sense of purpose. But since leaving the army he had drifted, much to Pamela's annoyance. He didn't know what he wanted. The most important thing in his world had been duty to his country and to his regiment. He failed to identify anything worthy of his attention in his vacuous life as a civilian. To keep the days ticking over, with some money coming in, and to keep Pamela from complaining too much, he would take some of the odd jobs his brother, Jonathan offered him: personal protection for well-known celebrities, politicians or rich business men, which earnt quite good money; transporting valuable commodities around the city, gold bullion, precious merchandise which carried a bit of a risk against the professional criminal, not such good money; round-the-clock property security, patrolling building sites, definitely the less glamorous end and not good money at all. Sometimes he found himself working alongside other ex-army blokes struggling to settle to anything just like him. Which was reassuring in a way.

At least he had not resorted to working in the prison service.

Over the last few weeks, he and a handful of other bored young men in their *Security First* dark green caps and jackets, had been posted down at the old Tate & Lyle sugar refinery on the East Thames. Expected to be a quiet job, supervising a peaceful protest by some dissatisfied workers. No problem, an easy ride, no sweat. A substantial site along the north side of the river in Silvertown, near the Thames Barrier and adjacent to the City of London Airport, been there over a hundred and thirty years. A vulgar mix of hot smelly warehousing, grimy Victorian blocks with corrugated roofing, storage tanks, cooling towers and steaming chimneys, it felt like a relic from the last century.

From the river side, it's a familiar landmark huddled in higgledy-piggledy fashion, its turquoise blue sheds, its blue and yellow derricks on the wharf, its white towers with its distinct blue and white logo and those two tall pencil thin black-tipped chimneys looking like used matchsticks, as recognisable as the Tower of London. One of the few remaining manufacturing sites in the once thriving Docklands with its river access, its own jetty, built on legs of oaken beams like a stiff centipede, thirty yards out from the bank to allow sufficient water depth for ocean-going vessels to draw up alongside.

Jarvis arrives on foot, as is his way, jauntily approaching the site from Pontoon Dock. Factory Road runs straight and narrow, for half a mile passing an endless wall of filthy brickwork and the old factory buildings on the right. On the opposite side, high fences and sharp wire discourage anyone moving over the disused railway lines. The main operations building is a bulky stone and corrugated metal hulk in the middle, with the company logo draped in pride of place from the roof high above. There are lorry and car parks at either end and an intermittent flow of heavy tankers and trucks regularly pass through the two main entrances.

Groups of men and women in coats and scarves waving banners are huddled together outside the workers' car park entrance, where a beam barrier is operated by an attendant. Cars are arriving freely for the mid-morning shifts, the park mostly full. The protestors chant quietly about fair pay for a fair day's work as they waive their placards at another car driving up to the barrier. A leaflet is passed through the open window as the driver is asked if he would like to add his signature to their protest statement.

It had all started, as these things usually do, as a grievance, a couple of workers being forced to change their work patterns. A handful of supporters had stood around the entrance to the staff car park looking self-conscious. One or two illegible placards, cheap strips of paper with a few headlines and cliched phrases, calling for others to join their brothers and sisters in their struggle with management, were waved and motorists encouraged to toot their horn to show support. Drinking tea, smoking, standing around in the cold stamping their feet, trying to find humour in the situation while moaning about the injustice of their pay and conditions. Disorganised, unimportant, nothing to get worked up about.

Then a union member starts a support group, which becomes a campaign and then a vote is called asking for strike action and suddenly shop stewards appear with official picket written in bands around their arms and the placards became more professional, printed properly with wooden handles. Staff are molested on arrival, and management starts putting out statements about the unacceptable behaviour of certain rebels that would not be tolerated. One of the original workers is sacked and that's when management decide they needed outside help: Jonathan's outfit, *Security First,* is drafted in.

There are more of them today than he has seen before, a few more hefty looking men with aggressive faces and voices. Jarvis realises, however fit and keen they might all be, that their total of nine security men cannot patrol the whole site properly. And if the number of protestors were to increase, they would be in trouble. He needs to remind Jonathan about this again.

Jarvis pulls his official cap on and walks past them, responding to a couple of faces he recognises. Someone calls out, 'Morning, Mr Collingwood.' Suddenly, a roaring noise worse than thunder, that makes Jarvis jump with surprise, jolting his mind back into the chaotic battlegrounds of the Middle East, explodes around them. He feels compelled to watch as another aircraft rockets up from the short runway that lies parallel to the river a stone's throw away. It hurls itself skywards at an acute angle, the sun glinting off its metalwork, so close he's sure he could identify the pilot on request. Thankfully it soon disappears through the low-level clouds.

He crosses the car park. Passing through a security door with his electronic id card on a lanyard, he wanders over to the reception counter.

'Hi, Rab. How's it going?'

The cheery Asian has a friendly face for anyone who comes past his desk. He has swept back jet-black hair and a dark neatly trimmed beard. Always polite and well-dressed, he must be late forties, been at Tates for many years, reliable. Jarvis has already shared a few conversations with him about the current situation. The manual workers use an entrance further round directly into the warehouses, but here, the daily routine is a little slower and more peaceful, where the testing laboratories are above them, the women employees and bright engineers and chemists pass by. They all tend to like Rab.

'Oh, all pretty quiet at the moment, Mr Collingwood, sir. Yourself?'

'Yeah, okay. Did I see someone from the press outside? A bloke with a camera round his neck. Chatting to the protestors with a notebook?'

'You could well be right, wouldn't surprise me, the things that some of the managers have been saying to the local newspaper.' Rab is leaning on his elbows over the desk, a copy of a paper in front of him, looking at the front-page story with his chin resting in his hands. He reads: "The company, under new management, is desperately trying to become more competitive under adverse rules from the European Community, which is limiting the quota of imports of cane sugar. The company is seeking to cut costs. This means trimming the workforce to suit demand." What it means, Mr Collingwood, is yet more job losses, pay freezes and banning overtime. No wonder they're not happy. Strike action is being planned, my friend, as sure as eggs is eggs.'

'Is the workforce unhappy? Really? Or are they being stirred up a bit?'

'Well, I think so. Lots of rumours about.' And raising his thick black eyebrows, he stares pointedly into Jarvis's face, nodding his head repeatedly. 'And seeing extra security people brought in from outside is not helping. They think it's management being heavy-handed.'

'Well, no: management see the unions beginning to take a stronger line, more unwilling to listen or negotiate, and can see problems with workers stopped at the gates, so they can't get on with their usual routine.'

'For sure, we know that, init, but it looks like a little panic.' There is a grin of regret on Rab's face. 'The manual staff cannot afford not to work, you know, they need to bring in wage at the end of the week, they got families to feed.'

Jarvis wants to know if the rumour is true about some of the big unions getting involved, even bussing in other protestors to picket the factory gates. 'I think they might,' Rab says after some thought, 'I can see that happening. There's a sense of grievance, that the board need to realise what it's actually like to work on the shop floor.'

Jarvis reports to Jack Appleton, Jonathan's appointed project boss, and they spend the rest of their morning wandering around the periphery of the site, recognising the weak spots, where the fence work might be breached or the automatic gates jammed by a determined outside force. They agree on some points that they will put to Jonathan to argue for strong reinforcements, for an extra boost to their numbers of twenty men minimum.

During the day Jarvis spends some of his time chatting to a few of the friendlier protestors outside, trying to understand their problems. A little before five o'clock, he heads home with the factory exodus of hundreds of workers on foot and in vehicles.

Later that evening, when Pamela is out on a food shop, he rings Joe Street. They have not spoken to each other since Jarvis's discharge ceremony February before last, when Joe had his mother with him.

'I'm still with her, in the same old house, it's ridiculous, I know, a man of twenty-five. But there it is. Me Dad died a couple of years ago and she appreciates the help and the company.'

'What are you up to these days, Joe?'

'Well, I have a job in a factory in Slough, engineered tools, car parts mostly.'

'Sounds alright. Good pay?'

'Not really, but I get by. How about you?'

'Yeah, fine. Work for my brother, on and off, security and stuff.' There is a pause, Jarvis unsure what else to say. 'Listen, Joe, I received a subpoena this morning, to appear in Washington, the Haditha business. Just wondering if you might have had one, or anything?'

'No, not me. You mean the shooting there, that was 2005, ages ago.'

'Yeah, I know, but these things can move very slowly, especially when it's army personnel. Appeal after appeal. And then the witnesses disappeared. I think someone has dropped my name in it and the lawyers want to get their hands on another story.'

'The longer it lasts the more the lawyers make. But still, four years, how are you supposed to remember everything?'

'The point is, Joe, I could still land in big trouble, when the truth of Sergeant Wosniak's death gets out. I mean, I won't involve you, I'll make sure of that, but I thought I would ask. And warn you, I suppose.'

They natter on for a little while longer.

Jarvis has to pluck up courage to ask: 'How's the arm these days?'

'Oh, it's fine. Lovely scar, but yeah, everything works fine.' There's slight laughter in his voice.

'Good. Listen, why don't we meet up on Sunday?' Jarvis suggests quickly on the spur of the moment. 'It's Remembrance.

We could meet in St Stephen's, for a pint or two. We met there once before, remember?'

They agree a time, after the Cenotaph service.

Joe had sounded cheerful enough, which pleases Jarvis.

Debriefing interview with Corporal Jarvis Collingwood. Captain Michael Malone, 1st Battalion Special Forces, parachute infantry unit.
December 12, 2005.

Early morning, Jarvis sits alone for at least an hour waiting in an unmarked interview room in an anonymous MoD building off the Aldwych. There was a light covering of snow overnight and he apologised to the man at the door for bringing in some slush from his shoes. He's been back in London a mere three weeks. Although dressed in a plain grey suit, he feels the need to stand upright and salute when the Captain arrives, but Malone smiles meekly and says no, no, Corporal, no need for any of that.

Malone slips his long raincoat off. Tall, nervy and trim in his khaki officers' uniform, shiny dark brown brogues. He promptly dispenses with the niceties and sets his pocket tape-recorder on the table in motion pretty much from the off. He has an urgency about him, keen to press on and get this over with. 'It's important that I have the details of our conversation, just in case. Don't want to be seen to be neglectful or cutting corners or showing favours, eh Jarvis?'

By which Jarvis assumes he means he wants to protect his own backside.

'Haditha, November 19th. We need to go over the events, from your point of view, so that we have your version, correctly recorded, to avoid any misinterpretation.'

Jarvis peers at the smart cleanshaven face of his battalion commander. He picks up a whiff of expensive aftershave. Malone's eyes keep shifting from Jarvis's regimental tie to his own little notebook in front of him, to the small black recorder between them, but never meets his gaze. 'In your own time, corporal.'

'It was shortly after seven, when Joe Street and I prepared ourselves for the day ahead.' Jarvis proceeds to recite the exact sequence of events of that fateful morning, something he has gone over in his own mind a million times, remembering all the details. The dead carcass on the side of the road, the vultures and the crows, the dogs barking, the herd of goats and the white Opel taxi, they all get their rightful mention.

'Were you aware of the IED on that road?

'We had been in-situ for sixteen days. During that time, I had never observed any group digging in such a device - it must have been placed before our arrival. I had no idea of its existence.'

'What triggered the device?'

'It was no accident but a planned attack, set off live by a hostile watching from nearby, using a mobile phone signal.'

'How can you be so sure?'

'The position in the road, the perfect timing of the explosion; their usual modus operandi.'

'They knew the convoy was travelling that route,' queries Malone, 'at that time of the morning?'

'I doubt it. Coincidence. These guys have dedicated patience, they would have been watching, waiting their chance.'

'Did you see him or them? Did you consider pursuing them?'

'No, sir. Joe Street, my spotter, detected no signs of anyone involved. We did not consider pursuing them, as we had no idea who or where they were.'

Malone, holding onto some deep inner anger, mumbles as an aside: 'So much for a coordinated approach. Supposed to be a working example of British troops providing support and protection for our American cousins.'

'We never had any forewarning of US convoy routes and

we had no means of communicating directly with the marines, even if we had.'

'Brilliant,' stutters Malone in a huff. He aimlessly lets an unnatural gap of many seconds develop before leaning forward onto the edge of the table, his neck protruding forwards, as his narrow eyes fix for once on Jarvis directly. 'This Wosniak chap, what was he like?'

Jarvis takes in a long breath. 'A bully and fitness fanatic, stubborn and inflexible. Not one to let his emotions get in the way of army routine. Not a cowboy as such, more an instinctive man of action. Someone who only worries about consequences after the event. In a challenging situation, potentially dangerous.'

Chapter 2
Saturday November 7

Just as they turn into leafy Colvestone Crescent, a clock is striking eleven and it starts to drizzle. Saint Mark's Church with its impressive English Gothic tower hoves into view behind wrought iron railings. The wipers screech across the smeared windscreen, as Jarvis tries to find a parking space along the packed road.

Jarvis is annoyed with Pamela, that she might steal the attention, when it is obviously Brenda's day, and thinks she should have chosen a more sober outfit. It is a Christening, after all, some restraint is called for. He hates to think what his mother will say. Jarvis is wearing pressed jeans and a clean white shirt. They have already exchanged some angry words. Pamela, quick to take every opportunity to show off her attributes, has got her way, as usual.

Silence prevailed during the short car ride: Pamela determined to feel joyous in her own style, Jarvis lost in his own thoughts. He's looking forward to seeing Joe tomorrow and is easily distracted by memories of their time together.

When he first heard of the plan for a coordinated operation up in Haditha, near the Dam, with US First Marine Division and Special Forces of the First Battalion working together, Jarvis was excited by the prospect of his skills being put to the severest of tests. The British Army would supply a support network with the US military in counterinsurgency, to serve as an operations and training resource for the demoralised and depleted Iraqi army. Here was a unique opportunity to show that these two major modern war machines could work together, that they shared the same values, had the same ambitions.

He was well aware of the reputation of the place. Al-Anbar Province, north-west of Baghdad, was a hive of Sunni Muslim and al-Qaeda insurgency. As if a reminder were needed, only two weeks before, a Christian priest, an Englishman from Shropshire, had been grabbed in a public street, tortured to death and distributed in pieces from the telephone poles across Market Square. The insurgents said he was a spy, working for the British. Other tales of cruelty against both Iraqi locals and coalition forces were becoming legion. The second Battle of Fallujah six months before, in which the US military had rampaged with vengeful aggression, causing widespread insurgent casualties and mayhem, following the slaughter of four freelance mercenaries whose bodies were mutilated and hung under a bridge over the Euphrates, was still fresh in everyone's minds.

'Some of the heaviest fighting of the Iraqi conflict so far that US military has been involved in since the Battle of Hue City in Vietnam in 1968,' commented Major Shawcross, in one of his gruff introductions for the chosen expeditionary few, which included Corporal Collingwood and Private Joe Street.

'The Blackwater mercenary force are a private army,' Jarvis was told, 'that enjoys total legal immunity as it kills Iraqi civilians in much the same way as the early American settlers in the wild west shot and killed buffalo, for sport and often while drunk.'

Collingwood and Street were thrown together with a dozen other pairs and so spent many professional hours in close proximity, learning to understand each other. For just about every minute of every day, night times as well, for several weeks at Basra British Army Headquarters, before moving up to the hot conflict zone along the Euphrates valley, close to the strategically vital Haditha Dam. They worked well, Jarvis the senior, the expert shooter with the dazzling reputation and Joe the young one learning the ropes and acting as spotter and radio comms man. They shared their worries and anxieties, sometimes the joys but mostly the misery of cold showers, the awful dried food rations, the lack of privacy, the primitive sleeping arrangements.

Joe appreciated Jarvis had extensive experience of his craft. He had the right mindset, understood the preparation needed and the outcomes desired. Jarvis was able to shut out the uncomfortable realities of the moment and enter the zone of pure focus, for long periods of time, with absolute patience. Joe was much less aware and new to the process; anyway, his expertise was communications, the radio man. He was always wanting to scratch or adjust a crease in his shirt or pull at his crotch, fiddling with his binoculars, wanting some action. His focus was easily distracted, and he was bored with his own company for too long. Lying close to Jarvis, with his sniper's rifle camouflaged with netting, foliage, the usual stuff, Joe with his high-tech binoculars was always desperately worrying that he would need a slash, even not drinking from his sucker to reduce the need. And just when he was desperate, Jarvis would offer a casual remark about what his Pamela might be doing at that moment. He would whisper in short outbursts personal things that Joe knew he would never tell the others in the squad.

'We've not been married long, but I've known Pamela a few years now. First and only girl.' They sometimes preferred to relax at the end of the day with their drinks, out on the open veranda of their hut complex, rather than in the mess drinking beers with the other lads.

'Really, what, childhood sweethearts?'

'Yeah, more or less.'

'Lost your virginity together?'

'Yeah, more or less.'

'What do you mean, more or less? You either did or you didn't.' Joe was amused.

'So, what's wrong with that?'

'No, it's cool. A bit unusual today, isn't it? Most blokes like to try their hand with a few girls, you know; get some experience in before they settle down.'

'You're an expert all of a sudden, are you? So, what's your sexual experience then, lover boy?'

'Oh, nothing exciting,' Joe admitted. This was Joe's chance to impress, but he knew Jarvis would see through him if he exaggerated his conquests, which didn't amount to much at all. His mother was always asking when he was going to go out with a nice girl from the estate, but he didn't fancy any of them, preferred to stick with his circle of mates, mostly from his school days, going to watch the Hornets on a Saturday afternoon, sinking a few pints in the pub afterwards.

Joe's blueish eyes brightened up, his spirit always lifted, at stories of Jarvis's marriage to a girl who sounded so lovely. He took it all in as gospel, although Jarvis was not so relaxed that he would freely reveal it exactly as it was, more his idealised version of how he wished it was.

And Joe was not entirely honest with Jarvis either. When telling tales of his love life, for similar reasons, he would not expose his inadequacies or lack of achievement. But Jarvis spotted the slight quiver of his upper lip when Joe told his little lies, delivered his exaggerations. And said nothing.

A bit of a lad, our Joe, he can hear himself saying. Pamela does not notice but clacks across the pavement from the car under a raincoat thrown over her shoulders. Once inside the tiled vestibule, she drops it onto a bench, to reveal a bottom-hugging trouser suit in olive green, the waisted jacket sufficiently low-cut to show off the tops of her pale quivering breasts. Lavishly made up with matching crimson eye shadow and lips, with a jaunty little saucer-like olive hat for good measure, she puts the droopy Brenda to shame.

Jonathan of course does not bat an eyelid, although Jarvis is certain of the mischievous thoughts that go through his mind as he welcomes his luscious sister-in-law inside the porch, his gaze fixing on her bare flesh as he kisses both cheeks. Jonathan had been pacing around, staring out at the street every now and again, swearing under his breath, to see where they had got to. Not that that made the slightest difference to the timing of their arrival, but it's what Gwendoline wanted.

The magnificent church in yellow brick and stone dressings

is Gwendoline's inspired choice, although ridiculously large for the small family gathering. And Gwendoline, bless her, has arranged the whole day for them, even though Jonathan and Brenda were not bothered either way. Amelia had been christened and Gwendoline felt strongly that this would be an important family occasion, a chance for them all to get together and to feel good about themselves. It would be a happy day - she cannot recall too many of those as she looks back, it all seems to have been funerals and disappointments. Although there was Jarvis's ceremony at Colchester Barracks last year, which had been ever so formal. She had enjoyed hearing the patriotic band music and all the fine words of Major Shawcross, speaking about the heroic paras that were leaving the service. She vividly recalls under the overcast skies sitting among the rows of well-dressed visitors bracing herself against the cold, wondering what she and Derrick would do if it had started to rain, they had left their raincoats in the car, imagining Derrick sitting cramped up next to her, even though he had been dead for the best part of six years. And then agonising images of her poor Edward being killed in action in Iraq bubbled up inside her head as the Major mentioned those they had lost or had had to leave behind.

She had insisted on a separate day from the Sunday service, on their being alone and not sharing with other families, and that godparents were an essential element of the service. A couple of Brenda's friends were kindly co-opted. At least her Jarvis would be there, looking impressively fit and straight-backed as always, doing the right thing, although he had vehemently turned down the chance to be a godfather. Why couldn't Pamela start her family, that's what was needed?

Pamela and Jarvis slip inside the vestry and join a small group of well-dressed waiting guests, huddled together patiently near the font. Happy smiles and handshakes are exchanged. Jarvis moves to kiss his mother on her cheek, while tickling little Amelia's chin as she sits obediently in a neat dress on her grandmother's lap.

The reverend Joshua Sashimba conducts the short service, smiling on everyone, so jolly that all their thoughts are on the little babe, Barney, who wisely sleeps through the whole procedure unbothered, anointment and all. Jarvis, while staring up at the lovely rose window above them, spends the time pondering his subpoena and feeling let down that his regimental admin had given the US court his details so freely. He misses the bible reading completely and then sees Barney grasping a little white unlit candle in his pudgy hand while his mother carries a lighted candle for him, to light his way ahead in the world. A quick burst of prayers for the parents and the godparents and all those who will support the child in his path of faith - hypocrites, the lot of them, Jarvis is thinking - then the Lord's prayer and the vicar's blessing and the whole shebang is over as quickly as it began.

They stumble out into the gloomy morning, where unfortunately, the overcast Islington sky is still drizzling, and everybody snuggles together under a couple of umbrellas for the photographer on the step outside. The newly arrived is draped in swathes of cream silk, the very gown Gwendoline proudly recalls she had used for all three of her children's christenings, much to Jarvis's embarrassment. Barney Adam, what treats he has in store.

Back at their Dalston house a couple of streets away, for canapes, champagne and presents. Stella is there, Ed's widow, in a dull navy skirt and blouse looking thinner than Pamela last recalled. Uncles and aunts are standing around politely making all the right noises, Ian, Derek's brother and the irrepressible Duncan. Jarvis is as aware of his late father's absence as he knows Gwendoline is and commiserates with her when they have a moment alone in the hall.

Uncle Duncan admires Jonathan's new groomed look, hair and beard trimmed along strict shaped lines, a film of gel giving it a doubtful sheen. 'Went up West, a new Italian barber in Bond Street, Giuliano's,' Jonathan intones proudly.

'How much did that set you back, then?' asks Uncle Ian, who regularly pays £2.50 for his fortnightly trim.

'About 65 quid,' says Jonathan. Brenda looks on horrified.

'In Kandahar, for 65 pounds equivalent you could have your hair cut every day for the rest of your life,' Jarvis murmurs.

'And still have change for a full-blown meal for a whole family of starving Afghans,' Duncan observes caustically.

'Well, it's only once in a while,' Jonathan pleads, trying to retrieve the situation with an innocent smile. 'Come on.'

Later, when they are alone outside the back door to the garden, Jonathan, sucking desperately on a cigarette that he is supposed to be giving up, checks with Jarvis on his latest job, on the East Thames. Jonathan knows the factory there has been under a slow siege mentality for a few weeks, disgruntled workers with banners, which is now threatening to break out into something bigger.

'We need to keep a lid on this trouble, Jarvis.' Jonathan is worried. 'It's our contract that might be at stake. The shop stewards last week threatened to increase the pressure with tougher picket lines. They want to cut down the number of workers getting through, reduce them to maintenance work only. They want the factory to stop, basically, so the bosses lose money. There's a rumour they're going to bus in a whole new crowd, to add weight.'

'Rent-a-mob,' Jarvis says. 'Still, the union have a right to picket the factory gates. There was a vote.'

'Yeah, but short of the needed majority, it has to be 65%. The vote was split. Management are insisting on better control. They're worried. I've had the CEO on the line this morning. He says the press have been snooping around.' Jonathan whips out a copy of Saturday's Newham Recorder from inside his suit and sticks the headline under Jarvis's nose, while exhaling smoke into the chilly air.

"TROUBLE IN STORE AT TATE & LYLE"
"Belligerent management not listening, as cost savings plan gets the go-ahead"

'I'm sending some more men down there next week, help Jack deploy them sensibly, will you?'

Jarvis knows Monday will be another testing day. 'We'll need more than that, Jon. Jack and me did a walk round the place. It's vast, so many entrances. We reckoned another twenty men at a minimum.'

Jonathan whistles and stamps his foot as he whips round to face Jarvis. ''Ow many? You trying to ruin me or something, know 'ow much that'll cost?'

Jarvis stares him out, giving him a reflex shrug of the shoulders, a pout of the lower lips, as if to say there's no alternative. 'If you want the job done properly?'

'Well, I can't spare that many. I'll be down there, Tuesday, we'll see.'

Jarvis does not want to drone on about the protest at Tates, he's got other things on his mind. He wants to confide with his brother over the US subpoena business. Shortly after Jarvis returned from Iraq, earlier than expected, he had briefed Jonathan about the Haditha shooting and Jonathan, ex-Army captain himself, had shown some sympathy. But Jarvis remembers well his brother's serious warning that Kilo Company were hardly likely to let it rest.

'This is official, from the Appeals Court. Someone must have fed them my name, turned with a plea bargain, revealing my role as a witness. One wonders how much they know.'

'Jarvis, the NCIS are everywhere, although nobody knows them, they're discreet. But they have contacts with armed forces, intelligence agencies, police forces, governments. They get what they want, especially in the UK – we bend over backwards to please them, not to upset them. They probably just asked at

BAHQ for your address, routine like.' Jonathan can sense his brother's discomfort and smiles indulgently, never surprised by anything the Army does.

'It arrived under BA cover, but even so, they sent it on without informing me.' Jarvis sounds irritated.

'Well, we do work with the US, generally speaking.'

'Great. And am I compelled to attend?'

'You would be wise to. Speak with your commander.'

'Shawcross? We never got on. Always thought he was a bit of a prat.'

After a moment, Jarvis mentions the Commemoration Parade tomorrow. 'You coming?' he quips, knowing his brother will be busy with baby duties.

'Not me, bruv, probably catch it on the television.'

They hear the dulcet tones of their mother calling and Jonathan stubs out his cigarette under the sole of his Italian loafers, before kicking it under wet autumn leaves on the path. He blows the air and waves his hands to disperse the smell. 'Good man,' he repeats, patting his brother on his outer arm before returning to the bosom of his loving family.

Debriefing interview, MoD, Aldwych.
December 12, 2005.

The room is utterly quiet, carpeted, heavily lined with oak panelling, a deep-set window high up on one wall double-glazed, with a metal grill on the outside. The wall lights are dimmed. The captain and the corporal are alone. A square polished walnut table sits in the middle with two matching padded chairs placed opposite each other. Whenever Malone is about to ask a pertinent question, he curls up the inner halves of his neat eyebrows and his eyes squint. He leans forward, both wrists on the edge of the table, a fountain pen poised between thumb and extended finger. Left-handed, Jarvis had forgotten.

'The official story from US Command, as stated in Kilo

Company's report, is that the marines were fired upon by insurgents from the adjacent housing, soon after the roadside explosion. How can you be so sure that that was not the case?

Jarvis is unable to hide a flickering look of scepticism. 'There was an odd stillness soon after the explosion. Even the goats seemed to stop bleating. We heard no extra gunfire. I saw the taxi driver and his passengers executed point blank in the road. None of them armed. The twenty-four dead were mostly women, old men and children.'

After another interval, Malone with his thoughtful stare and squinting eyes, asks: 'Why didn't the white Opel drive away?

'I've asked myself that many times. I don't know. I guess the driver was scared, that he would be accused of being part of the attack, that he would be fired upon if he appeared to be making a getaway. We will never know, but the driver and his passengers were innocent victims.'

Chapter 3
Sunday November 8

Comfortable in his old uniform, ex-para Corporal Jarvis Collingwood, bare-headed in heavy khaki topcoat and black polished boots, mingles with the crowds along Whitehall. It's a bright autumn day. He assumes a position close to the Cenotaph, opposite the entrance to the Foreign & Commonwealth Office, from where the Queen and Prince Phillip would emerge in due course in their winter coats to join the proceedings. He studies the fine Portland stone pylon, without any inscriptions to acknowledge the fallen without graves. Religious and political leaders and the commanders of the three British services gather in lines alongside royalty. During the ceremony, the top brass, including Prime Minister Brown and leader of the Official Opposition Cameron, stand agonisingly side-by-side with the suitable deadpan expression of the detached observer, before stepping forward to lay wreaths at the foot of the empty tomb. At the end Jarvis watches them retreating inside the big building for a hot cup of tea, or perhaps something stronger, in the warmth.

Jarvis drifts through the service without really hearing the words. His attention flits between faces in the parade, everywhere seeing his younger brother's anguished look, as he died in his arms, aware of the warm drenching of his fatigues. All the battle incidents of his life, it would seem, are rolling through his mind like news flashes. As he sucks at his imaginary water supply, warm and tasteless, he feels the desert heat pricking the back of his neck. He flicks away the persistent flies tickling his nose and eyes. His shirt is wet with humidity, but the gritty dust in the air leaves his mouth as dry as sandpaper.

They were perched, Joe and Jarvis, on a precarious flat roof, high up in the warehouse building they had taken refuge in, at the top of an iron fire escape. It was late the same day as the Haditha explosion, getting dark. The road below them, leading into Market Square, was crammed with noise and movement, hundreds of people milling about on foot and on cycles, car and truck horns hooting, dogs and goats wandering everywhere, cattle as well. If they craned their necks over the parapet, they could see the jumble of brick and concrete buildings that formed the square, with open traders in the street, selling their meagre produce, dates and potatoes and spices, cheap shoes and clothes. A few streets away, the slow-moving shallow waters of the Euphrates looked muddy and uninviting. The river was wide and only one undamaged bridge remained to carry all the traffic. A line of camel was crossing over with the trucks and cars. The once grassy slopes of the far banks were sparse and bleached, the terrain beyond flat and featureless as it merged into endless desert.

The heat of the day had been formidable, but it was ebbing slightly. The sun was sinking over the other side of the building, leaving them in comparative shade, but they were both sweating profusely. The noise below them was not too distracting, although clearly audible, with tinkly sounds of Arabic music from countless radios. Smoke trails of cooking were wafting through the humid air.

They crouched together in the narrow space, their shoulders knocking against each other. A flimsy wire antenna was thrown over some corrugated roofing and Joe twiddled the knobs on the Bowman this way and that, listening intently on headphones. He had 126 channels on 440MHz to play with and eventually achieved a reasonable signal, which he had been unable to do earlier from down in their dingy basement.

'Press the button to speak, release to listen,' Joe explained. Jarvis put

the spare headset on and half turned with his thumb raised when he heard Malone's voice. After identifying themselves, Jarvis had to explain their dilemma. Malone knew little of the detail of the earlier explosion.

'We can't risk putting ourselves at the mercy of the US. Street and I were witnesses to the innocent slaughter of Iraqis, I don't know how many, twenty or more.'

'If this is some personal vendetta, Collingwood, I will not be impressed.'

'No, sir. One Humvee was taken out and its driver killed, two other casualties. The company sergeant went berserk, slaughtering innocent inhabitants point-blank. Probably taking orders from higher up: I saw him reporting back on his radio all the time. We were witnesses. This was a war crime. They'll want to stop us talking.'

'The conduct of the US marines would not allow them to treat you improperly, and I for one ….'

'Hang on a minute, sir, if I may?' Jarvis was in no mood to be pushed off course. 'We were spotted by the insurgents and were attacked, we had to fight our way out. Private Street was injured, we only just escaped in a truck. We got down to the city, we're close to Market Square. We're catching a convoy out early in the morning, down to Baghdad. That's the only way we will get out of here. They would not hesitate a moment to eliminate us, more collateral damage…. I saw the whites of their eyes, the anger they felt. Street needs medical attention. We have to get out and I can't afford to return to Haditha Base.' Jarvis was hanging on in there, as he heard a buzz of static echoing around his head in reply. 'No way. Sir.' For a moment he thought Malone had hung up on him, but perhaps he had put his hand over the mike as he spoke to someone else at his end. Joe just looked bemused, listening but not quite understanding what Jarvis was talking about. Attacked by insurgents, injured? After a little while, Malone coughed and Jarvis carried on. 'We will be in a supplies convoy heading back to Baghdad. We'll need a flight, to BAHQ Basra, sir. That's the only place the US will not be able to touch us.'

Once again there was a pause and they could sense Malone's irritation drifting through the static. Malone was rattled. Jarvis always thought he was a bit weak. Sounding distant, although he was actually about two miles away, Malone stuttered: 'You are asking a lot, Corporal. You'll need to be on a reconnaissance flight. You'll need protocol clearance, et cetera. I will have to sweet talk Major Shawcross. That won't be easy, he's rather techy at the moment. Can't promise anything, Corporal.'

'Sir.'

And the line went dead. Then the crisp Welsh tones of Lenny Bagshawe, Royal Signals Corps, communications expert and jolly fine bloke, came on the line, as clear as day, only a mile away apparently in his transmission vehicle. 'Blimey, Collingwood. What a caper, eh? You alright, you two?'

'You heard?' Collingwood tried to sound indignant.

'Well, I have to maintain the quality of the signal for communication purposes, as you well know, Corporal.'

'Yes, Lenny, we're fine. Just need safe passage down to Basra.'

'You'll be fine, they love you at HQ, Jarvis. Valuable cargo, Mr Superhero, you are. Sun shines out of your ...'

'Yeah, yeah, that will do. This is a bit embarrassing, you know.'

'Not half as embarrassing as the US will find explaining their actions. You wait till it gets into one of those American news journals or whatever. Blimey.'

'It won't, they won't let it,' Jarvis insisted.

'Oh, these things have a way, boyo, a habit of appearing when you least expect. Bet someone had a camera on that scene. What about the bastards who set off the bomb in the first place? They would have filmed the whole thing for their own propaganda purposes and they'll soon make sure it gets to the press boys with suitable taglines attached.' Lenny sounded excited, enjoying his role in the day's activities. Jarvis was marginally encouraged by his enthusiasm. Of course, he was right, the local Iraqis would be desperate to show the world what monstrous law breakers the occupying forces of the USA really were.

Joe was packing up, reeling in the aerial line, folding the headphones away. He had done well with his radio ops using Bagshawe as an intermediate relay. 'Well done, Joe, good work.'

'So, what's all this about being attacked? And Street being injured?'

'What?' Jarvis was thinking with certainty that they had no chance of getting out without Shawcross agreeing to putting them on a flight home.

'That's what you told Malone. What was all that about?'

They stored the equipment away in Joe's backpack. Jarvis led the way gingerly down the zigzagging metal staircase inside the warehouse shell to the ground floor, and then down to their basement. He closed the door behind them and made his move.

'Sorry, Joe, but I have to do this.'

Jarvis enjoys military bands, can listen to them all day. He silently says a prayer for Edward, remembering how he had closed his brother's eyelids before handing his body over to the medics in the chaos of that rubble strewn Baghdad backstreet, wanting to stay with him but having to fight on with his remaining troopers. He had their safety and destinies in his hands and had no time to mourn. He chased three fleeing insurgents waving their Kalashnikovs about and ruthlessly took them out, from a roof top, head shots from two hundred yards that killed them instantly; and shamelessly he felt the better for it. He can remember his team full of admiration afterwards.

Prayers are delivered, announcements made, and more marching music follows. The massed ranks and military groups start to shuffle along Whitehall towards Parliament Square in formation, the older veterans in wheelchairs, some in step, all in their crisply pressed uniforms, their lapels glittering with medals. Stirred by the music, Jarvis lingers to watch the thousands march past, everyone a survivor of some war or other; followed by relatives and others with special permission. They shuffle like a river on the ebb, while the crowds that line the street and spill over into the square dutifully clap and cheer. He listens to the chatter, at ease among these people, a swell of loyalty and a sense of duty rising like a wave from deep inside him, which he has to gulp back before it causes any embarrassment.

He stands beside a veteran, regimental tie, blue blazer, neatly pressed grey flannels, polished black shoes. He is wearing his War medals: the 1939-45, the Korean. 'Royal Artillery,' the old man replies proudly when Jarvis searches into his rheumy eyes. He wants to shake his hand.

The sun remains bright and low in the sky, reflecting off the wet roads. He follows the movement of the crowds and then turns down Canon Row, squeezing his way through the heaving groups of punters at the entrance to St Stephen's Tavern. There is a general hubbub of rowdy noise inside with the smell of warm beer and bodies. The brass fittings are shining, orange light streaming in through large windows to one side.

Jarvis edges closer to the solid mahogany bar, ornate glittery chandeliers and gilt edging everywhere. He has to shout his order. The noise level of people talking, mostly men in uniforms, ex-service people, with memories to share, is almost deafening. He scans their faces, some at the bar, coming and going at the open doors, filling the ground floor space, but he does not find Joe among them. He perches on a stool away from the bar in a corner by a window, where he can raise himself up with his boot on the crossbar, to scan faces over the heads of the people pressing around him. He waits for ten, fifteen minutes, but still no sign of Joe. He tries his number on the mobile but gets an immediate no response. There is lots of movement and calling out, drinks being passed back to waiting hands from the heroes at the bar. At one point, at the open door, Jarvis sees a face he seems to recognise although unable to put a name to it or a location. The man is short with a slightly comical look as his hat presses onto his flappy ears, which are made to stick out while the nape of his neck and the sides of his head are excessively shaven. Clutching a green glass Budweiser, he appears to be alone, looking out for someone. The fawn mac and trilby look a little out of place.

Jarvis, wracking his brain all the while to remember, follows the man's turgid progress through the swarm of people. He looks American, he's convinced by the button-down, the lazy look of his hooded eyes. By the time he gets over by the door he's lost sight of him. He squeezes his way outside and glances up and down the road, amongst the melee that is beginning to thin, but he cannot spot Joe or the supposed American among them.

As he turns back towards the entrance, it flashes across his mind. 'Shorter, that's who, John Shorter,' he murmurs to himself, suddenly remembering the little man at Wozniak's side at the chariot races in Haditha, in his toga, bare arms and legs and stupid helmet. His legs were like solid tree trunks, rough and thick. He was among the marines at the shooting as well. They all called him Shorty.

With absolute certainty, he knows what Shorty is doing in London. But to be seeking Jarvis among a huge crowd in Whitehall is a bit of a shock. The Americans must be already here, preparing their plans against him, watching him. Jarvis is not sure that Shorty identified *him*; perhaps he left when he thought Jarvis was not there. Jarvis stays by the main doors, finishes his drink, glancing at everyone that comes and goes, and thinking that something must have happened to Joe, to prevent him from attending. He does one more circuit of the two bars inside before deciding that his once spotter and friend is not to be found. Perhaps Joe has not forgiven him properly for the injury he had caused, the special surgery he had needed, the nasty scar that had been left behind, although he made light of it on the phone yesterday.

Outside Jarvis tries the mobile number a few more times, but only hears Joe's voice: "Can't talk to you right now, sorry, leave a message and I'll get back to you when I can."

Joe dumped his pack and turned to find out what his partner was referring to. The fist caught the side of his forehead, hitting him hard. His head jerked backwards alarmingly, and he stumbled onto his knees, knocking against the back wall. Jarvis had his hunting knife in his right hand, and a peculiar teeth-clenched expression that Joe captured as the flash of steel ripped across his outer arm, slashing his shirt. Joe yelled something incomprehensible before fainting for a moment, a blip of weakness as his consciousness wobbled and the room became distant and hazy. His head was spinning, feeling the wetness of warm blood gushing from a single deep cut along the deltoid muscle. Big drops bombed the dusty floor beside him.

Jarvis dropped the knife and grabbed a thin tee shirt from his corner rug where he had been sleeping. He darted back to Joe slumped on the floor and set about stemming the bleeding with the tee shirt pressed hard against the clean cut. He tied it tightly around the upper arm as best he could. Then he fetched a bottle of water from one of the fridges and splashed Joe's face, getting him to gulp some down. Joe revived enough to feel the pain and started to shout obscenities.

It didn't take too long for the blood to seep through the makeshift dressing. Jarvis continued pressing hard. Then he found another shirt among Joe's things and folded it into a thick wad, to be applied with firm pressure for as long as he could before his own arms started to ache.

'Sorry, Joe, I am sorry,' he muttered several times, with meaning. 'We have to have a convincing story, an excuse. You were injured in the fight with the two insurgents. I shot them both and dragged you away. I packed up our things. We found Rahim, who took us away to safety, before anymore ugly al-Qaeda thugs turned up.'

Joe was moaning, dazed and hurt. He was clutching at his arm, his face contorting with anger and pain and he wanted to cry out. Was he listening?

'Lie still, Joe, and shut the screaming or we'll have all these other guys onto us. Stay quiet. I'll hold this, it'll be alright. Lie still, damn you.'

For twenty minutes Jarvis wanders around Parliament Square, doing a circuit clockwise, then anticlockwise, each time returning to the entrance to the pub. All the time thinking of poor Joe, trying to form a strategy in his head for dealing with the impending threat. He scans the faces again downstairs and in the adjacent bar but still has no sightings of his friend or of that man, Shorty. On the spur of the moment he decides he needs to go up to Watford, to find Joe's house and to find Joe. He is filled with suspicion; something does not feel right. The coincidence of John Shorter being there is too much. And if Joe is in trouble he wants to help. He'll nip back home first, get changed. Pamela is out all day with her mother. He'll take the car, drive up through Holloway, take the A1 and M1, it wasn't too far. He could do it in an hour, talk to Joe, have a drink, be back home in no time.

From Old Street Jarvis heads north along New North Road, striding purposefully by the railings of Shoreditch Park, a generous expanse of wintery green. Not many people about, a few keen fitness fanatics on a group workout, a few joggers and walkers with their dogs. Over the canal bridge, he turns into Baring Street, a non-too prosperous-looking bus route with an eight-story council block on the corner. There are rows of terraced buildings on his left, and running full length, two hundred and fifty yards up to Southgate Road, along the righthand side is a featureless brick wall with a tarmac pavement. A couple of gaps at either end break the monotony, wrought iron gates leading down steps to the canal towpath. The one distinguishing feature of the street is its quiet crescent of terraced housing that branches off to the left and loops round to emerge back onto the main road via Wilton Square up at the far end. The buses don't go up there and it is really a different street, but is still called Baring Street, which must confuse all visitors and the postmen from time to time. Quite why this semi-circular arrangement keeps the same name as the main road is a mystery.

Jarvis lives on the crescent, in the north side terrace, half-way along. There are double yellow lines and residents' parking everywhere, and no off-road or garage parking. His instincts are alerted by a black shiny Ford hatchback that he has never seen before, ordinary plates, sitting illegally at this end facing up the road. Out of the corner of his eye, he can make out the individual shape of a man at the driver's seat, looking away, waiting for something. In his army greatcoat and heavy black boots, Jarvis is a give-away. Too late to stop midstride, he walks on perfectly normally, without hesitation or any tilt of his head to see who's in the car, and continues on past his front door as if it has nothing to do with him, up to the end of the street, where he turns left and out of sight.

On the corner is a neglected block of flats, squat and drab. But around the side, there is a weedy paved driveway into an open yard, strewn with rubbish and leaves. Occasionally someone parks an old Bedford van in the space, but it's not there now and there's nobody about on this Sunday afternoon. Under overhanging branches with autumnal leaves, he squeezes through a broken gap in the slats of a wooden fence. This is what he calls his back route. He nips across one tiny garden, over a wall, across a second and then a third, before he vaults another brick wall into his own backyard.

An hour later, with a scrap of paper with Joe's address in Watford in his anorak pocket, using his back route in reverse, he nips over the walls into Wilton Square. Around the corner under the trees is where he habitually parks his red Astra. After an uneventful drive out of London, he turns into Vicarage Road where he stops to ask a woman out with her dog the way and in Brightwell Road, he walks along the car-lined street checking the numbers for the little semidetached he's after.

Doris Street answers the door and is taken aback at seeing this tall young man in a Parka and jeans on her front doorstep. It takes her a few moments to realise who it is, after Jarvis politely introduces himself. She grabs at his offered hand with both hers, chubby and warm. And then suddenly withdraws them to pull an apron from around her waist and apologise for not being made up or anything.

She's a plain-looking woman in her mid-fifties, with a well-worn rounded face that's seen plenty of hard times. She pats her bundle of mousy hair and scratches the back of her neck in embarrassment. In a lurid purple pleated skirt and green patterned cardigan that date back to the 1980s, she looks like the millions of other anonymous working-class women just about managing.

Retreating into the narrow corridor, Doris takes him into the front parlour. 'Would you like a nice cup o' tea, Jarvis, Corporal, I'm sure you'd like something? Have you come all this way just now? In the car?'

'I'm fine, Doris. It's Joe I came to see.'

'Well, would you fathom it? Joe's not here just now. He hasn't been home since yesterday.' She looks worried, holding an arm across the droopy bulkiness of her chest.

'Oh. Where's he gone? He's not answering my phone calls.'

Doris returns from the back kitchen with two mugs of hot tea and settles down in a tatty armchair. In the middle of a low table between them she places a plate of assorted biscuits. Jarvis takes his mug gratefully. 'Haven't seen him since yesterday. He went to the Watford game, met up with some friends at lunchtime. He come home after dark, had been to the pub but went out soon after that, with some of the lads, he said. Not been back since.' She does look concerned, her lip turning down as she explains. 'I was worried, this morning, like, called Jake, his best mate. He said they had been in the park along the river, its down by the Arches Retail, they muck about down there; its where the local druggies gather, I don't like it but what can I do, Mr Jarvis?' Doris's eyebrows knit tightly, as she fiddles idly with the buttons of her cardigan. 'Joe met some blokes there, he said, foreign he thought. Big bruisers, wanted to talk to Joe, they went off in a big black car. Joe said it was fine, apparently, he'd see Jake later. But, nothing doing, nothing since.'

'And this was Saturday, last night; what, late, nine, ten o'clock?'

'Yes, not called or nothing since.'

'Where can I find this Jake, need to talk to him, Doris?'

'You worried, Mr Jarvis? He'll be alright, won't he?' Her lips wobble a bit and she raises her mug to her mouth to disguise the fact, to give them something to do.

'Now, don't you fret, Doris, there's probably a simple

explanation. I need to talk to Joe and Jake might be the man to help me find him. Joe can look after himself, you don't need to worry about him.' Jarvis tries to sound convincing, but inside he is not so certain.

As it happens, Jake only lives a few streets away, with his girlfriend, and he finds the place straight away. It's an unimpressive nineteen-sixties terrace, and they're in a small flat at the top of a steep flight, with a narrow corridor, one room at the front, a bedroom at the back and a kitchen area in the middle. Everything the neighbours do and say, the TVs mumbling on both sides, can be easily heard.

'Jake, I'm Jarvis, friend of Joe. I gather you were with him last night when he met some blokes - and went off with them?' They're standing just inside the open front door, Jake in a white singleton vest and a half-naked baby on his hip. He's holding a feeding bottle in his free hand and looking a bit bleary-eyed.

'Yeah. Alright? Anything wrong?' He's a Scot, Jarvis notes.

'Well, we haven't seen him since. I need to talk to him. Any idea where he might be?'

'No, he not at home with his mum?'

'No, Jake. I've just been there. Describe these two men to me.'

'Well, big guys, broad, in heavy overcoats, I mean it was a bit chilly, November. American accents, I think. They drove a Chevrolet truck thing, you know, the MPV.'

Jarvis concentrates. 'With sliding back doors?'

'Yeah, that's the one, shiny big bugger, with blackened windows all round, couldn't see a thing inside.' Jake gets quite animated for a second. 'Come in, won't ya?'

Jarvis doesn't really want to, wants Jake to take him to where they had last seen Joe down by a river, Doris mentioned. 'Joe wanted to go there to meet them, did he? I mean he had been called, had he, what, on his phone?'

'No, we were under the Arches, retail park, we often loaf around there under the trees, along the canal, a bit of a social, you know,' and Jake winks at Jarvis, as if it's all a bit of innocent fun. 'This black car stopped in the car park, and a big bloke got out and called over to Joe, he knew his name. Called him Private Street. Joe seemed to recognise him, I think. He walked over, spoke for a bit, they shook hands, and then called out to me that it was fine, I should go home, he had to go with the two guys. He stepped inside the back of the car; the doors closed. I went home on my own.'

Jarvis listens with interest but has no clue as to where he might start to look. 'Did they force him, threaten him?

'Didn't see really, it was quite dark, but they kinda stood over him, muscled him inside, yeah.'

'Don't suppose you remember the number plate?'

'No, mate, no chance; I was seeing double by then as it was. The Hornets lost, badly you know, and we downed a few, I was a bit wobbly.' He mimes his disappointment as a waif of a girl with acne appears beside him, in a tee-shirt and jeans, and takes the baby off him. 'Come in for tea, if yer like?' she calls.'

'No, thanks, need to get going.'

'No point going down there now, you won't see anything,' Jake says.

'You've been helpful. Give me a call if you hear of anything or see Joe. Tell him to ring me, Jarvis Collingwood.' He scribbles his name and number down and gives Jake his bit of paper.

It was barely a sound at all. But, like a dog with twitching ears, Jarvis was attuned to pick up such sensations. And a week hiding in the open scrub overlooking the western edge of the city meant they were both familiar with their surroundings. A slight snapping of a footfall on the twiggy ground nearby. He listened, holding his breath. He reached out soundlessly in the darkness to touch Joe's knee. A long pause, over half a minute. Another snap, as someone or something stepped closer.

Joe was gently stirring his army gruel with a wooden spatula making a slight scraping sound on the inside of the pan. He was hungry, anticipating his austere repast after another day of routine boredom in the debilitating heat. Now that the night had settled all around them, they could relax a bit, spread out a little, enjoy the cooler air clearing the sweat from their bodies. They had dug themselves into a little culvert on a rising patch of sandy scrubland below two twisted palms, which offered some natural protection from the midday sun. It was not an area that attracted anybody, far from the main road. Sometimes kids took a short-cut through the thinner scrub running from their schools across to the slum of breeze block housing that sprawled over the far brow; men on their way home during twilight hours would often take a leak or dump among the bushes by the road, but Joe and Jarvis, lying concealed all day in their camouflage ghillie suits, hot and uncomfortable, were safely positioned well back on the edge of the thicker scrub. Jarvis said they were more at risk from the wolves and hyenas that would be scrounging around at night, than from the locals.

Joe was leaning on one elbow, his head and shoulders risen above the ground. Now he too held still, stopped moving and listened without breathing. Orchestras of cicadas had started their nightly ritual and a few stars had appeared to twinkle. No one had ever come this way before; and not at this time of night.

The ground was soft and sandy underneath them, but the surface was covered with wooded debris of fallen branches, bark and fronds. There was no street lighting anywhere. The city lay ahead and below them on the dry slopes to the west of the Euphrates, and only a few lights were visible, concentrated mostly around the market square downtown. A few flickering candles and burning torches were scattered about the surrounding neighbourhood.

Another twig snapped, another step closer. They both heard it. Twenty paces away, behind them. Joe cocked his head to one side, looked around like a trembling mouse poking his snout out of his hiding hole. But he saw only the darkness that enveloped them and the outlines of the statuesque date palm trunks that were dotted about. He placed his pan silently to one side and lowered himself face downwards until he could smell the coolness of the sandy earth beneath. His netting camouflage covered him like a shroud. Jarvis was already flat and motionless but lifted his head just enough to give him some space for watching and listening. If someone were stalking them, his guess was they did not know exactly where to look or they would have challenged them by now. Perhaps it was a wild fox or a cayote that had picked up their human smell; or a dumb goat lost from its flock. If they kept absolutely still, Jarvis and Joe, they would probably not be discovered at all and their predator would give up and move on. Whatever, whoever it was.

Jarvis picked up a movement through the semi-obscurity of the layers of his disguise: over to his right, only ten paces, a figure in white behind a trunk. He held his nerve, his eyes darting between different shadows. Joe was quite still and all he could hear was his own heartbeat. The figure moved again, its head covered by a dark shawl but then as it turned towards them a drop of freak light, moonlight perhaps, caught its features: a young woman, he thought. She must have been watching them. She must have spotted them before, gained enough reassurance to approach them. She looked friendly, curious. She must know they were British, as she would not risk bumping into US marines or suffering the trouble she would be in if they were insurgents. The al-Qaeda were notorious for their viciousness towards anybody local meddling or just being in the wrong place.

He reached slowly for his Glock, in its holster beside him and brought it up beside his face, the coolness of the metal reassuring on his cheek. All the while watching the girl. She moved, more firmly this time, still approaching. She was carrying something in both hands. She called softly: 'Hey, you, British soldiers? I know you there.' Her voice was small and whispering.

Jarvis waited a little longer. He remained cautious. Could she be a foil, a trap for them to reveal themselves? She knelt to place two ceramic bowls on the ground. 'I know you hungry. I hear you, scraping, mixing food. Scraping, scraping. Here is hot food for you, from my house.' Joe could not believe their luck, a hot meal dropped in from Heaven after endless days on dried biscuits and cold oatmeal.

She did look straight towards them. She seemed to know where they were and Joe felt she was looking directly at him, although convinced she could not actually see him. She smiled. 'I know you there. I am alone, there is no one else. You are safe. Here,' and she pushed the bowls forward across the sandy ground. 'My grandmother make this. Is good. Is spiced baba ganoush and kubba haleb with basmati rice and flat bread.'

Joe had no idea what she was offering but it sounded good and he was starting to pick up the warm aromas. Jarvis knew that Joe's mouth would be watering, and he could discern his partner fidgeting in the undergrowth. The girl was alone, he was sure of that. They broke cover slowly together, emerging like the dead from their graves. The girl looked startled and wobbled backwards on her haunches and laughed. 'Ya alhi. You like monsters.'

'Nice monsters, I hope.' Joe fumbled for a small torch and shone it carefully behind the palm of his hand onto the food bowls. 'Gosh, look at this, Jarvis. Grub, real grub.' He dropped the small torch onto some grass, giving them enough light to see by. Jarvis returned his pistol to its holster. Using his fingers, Joe started nibbling at the hot meat, tentatively at first, not sure of the spicy tastes. He sat awkwardly on the ground, holding his bowl up close so that he could scoop more directly into his mouth. The girl explained that it was minced lamb with aubergines in yoghurt and lemon.

'Thank you,' Jarvis said. He picked up the other bowl, taking the piece of warm bread from the side which he used as a shovel to stuff the food into his mouth, while still watching the girl. 'Tastes good. Good.'

'First time in weeks we've had proper food,' Joe mumbled with his mouth full.

The girl shrugged her shoulders and tossed her shawl off her head. She looked young, pretty too, even in the poor lighting. With their ghillie suits draped over them with twigs and leaves sticking out at all angles, they must have looked a strange sight to an Iraqi girl. They smelt ripe, too.

'What's your name?' Joe asked almost in a whisper, between swallowing mouthfuls of warm lamb. 'This is delicious, by the way.'

'Jahinda.'

As the only excitement of the day had been watching an American troop carrier drone across the sky, flying directly over them on its way south to their Al Assad airfield, the chance to talk to a local girl was awesome.

'And where do you live?' Jarvis this time, looking around furtively, not entirely relaxed.

She turned and pointed through the trees in the almost complete darkness across wasteland to a row of concrete block buildings that they knew squatted along a ridge of land towards Route West, even though they could not actually see them at that moment.

'The end house there, with garage.' She continued to point. 'You see those lights, that's our yard. They working in garage, you see entrance there.'

They looked vaguely in the direction her arm was pointing and nodded. 'Yeah. With your mum and dad?'

'My father and grandmother. My mother died in childbirth.'

'Oh, sorry. Is your father cool about you talking to soldiers?'

She shook her head. 'He not know, I think. But he likes British; says they will restore everything to order again, like it used to be.'

After a slight pause, during which all Jarvis could hear was the sound of Joe munching happily, he said: 'We hope so, Jahinda, we hope so.'

Jahinda had been watching them apparently for a few nights before she approached them. She heard their voices, knew they were British. Her father told her the British were there to help, so she should not worry and not disturb them. Meeting with her over the next few nights was something of a treat that both soldiers looked forward to, although Jarvis instinctively worried about potential danger. If she had found them that easily, what of some vicious insurgent, native of the area, or just a suspicious neighbour picking up her leaving her house after dark regularly, something a woman would never be permitted to do. Suppose she was followed, with unthinkable consequences: within a trice, a band of merciless friends would be gathered, and they would not be asking questions. Jarvis began to feel the urge to move, to vary their position, to ring the changes and reduce the risks of falling into a predictable pattern.

Jahinda would wait until late, well into the night and wore black at Jarvis's request, her head and face covered. They never saw her coming, so furtive, so petite. She always brought hot food that her grandmother made. They would relax in the darkness, eat gratefully and whisper about Haditha life, the cruelty of al-Qaeda and the desperate lack of water in the city, leaving crops ruined and livestock dying from dehydration.

'We wait for November rains to begin, but no signs yet.'

'Your English is good, Jahinda,' Joe said, 'where did you learn?'

'At school, of course.'

'Are you still at school?'

'No, not now.'

'How old are you, if you don't mind me asking?' Jarvis asked.

'Sixteen.'

'You sure your father is happy with you being here?'

Jahinda repeated that he was alright with it. 'He suggested you come to the house, meet him, one evening.'

'Maybe I'll take a look,' Jarvis told Joe later. 'The advantages of the roof position might be good.'

A new routine developed after a few of her visits: once they had eaten and sat chatting in the complete darkness for an hour or so, Joe would walk back with Jahinda, up to the edge of the natural cover of bushes and thick undergrowth. She would pull her hijab tightly around her head and neck, ruffle up some more scarf over her face, and they would creep away through the harsh scrub. Jarvis would watch them for as long as he could still see them, which was never for long, and noticed the easy casual friendship that was developing. They had begun to lean into each other, knocking shoulders and hips as they walked. He was waiting for the hand holding, God forbid.

After a few such visits, Joe said they should go back to her house to meet her father, who was keen to help apparently. Jarvis worried they were being lured into a trap but still made the trip, alone in the dark one evening, leaving Joe in charge. He returned an hour later saying that Rahim, Jahinda's father, seemed a genuine sort of chap and his rooftop position over his garage offered some advantages, safer, more protection and a better direct view along Chestnut towards the city or the other way across towards the western approach road.

That was how they came to change their lair, clearing up all traces of their existence from the scrubland area and spending their time confined to a flat concrete roof, fully exposed unfortunately to the boiling heat of the day and the frequent freezing drop in overnight temperatures.

Their new sniper position was protected on all sides, three of them behind a waist-high parapet wall of breeze block topped with a few levels of brick. It was attached to Rahim's narrow two-storey house and there was a concrete set of steps running up from inside the garage to a landing and a wooden door. Every day was washing day, and Mahdiya, the grandmother, was forever *hanging out sheets and robes on lines to dry. Rahim erected a simple covering with a coloured sheet and a few wooden stakes used for clothes lines, so that they had some shielding from the sun. He found an old metal-framed bed with a couple of thin straw mattresses, which were lumpy hard and smelt of cat's wee, but did the job. He also fixed up some hessian sheets to hang inside the parapet on each side which would interrupt anyone's casual view from outside looking up through the gaps in the brickwork. So long as they kept themselves low and quiet, no one would suspect.*

Rahim seemed an easy-going sort of a bloke and Jarvis rather liked him. On the first evening they passed the time sitting on the oily floor of his garage, sipping black tea and moaning about the rotten ways of the world and life in Haditha. Jarvis explained why they had to be there. 'The US have to protect the Dam and the hundreds of workers up there. The insurgents want to destroy it and flood the whole Euphrates valley, which would threaten Baghdad. It would cause massive disaster, villages swept away, lots of people dead.'

Rahim seemed to accept the presence of the soldiers from the West, understood the need. 'They keep the insurgents down, at least for a bit. I support the coalition forces, the US and the British working with the Iraqis, they here to protect us. Those bastards in Sunny al-Qaeda and all the other insurgents, they just want to cause chaos, so they can grab anything they can, some land, some oil, some weapons, whatever. They want to destroy everything in this country so no one else can have it.'

Jahinda had to share a room with her grandmother. A rotund short lady, always dressed in black, who pulled her head covering over her whenever anyone came around, she did all the cooking and never spoke a word of English. Her wrinkled face, with sparse dark hairs sprouting over the outer parts of her upper lip, invariably broke into beams of pleasure when she saw the two British boys eating her food; and they always smiled back to ensure they got second helpings.

Now whenever Jarvis thinks of Joe, all he sees is the anguish on his young face, his screaming as he grabbed his upper arm in shock, trying to stem the bleeding with his bare hand, and Jarvis bending over him still holding the sharp knife. He had to smack him to shut him up, before tying a dirty strip of tee shirt cotton under his armpit. Blood soaked all down Joe's sleeve, spattered across his face. He looked suitably battered as a wounded soldier, enough to convince the bosses. But his palpable expression of confused revulsion has stayed with Jarvis ever since, even as he tries to recall a happy Joe, a smiling Joe, a couple of army mates going through some good times together. But the only Joe he sees is Joe with a sneer of venomous hatred.

By the time he returns to Hoxton and parks his car in Wilton Square, he has gone over the scenario countless times and still does not understand it. Why would Joe get into the black MPV with three suspicious-looking American strangers? What had lured him in? And how did the Americans know where Joe lived? Thinking about it, Joe was for ever chatting to the US soldiers over there, sharing stories and stuff about his home life: they thought he was cute. He was friendly, offering any time, if any of them were around good old England, give him a call, pop in: that was Joe. The chances are he had distributed his address to all and sundry. Not Jarvis, he would never have shared anything personal with any of them.

He reaches his home again via the back route to be safe, slips into the kitchen with his key and finds Pamela in full cooking mode, lovely smells of onion and sage gravy filling the house.

Debriefing interview, MoD, Aldwych.
December 12, 2005.

'So, you moved your camouflage site from the scrub on the ridge to a nearby garage roof, befriending a local Iraqi? Malone adopts a look of bewilderment, as if Jarvis had taken leave of his senses. 'Were those actions within your remit, Corporal?'

'There were a number of advantages from our new position. We were higher up, giving ourselves a better view through the

Subhami neighbourhood. Plus we had views both ways, to the east and to the western approach road, where the US often had a roadblock. The view from the scrub was not so good, so I thought the move was justified. We made friends of a local garage man and his daughter - they gave us an insight into the neighbourhood, the behaviour of local groups, the movements and activities, likely targets of insurgents. All invaluable local info. I thought the move was justified on those grounds.'

'How did you meet him?'

'Through his daughter. She had been watching us and approached with food from her grandmother. I recced the house: thought the roof of the garage would be suitable.'

'And this garage man, Rahim. How did you know if he was secure? Could you trust him or was he just another of those oily Arabs on the make?'

'Rahim was a solid supporter of the coalition and hated the insurgents and al-Qaeda. He was totally loyal and became someone I trusted. He saved us from the marines when they came searching. In fact, he took a hit through defending us. I remain deeply grateful for his help. We owe our lives to him.'

'You could easily have been caught out.' Malone mutters, unimpressed. 'You were lucky they were not part of a clever trap, using food as an enticement.'

Chapter 4
Monday November 9

No sign of a black Ford this morning, on the crescent. Maybe Jarvis imagined it, seeing potential trouble everywhere he looks. Watchful, as ever, he sets out on foot to Old Street and via DLR to Silvertown, his destination, to secure safe passage for the workers of Tate & Lyle, which is where his thoughts are now focusing, putting aside Joe's disappearance for a while.

As he approaches the refinery site, he can see immediately that the size of the problem has increased. There are many more people crowding about, in groups around all three entrances of the site along Factory Road. The works seem to be ploughing on as usual, steam pouring out of one of the main cooling towers, streams of white smoke puffing from the chimneys, squirting like jets out of some of the pipes. There's a background humming of machinery and the revving of transport engines as usual. A couple of minibuses are parked up the road. Outside the near car park, there's a white Bedford van, its sliding door wide open, a chunky aerial dish on its roof and ITN in large orange letters painted on its side. The crew are chatting as they check equipment, blow warm breath into their hands and pull their coats and scarves tightly round themselves, sipping at mugs of steaming coffee. Settling in for a long day, by the look of it.

The atmosphere last week was friendly and all fairly tame, just a few rude words shouted out, with vague threats in the air. There are a lot more demonstrators now waving placards demanding fair treatment, pay rises, worker solidarity, the usual. Some are printed quite professionally, others scrawled childishly in paint on home-made boards.

Several of the old hands have white arm bands with 'Official Picket' on. The protest seems rowdier, a few persistent rebels dotted among the crowd to incite more fervour, inject more aggression into the proceedings; who raise their fists and raise the volume of the protest, shouting the loudest, often obscenities, especially at the managers in their smart cars.

A few blows have already been struck, vitriolic words and rotten fruit in anger hurled, a few raw eggs, too. Jarvis can see that if the numbers increased any more, or the level of anger swelled and the strikers became a bit better organised, trouble could easily escalate out of hand, especially if they coordinated their action at all three of the entrances at the same time.

The security team, mostly ex-police or ex-army themselves, are all effective in their use of brute strength, when needed. Each time a lorry arrives to deliver onto the site, or a distribution lorry wants to leave, and the gates are opened, there is uproar and a lot of shouting and shoving as the protestors surge forward. The security line shoves a wedge between the crowd to push them to each side, creating a way through. Then the gates are closed as quickly as possible, which is not quick enough for Jarvis's liking, the ancient mechanisms too slow and clunky. But robust once closed tight.

Jarvis hates confrontation, the ugly shouting faces, the grotesque gestures and looks of hatred. Even if no blows are thrown, he still finds the whole thing of grown-ups behaving aggressively towards each other unattractive. He is on his feet all day, watching for trouble up and down the long road at different entrances. Several times, he is in the line pressing a crowd back, holding them steady as they want to surge towards a lorry driver, their abusive voices loud in his ears, their spittle felt over his face. He takes a blow or two across the back of the head. Having to be always alert, looking out for his colleagues, trying to keep in touch with the other teams on the site, it all adds to the strain, but he copes mostly in a calm fashion.

A group of half a dozen extra men in crisp new green jackets and caps turn up during the morning and are immediately deployed at the different areas, which help even out the level of control. Around midday, a couple of police vans arrive with all the trimmings, the overhead strip flasher lights, the blue and yellow reflectors, the metal crowd guards across the front, the shrill voice-overs on their radios. A mixed bunch of officers, in their usual dark uniforms or yellow combat jackets, pour out with juvenile enthusiasm. A few bikers join them, in leathers, crash helmets and goggles. They huddle near the television van, where the crew seems happy to loll about, some playing cards inside or whatever they do when bored. Not much different really from controlling a crowd of football supporters.

Late in the afternoon, the demo boys have mostly stepped back over the far side of the road, to reconsider their tactics, the placards put to one side, the thermos flasks now empty. The low western light that has been bouncing off the turbulent waters of the Thames, is cautiously beginning to fade. It's been an arduous day, but everything has quietened down, both sides remaining about even in strength of numbers and determination, a day when the status quo was maintained. By the time Jarvis slopes off a little after the staff rush for the exit, he is feeling drained. He sets off on foot at least unscathed. Tomorrow will be another day of huffing and puffing, with the hope of more reinforcements.

Had he been going home to Hoxton, he would be getting off at Bank and tubing it to Old Street, walking the rest of the way. But with his thoughts drifting back to a potential American menace, as he sees it, he heads for a workout at Sid's place, so changes at Shadwell for Whitechapel. Hoping for some time to himself, to weigh up his situation and Joe's, while going through his usual fitness regime. Joe not available on the phone, not turning up at home, not turning up at the Ceremony yesterday, disappearing seemingly after meeting with some big lads from the US. Odd, hardly coincidental.

Although not often seen there these days, Jarvis remains a popular figure at Sid's gym and Christoph The Greek welcomes him as usual with a tight hug. Jarvis's father had been close mates with the larger than life, Sidney Price. For a while the two of them had worked together, collaborated was the way Sid put it. Which explained Sid's continuing interest in Jarvis's wellbeing. Although Jarvis's mother had always been convinced that he was up to no good and disapproved of her Derrick associating with a crook. Jarvis remembers Sid at his father's funeral trying to embrace Gwendoline: he had eased his overlarge figure close to her, stretching a pudgy arm around her whilst she closed her eyes and braced herself with a grimace, her face turned away from his wobbly cheek in abhorrence. No love lost there.

Christoph also has a soft spot for Jarvis, the hero figure fighting for queen and country, whom everyone respects. He has watched Jarvis over the years take on most people in the boxing ring, giving them a good testing, a pasting if they were not careful. Jarvis's tall and solid frame was always hard to knock off course and that long reach of his, the constant jab from the left with a characteristic sharp and straight right, invariably surprised even the best.

Christoph, his mouth working his chewing gum with noisy relish, smiles hugely and lifts his arms up. 'Come, come to me, man. Long time. Where you been?' He squeezes Jarvis, crushing the breath out of him. He has a mop of floppy dark hair and a grisly beard turning grey. He is like a great bear with a shaggy coat of curly black hairs over his torso, front and back, and not even Jarvis is able to wrap his arms around his bulk. He wears a stinking tee shirt with *Sid's Hut* emblazoned across the front. He's a lovable rogue with stinging body odour and Jarvis respects the man, who has so often in the past looked out for him.

'Some people been asking for you, Jar. Couple of Americans, judging by the accents.' Giving nothing away, Jarvis's heart sinks, but he's alert. 'They try all casual but is acting, they a bit tense. Didn't say who they were, asking about you, where you lived, how often you come in here. I not trust them. Said I hadn't seen you for ages, that you lived out East somewhere, Romford or somethink.'

'Good man, Chris. When was this?'

'Yesterday, my friend, Sunday morning, like; I was here. And now you show.' He chuckles.

'How much do they know, you reckon, or was it just fishing?'

'They wanted to see register, names of members. I say that none of their business. I say you not a member, you come and go whenever.' Christoph suddenly stops his crazy chewing and fixes Jarvis with a serious worried look. His thick eyebrows bump together. 'Who are they, Jar, you in trouble?'

'No, nothing I can't handle, but keep an eye out for me, will you?'

In the changing rooms Jarvis strips off into vest and silky shorts. His routine in the stuffy gym takes him from skipping exercises, through hanging punch bag to the treadmill and after half an hour, he is sweating profusely. A couple of ex-army trainers are barking orders at the young kids pummelling, dancing, jumping or running round the periphery, mostly black guys with bulging pectorals and expectations, searching for their lucky break, convinced they have the raw talent. One of the supervisors nods to Jarvis and comes over wiping sweat from his face with a towel.

'Yo, Jarvis, how's tricks?'

'Good, thanks, Benny. Yourself?'

'Yeah, yeah. You're looking good, man. You out the army now, yeah?'

'Oh, yes. Working security for my brother, here and there.'

'Good, sounds good. I'm still trying to keep up with these young whipper-snappers, init?'

'You see these strangers Christoph talks about, in here yesterday morning, Danny, asking for me, Americans or something?'

'No, but I saw a new guy up with Sid, solid man built like a rugby player, crew cut, shaking hands together, clapping each other on the backs, I mean showing respect. Could be American, definitely.'

'They looked friendly, you mean?'

'They did.'

'Sid here today?'

'No, rang in first thing, busy he said.'

'Okay, thanks, Benny.'

Joe was awake, confused and sore, his expression caught between pugnacious resistance and childish submission. Jarvis sat with him, sharing some lukewarm stew that had been left outside their door. Since his injury Joe had not spoken to him, except to swear and scowl at him. They were expecting to move out later after midnight on a carrier flight, returning other wounded soldiers to the UK.

Jarvis was obviously sorry to have caused Joe such pain, but it was important to stick to the story and be consistent. Jarvis could be under grave suspicion of improper conduct and assault, if there were doubts, and they would certainly not be on their way out back to the UK. He had tried to convince Joe several times, but Joe remained unsure, determined not to believe him.

'How about the truth, Jarvis, that might have worked.'

'Not so sure, Joe.'

'I said it was suicide,' Joe moaned.

'Well, it looks as if we are going home, hopefully we'll get away with it.

And without the Yanks on our backs.' But Jarvis knew that that sentiment was probably wishful thinking. While Joe simply shut him out of his mind, tearing himself dreamily back to images of Jahinda's black hair and petite Arabic face, that he much preferred. His mind was wracked with how he could find some way to return to Haditha to see her, but he was overtaken with sadness, realising that the chances of their ever meeting again were remote.

During their time at the Army barracks in Basra, restricted to the medical quarters, virtual prisoners really, Jarvis found himself waking in the early hours, as first light eased serenely over the city and the first calls to prayer warbled in the distance. He had bunkered down out of sight in a storeroom at the end of a corridor in the hospital, a single-story hut. He spent the days alone, frustrated among crates and boxes of stores, bedding, uniforms and medical supplies. Food was brought by an orderly who spoke little. He had access to drinking water from an upturned plastic barrel in one corner. A feeble overhead fan noisily pushed the warm air around. Through the round glass window in his door, he could see the laundry opposite, that hummed away most of the time. He would occasionally see soldiers walk past: they paid him no attention at all, did not even glance his way. The door was locked from the outside, there were no outside windows.

In a single room next door, Joe slept heavily, recovering from his surgical wound stitch-up operation, his left arm bandaged. He lay on his back, snoring, all covers thrown off in the heat.

One evening Captain Mike Malone appeared unannounced. Surprised, Jarvis leapt to his feet, stood to attention, in his socks and baggy shorts, not wearing a top.

'You have no idea the headaches you have caused me, Collingwood.'

'Yes, sir.'

'At ease, Corporal.'

In ponderous mood, he weighed up the difficulties for Jarvis's benefit, being clear about the extent of the embarrassment he had caused the British command. Malone wanted to ensure that Jarvis understood how hard he was working on his behalf. He had a neutral sort of face, except when he was angry or anxious, when his pale brown eyes would shrivel up. He started to pace around the confined space, kicking the boxes, knocking into things. His hair was not its usual immaculate groom, but slightly uncombed. His shirt open, no sweat marks under the arms, he folded his sleeves up to his elbows as he interrogated Jarvis further.

'And this man you said helped you, was he a witness as well? Will he come forward, vouch for you?'

'No.' Jarvis hesitated: 'He won't want to be involved.'

'Reliable, or another sneaky grass, working for the other side?'

'He was our saviour, a good man.'

The Captain returned after another day in a more friendly mood. Secretive but triumphant, pleased to show Jarvis what an influence he was, but probably relieved to be soon seeing the back of them. 'Success. I have got the two of you on a flight home. Tomorrow, in the early hours. Shawcross has given the say-so. Brize Norton, you will report to Major Philip Robertson. And then a full debrief with your battalion commander, Colchester.'

Jarvis was elated, smelling victory at last, sensing a safe passage out of their predicament. He could look forward to getting home. He knew Malone had worked hard for them.

'We need to keep this absolutely quiet, deny all knowledge; assume Uncle Sam doesn't want to pursue it. Officially the reports all say that Kilo Company were attacked by insurgents, they returned fire, engaged with the enemy and the dead Iraqis were the result. But some photographs have appeared, from a Newsreel reporter taken on site after the shooting apparently showing the extent of the injuries. As you described, Collingwood. The US Army will want to keep this quiet. Jim Mattis was defiant. They will be embarrassed enough, they won't want to expose any more damaging stories.'

Before Malone left, he offered Jarvis his handshake, in a paternal sort of way. 'Well done, Collingwood. Good luck. And give my best wishes to that young soldier, Street.' He clipped his heels together and swivelled. At the door, he had another thought: 'If the true evidence officially gets out, if the story goes wider, the US will have to hold an inquiry, the pressure would be too great. What happens in that circumstance? Well, I don't think any of us can predict.'

Outside there's drizzle and gloom. In the lobby of the gym, Jarvis tries to get through to Pamela. His unshaven chin is rough to his fingers. He's pacing the enclosed area, worrying that the Americans will have his home address, just like the officials. And they might be watching it now, like from that unfamiliar black Ford parked in the crescent. He must get Pamela to leave, go to her mother's house, not to run the risk of being threatened or hurt.

He tries again to get through, leaves another message for her. As he sets off across Whitechapel and heads up Brick Lane, he is thinking how he might cope with a concerted attack by at least two, maybe three, beefy marine-trained thugs, probably with weapons. They will want to take him out cleanly, no fight, no mess, quick kill and dispose, no witnesses - so they can depart London unnoticed; there'd be no immunity here for them, not on this mission. Entice him to a remote spot, perhaps, done quietly. No blunderbuss at his home. No explosion under the car, letter bomb through the door. What about a stabbing by umbrella tip in the rush hour, radiation poison in the sugar? How about a garrotting in a backstreet, something soundless, that leaves no traces?

Don't make it easy for them, stay out in the open, with people around all the time. It would probably be at night, under cover of darkness. They would want darkness and quiet.

He needs to move out of the house. Thinking about his brother's place, although he wouldn't want to bring any danger to Jon and Brenda. He might turn to some of his workmates, they're a tough crowd, they could be his protection. Maybe his army mates would be better, they would understand the situation. Skilled in self-defence, able to make a quick kill themselves. This is all about the Haditha massacre. And the shooting of Wosniak. Joe said it would be suicide. Someone must have turned, giving evidence under a plea bargain and the remnants of Kilo Company want to make sure there are no witnesses to their atrocity turning up in Washington to tell their side of the story. And they want revenge, all neatly rolled into one.

He knows they have come for him. He had always understood it was a probability, just a matter of time.

He's thinking of Joe as well. He keeps glancing over his shoulder, watching everyone on the street, looking into the shadows in doorways, up at first floor windows, down alleyways. He walks swiftly, taking a zigzag almost random route, twisting and dodging between pedestrians. A ringing tone comes through, and Pamela answers, sounding distant and preoccupied. 'Hi, I'm home a bit earlier, making supper, burgers and chips. Don't be late.'

He must keep his paranoid feelings out of his voice. 'Pam, listen to me, will you. Just listen.' He steps into a doorway, his palm covering the mouthpiece. 'I'm not certain, but I think they've come for me. The subpoena is for me to be a witness to their acts of atrocity, official like. I think some guys have been sent over here to make sure I never get to testify. Don't ask me how I know, I have an instinct. And I'm worried that they may … get to me through you, Pam. They may know our address, I don't know. I want you to leave tonight, just in case. Go to your mother's, for now. It won't be for long.'

'What the hell are you blithering on about?'

There was an eerie pause, as they seem to lose connection.

'Jarvis, Jarvis, what is this?' Pamela sounds annoyed.

'You need to get out of the house, Pam, tonight. Serious. Don't answer the front door, make sure it's properly locked. Don't answer the phone, unless you know who it is. And ring your mother, now.'

'Jarvis, stop it. This is ridiculous, we're in London, for Christ's sake.'

'Pamela, I don't care. Do this, for me, trust me. I wouldn't want anything, you know, … I want you to leave tonight. I'm on my way home, walking, it's quicker, I'll be fifteen minutes.'

'And what about you? Are you in danger?'

'I'm going to keep watch, from outside, lie low. Call a cab to the front door, Pam, get straight in with an overnight bag, okay. I'll get in the house round the back. Do it now, please, Pam.'

When he is satisfied that he has got his message through to her, when she mutters a bleak alright, Jar, you take care, only then does he ring off and resume his trek at a fast clip.

Taking no risks with watchers in parked cars, Jarvis follows his back-route approach, over the neighbours' walls and through their gardens into his own yard, unseen. He has a nodding acquaintance with most of the residents down this part of the crescent: most of them are older, slower and seem unaware of his skipping through their unused yards - none of them have children and they never seem to be outside. No one has ever said anything.

There is a light on in the kitchen, shining bleakly through its glass panelled door, and he lets himself in with his key. In the narrow hallway by the bottom of the stairs is a black zip-up bag with shoulder handles, and a supermarket plastic bag with stuff in. Pamela has obviously taken his words seriously and prepared herself. He calls out gently. She's upstairs, finishing her make-up. She appears in trousers, ankle boots and a three-quarter length belted suede coat. She hurries down and falls into his arms. They cling to each other. 'You scared me, Jarvis. Why can't we stay together?'

'Too dangerous.' Looking at the bags, 'Good, Pam. That's good. Does your mother know?'

'Yes. The taxi's coming, be here in ten minutes.'

'Good,' he keeps repeating. They hug and kiss each other. She moans as he holds her tight for a second more. 'I'll be alright, I'm going to try Sam's place, over the road, watch this house from one of his upstairs rooms.'

'That weirdo.'

'He's okay, pretty harmless. He'll appreciate the excitement, the cloak and dagger.'

'Not so sure his wife will.'

'No, we'll see. What's her name?'

'Elfie? Delphie?'

'Debbie? Whatever. I'll be able to watch the front for a couple of days - I'm sure they'll show themselves.'

'What, US agents? What makes you think?'

'I told you. Joe Street has disappeared, I saw his mum. Apparently, a couple of Americans came looking for him near his home, took him away. And a couple of beefy guys were asking about me at the club, yesterday. Looked like ex-marines.'

'Oh, God. They must know where we live. The letter came here, the subpoena, they must know.'

'That came from official sources, the NCIS. These guys will be working a different agenda, below the radar, they won't have access to NCIS information - unless they have someone on the inside. These guys will be unofficial.'

'Seeking revenge or something?' Pamela looked angry, her brows knitted, her mouth pinched. 'I don't understand. Just to stop you talking?'

'Yeah, kind of. But I don't think they know the address. Joe didn't know where I lived. Unless Sid Price has given it to them.'

He's planning to go see Sid as soon as he can. Priorities first.

They wait in the darkness of their front lounge, sullen, not speaking. 'Supper's ruined,' Pamela moans flatly.

'There is something else, something that explains the marines' presence, their chasing me.' He gives her a thin almost apologetic smile.

Pamela turns to face him and Jarvis places a large hand on hers, folded in her lap. 'Oh, like what?'

'I told you about Bob Wosniak, leading the manic slaughter of all those civilians, after the roadside IED?' She nods slowly. 'There was only one way I could stop him going on with his slaughter, causing even more havoc, committing even more crimes.'

Jarvis lifts his head and for the first time for a long time, he engages directly with Pamela's warm eyes, her huge pupils, as if this is the most important moment in their lives together. 'I had him in my sights, it was the obvious thing to do. It was the only thing I could do.'

Pamela's eyes widen a fraction, her mouth opens. Suddenly, as she sees it all, she feels the colour draining from her cheeks. 'Oh God. You shot him.'

A statement. She knows it's true.

Jarvis nervously flexed his fingers, tapping on the barrel, tracing the outline of the trigger guard. From the floor, he reached for a magazine, the size of a cigarette packet, and automatically inserted it into the underside of the stock, clicking it home. He nestled the butt into his right shoulder, steadied himself, widened his legs a touch, moved his elbows on their thick rubber pads to ensure his stance and balance was right. He squinted firmly along the sights.

He could not take much more. His agitation was apparent. He and Joe were witnessing the slaughter of the innocent. It was more than uncomfortable, it was criminal, cruel and unnecessary. These inhabitants were of no threat, unarmed, women and children mostly. An elderly man who could hardly walk was slaughtered at his front door as more marines came to knock it down. They threw grenades inside, turning themselves away to avoid the shock before rushing in, all guns blazing. Jarvis was desperate to stop it. He had no means of contact directly with the troopers down on Chestnut, although he could ring through to Mike Malone, his commanding officer at US base camp. Captain Malone could communicate with his equivalent command on the US side, but would they get through to Wosniak and order him to stop? Would Malone carry any clout? And how long would that take? The US would not want to take it from a British officer and would dispatch observers to the scene for first-hand reporting before they did anything. By then Wosniak would have ceaselessly continued to wreak more havoc - he looked as if he wanted to challenge the whole of the Iraqi enemy on his own.

He was not facing the enemy of course, but the poor innocent civilians who happened to be living there, the only easy victims Wosniak could get to.

It did not take Jarvis more than a moment to realise that he could do only one thing. He needed to take the sergeant out of the equation.

The only way to stop the crazy Bob Wosniak from running further amok among these innocent people was to snipe him out.

From the moment they first met, Jarvis knew they were not going to get on. The British soldiers arrived at an obviously inconvenient moment in the daily routine of the maverick marines who ran the Haditha base as they wished. In the yard at the back of the mess, Sergeant Robert Wosniak was pretending to be some kind of Roman Emperor, in toga and bare chest, holding a long spear, while his acolytes raced around on two-wheeled trolleys pulled along by men in flimsy loin cloths and bare feet, with ropes lashed around their upper bodies. The racers were screaming at their 'ponies' to run faster, pull harder and they had thin bamboo whips to use across their bare backs to persuade them. The course was a narrow oval run in dirt around a kerbed flowerbed at each turn. Around the outside were loads of marines in tee shirts and shorts, shouting and cheering, while one large bloke in a cowboy hat on the far side was taking bets, chalking up odds on a blackboard. The finish was close between two tough looking marines who both managed to stand upright in their 'chariots' and keep their balance; they appeared to cross the line together. Wosniak held his spear aloft and declared one of them the winner, much to the derision of the other's supporters.

Jarvis, wearing his regimental maroon beret and silver wings, stood unaffected by all the noisy jeering and ribald language, much disturbed by the obvious suffering of the poor 'ponies', who were clearly not American marines, but looked like Iraqis, prisoners presumably. They lay sweating and too exhausted to worry about their exposure around the grassy periphery, their feet sore, their backs marked with red weals, their chests heaving to catch their breaths. A private whispered into Wosniak's ear and he sauntered over toward the British contingent, hauling his toga over a shoulder. There was a glazed look in his eye and Jarvis considered whether he was on something. The sergeant was perfectly briefed about their arrival: the Brits were expected to fit into the routine with the marines, to work within a new cooperative exercise to help with policing the dangerous streets of Haditha, tracking insurgents, finding their bomb-making factories, generally providing protection and keeping the peace.

'Corporal Collingwood: First Battalion Special Forces Support Group, Parachute Regiment,' Jarvis called out when it was his turn.

Wosniak did not look as grateful or welcoming as Jarvis would have expected and his voice was mocking. After the last of the introductions, he paced ponderously along the line of smart-looking British soldiers. 'From Little England, they send us Specials, so very educated; posh boys, yo?' he smirked. At the end of the line he stopped and whipped around. 'Well, I'm Sergeant Robert Wosniak and we are Kilo Company,' he called out and his fellow men all repeated loudly "Kilo Company" after him. Wosniak continued, '3rd Battalion and we are the best in the US fucking Army. The best,' he roared. There were more whoops and cheering and some serious fist pumping. 'Yeah. Just so's you know, this is a US base, run by the US. You are here at our convenience. What we say goes. Geddit?'

Wosniak looked pleased with himself, a supercilious smile across his stern face. He wore a silly black pencil moustache, split in the middle and the two pieces wriggled with the curve of his upper lip, like two worms facing each other. He had crooked front teeth. His supporters with angry looks and arms crossed, circled Jarvis and his companions, staring at them aggressively. Jarvis could not understand the hostility. He had heard stories of their recent battles in Fallujah, where the vicious fighting had been relentless, although the insurgents had definitely come off worse, with extensive loss of lives and countless injuries. The marines' fighting under Colonel Jim Mattis had been unforgiving, merciless, and Jarvis could detect their pride in that, but it cut no ice with him.

Later they eyed each other suspiciously from opposite sides of a canteen table over their evening meal, the two groups showing few signs of the mixing and cooperation that the top brass were hoping for. Jarvis was invited to join the officer marines for an evening of fun with some local lady entertainment and a good lay would be had by all, if they were lucky. And the drinks were on them.

Jarvis wiped clean the round glass eyepiece of his sights, where his eyebrow had smeared the surface with sweat. Through the swirling smoke, he was able to study Wosniak again, mentally giving him one last chance to change direction, to cease his senseless slaughter, or for one of the troopers under his command to see the awful wrong and to intervene. But the other marines were shouting as well and seemed to have jumped aboard this mad mayhem with abandon. Wosniak, magnified hugely in his sights, was still rampaging, gesticulating and rasping out orders. Jarvis detected an intensity about his black eyes, a determination in his square jaw and cruel lips.

The marine sergeant was at his mercy, if he only knew it. Snipe him. Consequences: the other marines would think they were under fire, would stop trashing the houses and would take cover; would realise that this was sniper fire from a distance, and presume not from an insurgent, as their equipment and skills were not up to that. They would soon calculate direction and identify the sniper position. Likely they would be aware who manned that position, since the sniper teams were collaborators, well-known to the marines; their positions around Haditha had originally been identified by US command for their key vantage points. It would place him and Joe on dangerous ground, like they had grabbed a tiger by its tail.

The angry and vengeful marines would come looking, while reinforcements would be on their way. Joe and Jarvis could stay put and remain out of sight in the hope they would not be found. But the marines would conduct a wide search, and they would surely be discovered. That would place Rahim and his family who had helped them in grave danger too, either beaten up by the US if they didn't tell them where the British soldiers were hiding or later murdered by al-Qaeda thugs when they found out they had been assisting coalition forces.

They would have to leave immediately and escape Haditha. They would need to leave no traces. The problem that was worrying Jarvis the most was that there were no British Army bases within a hundred miles; their only route out was through their local US base. Rescue, indeed survival, would be hazardous and not at all easy.

Nevertheless, his decision was made. The stimulus dictated the response, without question. Jarvis was ready to carry it through. After all, he was but a loyal servant to the Army, ultimately a mere instrument, an allegiant of State. He turned to look Joe in the eye. 'I'm going to take that idiot out. We will have to exit pronto afterwards.'

Joe looked perplexed. 'Blimey, Jarvis, what?'

'What else can we do?' He was already preparing his shot, breathing carefully with rhythm, while keeping the sergeant in his sights.

'You can't. It's ... it's against the law. He's on our side.'

'He's a murdering criminal, he deserves it,' Jarvis muttered under his breath.

After a short pause, Joe was hit like a knock on the head, as he realised he would not be able to see Jahinda again. As he reached out, as if to touch his corporal, to achieve better understanding, a picture of the young Arab girl he had come to know dances before him. He thought about dashing downstairs to find her next door. But he withdrew his hand as he sensed the other man's resolve. 'It'll be suicide, that's what.' He got Jarvis's point of view and his assertiveness told him that his more senior and more experienced partner, his cool buddy, the best there was, had made up his mind. Not for a moment did he doubt Jarvis meant what he said; there was nothing Joe could say to alter that. 'Suppose so.'

Jarvis's intention was clear. Joe knew that his professional job was to watch and spot, and to support his partner as best he could.

He needed to do it. Jarvis needed to take Wosniak out with one shot, but he was wearing a ballistic vest and steel helmet. He did not want to merely wound him, which would have incensed him even more to act with anger and uncontrolled aggression. He set his sights, relaxing his grip. His hands needed to be just firm enough to ride together with the stock. It was all a matter of feel. He drew back the bolt and rammed home a Lapua Magnum 8.59 mm bullet. He picked the spot for his hit and increased magnification to twenty times, matching up the graticule. He repeated his breathing routine, letting the barrel settle in a slow downward movement until the spot was in the crosshairs on the sights. His Schmidt & Bender had never let him down. He gently compressed the trigger, with its two-stage action, to the first point. It was all in the feel, to reduce absolutely any chance of the minutest unwanted movement.

His pale eyes were dryly focused as he concentrated wholly on his target. There was a slight quickening of heart rate and nervous fluttering in his belly, but deep down he knew he was doing the right thing. His lashes stopped blinking. He was no longer aware of the hard pressure on his knees or the points of his elbows on the lumpen mattress. The sweat around his neck, under his arms and running over his spine, the flies buzzing around his face, the glancing heat of the sun across the back of his thighs, none of these things were any longer of any concern to him.

He narrowed both eyes. His decision was made, he had entered his own bubble, a mindset of ruthless concentration with only one goal in sight. He caressed the trigger lovingly with second pressure. His four-hundred-yard target range was straightforward. With his AI precision L118 firmly in his hands, held like it was part of him, he had exceptional accuracy up to about a thousand yards.

There was a thwack as the rifle juddered and puffs of smoke trickled from the barrel vents on both sides. He retracted the bolt and the empty cartridge flipped out, tinkling across the concrete floor. The next round was loaded as the bolt thrust home. Joe had put all thoughts of Jahinda to one side. He was watching in his binoculars and gave a quiet commentary: 'A hit to the thigh, he's down, crouching, looking for help. There's blood, he's hurt.' Joe paused, watching keenly. There was another juddering thwack. 'Second shot to right neck, direct hit, he's down, blood loss. He's struggling, kicking his legs. He's down.'

Joe paused again. 'He's stopped moving.'

A head shot would not have been certain, with a Kevlar steel helmet to penetrate, so Jarvis chose to immobilize Wosniak first, allowing him a surer second hit to the neck. He reduced magnification to watch the result through his sights for a few more seconds. The marines nearby saw their sergeant felled and stopped where they were, calling to the others to take cover, shouting aimlessly. They all scattered to be behind walls, around corners. A couple prostrated themselves near the body and readied their rifles for action pointing vaguely outwards. Then they scrambled over to Wosniak, grabbed him under the arms to drag him away to one side in the lee of a house, leaving a trail of blood and scarred gravel where his heels have scraped along the ground. They crouched in positions of uncertainty. They screamed at Wosniak, slapped his cheeks, pressed on his warm slippery neck which splashed them. They were shouting angrily, with fear at their own hopelessness.

As always at those moments, after a successful hit, adrenaline swarmed through Jarvis's system, creating a bursting sense of elation. In truth, he could have taken out four or five more of the marines at will had he so wished. He had to suppress his pleasure. He knew of no greater exhilaration of power within a man's grasp.

Pamela is nervous, her pulse has quickened. She is frightened by the feeling that everything seems to have changed dramatically over the course of two days, their lives apparently turning upside down. She grasps Jarvis's hands with a desperate grip.

When the car comes and the driver hops out and uses the brass knocker at the front door, Jarvis sits still watching from behind the nets as Pamela stumbles out with her bags straight into the back. The car moves off and all is quiet. He stands back, straining to see up and down the street for any shadowy figures sitting in parked cars, cigarette buts alight, any foot soldier lurking in the shadows. But there is nothing untoward, that he can see. He bolts the front door. He retrieves some cold chips from the kitchen while sitting alone for a while, with diffuse streetlight filtering through the nets.

Upstairs in the dark, not switching on any lights, he changes into fresh clothes, black jeans, boots and a tight Parka. He packs what else he needs into a brown canvas holdall, including his security uniform and cap, a couple of shirts and a wash bag. From deep within his chest of drawers, he digs out a pair of binoculars and a hunter's knife in its leather sheath.

Another oddity about the crescent off Baring Street is the way the house numbers seem to follow their own peculiar sequence. The Collingwoods live at number 15; and not quite opposite, ten yards further up, is the house he is interested in, number 59. Both odd numbers, on opposite sides of the same road, which is odd in itself. Which has no obvious explanation. Number 59 is a rather dilapidated two story terraced house in need of attention, part brick part rendered a dirty cream, streaked with lines of rain water, which has its main door onto the crescent itself, whereas, unique to this house for some inexplicable reason, it also has a back entrance, a small yard and a solid wooden door set in an unremarkable brick wall that gives out onto the main Baring Street, right by the bus stop. Which of course could be its front entrance, as it opens onto the main road, but there we are, it's not. The crescent is really one side of a narrow wedge, with its point at the New North Road end and the base at the other. It should be called Baring Crescent or something, but it isn't, it's still Baring Street. And the numbering is all over the place.

Sam and Delphie's house is in the middle of the wedge, so it has entrances from both aspects, front and back. To the great advantage for Jarvis, who is assuming that if the Americans are waiting for him to appear on the crescent, they will be unaware of the back entrance to Number 59 out onto the main street. As he also assumes, they are unaware of his own back-access route to his own house over the neighbours' gardens.

Jarvis scampered up, his sense of achievement giving way to urgency, to pack up and run. He started to dismantle the rifle: stock and barrel, folding bipod, magazine, silencer, grabbing the spares and his ammo bag, packing them away. He retrieved the two spent cartridges. They both worked quickly, keeping their heads low below the parapet, picking up everything they could, folding away their kit. Within sixty seconds of Jarvis's well-aimed hits, they were ready to descend the inner stairs into the workshop below, gripping their bulging backpacks, tying their helmets through a loop.

Jarvis was planning to make a dash along to the checkpoint on Route West, where there was bound to be some transport over to Haditha US base, only a couple of miles away. Mike Malone would be out there, he'd help them. They would cadge a lift down to the nearest British base, in Baghdad, a hundred and fifty miles south.

At the bottom of the stairs, they greeted Rahim. The Iraqi owner and his young assistant have been working on a motorcycle, its main components stripped out and strewn across the greasy floor by the open doors. Rarely seen in anything but a white ankle-length dishdasha with long sleeves, his head well-wrapped in an orange and white shemagh, with its black cord agal, Rahim over, as they hung back in the shadows. Jarvis quickly explained that they had to leave immediately, trouble over on Chestnut. He told Rahim to remove all traces on the roof: pull down the muslin, push the frame to one side, make sure there were no sweet papers or anything lying about. US marines might come looking: deny he ever saw either of them. He apologised, thanked Rahim for all his kindness. Rahim helped them both heave their backpacks up. Jarvis had the extra weight of his folded rifle; Joe had his radio set and binoculars and carried his assault rifle.

With his weather-beaten leathery face and friendly hooded eyes, Rahim anxiously watched the two British soldiers, who he had been hosting, unknown to anyone else, on his flat roof-top for a couple of weeks. He raised his palms upwards in an expression of incomprehension. 'You boys, really.' He spoke good English with a thick accent. They could smell garlic on his breath. 'Not content to fight the insurgents or al-Qaeda or Ansar al-Sunna, you now take on the US bloody Army.' He shrugged, knitted his thick black brows. 'But I am sorry, too. It good to have you, Jarvis; and you, Joe.' Rahim wanted to shake their hands. In the shadowy light he offered them a lift in his Dayun truck. 'You need to disappear, I take you.'

Jarvis had his doubts when he looked at the rusty heap Rahim called transport that was parked outside the front of the shop. It was basically a Chinese three-wheel motorbike with a pick-up and dump platform the size of a double bed on the back. Without any of the comforts. It was painted red and had a lightweight frame supporting a metal roof, the sides wide open. An alternative plan might be to ride out the storm, hide away in the wooded valleys of Guadalahasha to the west of the city, where beyond the rocky outcrops the land rose gently up onto flat plains before the desert began — scattered farms and deserted-looking grazing fields would surely provide them with cover. From there they could contact Malone, although he had strong doubts about the abilities of their radio equipment.

'Yes, that would be good,' he smiled, taking up Rahim's offer. They shook hands warmly.

'Let me get keys. You need to fill up with water. Any food?' They used the cold water tap at the back of the garage, which they knew was safe, filling their camelbaks. Rahim found some bread from the day before in his kitchen, wrapped it in a dishcloth. In the door frame Jahinda appeared and called softly to Joe, wanting to know what was happening. The lad greeted her with a smile and sidled over to her. Touching arms, they nervously stared at each other, Joe explaining the problem in whispered tones. Jarvis hears him say they were in trouble with the US marines. She must go onto the roof for them and make sure all the signs were cleaned away. She agreed, but appeared desperate, pulling him back by his sleeves. She was worrying for his safety, her brown eyes searching for something, and he reassured her as casually as he could. 'You be safe, alright,' he teased, 'act normal.' He mumbled something about finding a chance to visit her again. 'Soon, you see.'

Rahim reversed his decrepit truck up into the wide shaded entrance of his shop. He jumped out to release the tarpaulin cover for them. Joe tried to tear himself away. Jahinda hooked a hand around the back of his neck to pull him down to her to exchange a fleeting press of dry lips. Joe's inner spirit was lifted, as Jarvis bundled him towards the truck. 'Come on, Joe, we have to leave.' Twisting himself round to grab one last glance, a fluttering somewhere inside of him, Joe was desperately thinking how he might take Jahinda with him, before crawling into the back of the truck with his backpack, to lie flat on the hard metal floor. Despite the suddenness of departure, a touch of pride inflated his chest and a euphoric smile formed along those flaky lips.

A fleet of US personnel trucks buzzed past the entrance fifty yards away, they lost count of how many, heading towards the roadside bomb incident on Chestnut. Noise and dust erupted around them and everyone stopped to stare as one vehicle after another roared by. 'Reinforcements,' Rahim muttered.

'Perhaps it would be better to head into the city,' Jarvis asked Rahim, squinting towards the bright sunlight, 'less expected. What do you think?'

Looking at the multiple wrinkles and deep creases that decorated the Iraqi's face, he realised he had come to trust the man.

'Yes, maybe. I know two brothers who have logistics company, transport trucks, they run to Baghdad every week, most days, I think. That give you best chance out of here.'

'Would they help? Would they want money? It might be risky for them.'

'Yes, no, no. They support the coalition, they like the Brits. They're cousins. Let's go ask. We're inside city perimeter, no roadblocks on the way.' A confidant look erupted across his face as he bundled Jarvis onto the steel platform beside Joe, pushing his backpack alongside him.

Rahim slammed the tailgate up and fixed the edges of the tarpaulin cover down with studs and a couple of rope ties before climbing onto his bike, adjusting his headdress. He waited for the roadway ahead to quieten, the traffic to move on as the convoy disappeared out of sight and hearing. He fired the engine into life and although it did not quite remind Jarvis of the Triumph Scrambler he once shared with his brother, the sound was sufficiently deep and throaty to give him some hope that the contraption would at least get them down to Market Square. The whole structure vibrated and rattled alarmingly, but Rahim happily steered his much-loved machine away from the shadows and over his sloping backyard. Watching with anguish on her face, Jahinda saw her father rev the truck down the driveway and turn confidently towards the city centre across a break in the traffic, mingling easily with the other cars and bikes and assorted trucks.

Soon after seven, he leaves quietly by the kitchen door, tugging a black baseball cap firmly onto his head, carrying his holdall. He repeats his back route, over the walls and through the fence out onto Wilton Square, which is thinly lit by lamplight filtering through overgrown wavering branches of the wintery sycamores. A few strides around the curve of the road and he crosses over to the pub on the corner, at the thick end of the wedge. *The Baring* is small, run down and out of the way. It does not do much business and is of no particular interest, except that it does offer a good selection of independent brews, and Jarvis vaguely knows the guys that run it. They have ambitious plans for taking it up-market, apparently, but just haven't raised the necessary cash as yet.

A handful of customers take it easy inside. A couple of young lads at the pool table, a flat screen above the long bar showing football has a few blokes clustered round on stools. A couple are sitting at a table at the far end with their beers, eating chips with their fingers. There is nobody that fits the description of an ex-US marine in search of adventure.

Sauntering over to the bar, he nods to the young man behind with a towel and a glass in his hands. 'Gerry, isn't it?' He asks for a tonic water. 'You seen any strangers in here, last couple of days, Americans, heavy guys, looking for me?'

Gerry stops wiping the glass and squints at Jarvis through spectacles before recognising him. 'Oh,' he says, in a friendly manner, 'hi. No, absolutely not, although I've only been on since five. I'll give Harry a shout, hang on a mo.'

After a moment he returns shaking his head. 'Nobody, he says.'

Jarvis relaxes and wanders over to the far corner with his drink, drops his bag and settles in an armchair, thinking about his next move. A young barmaid comes over, Jules, in a tight orange sweater that clings pleasantly around her chest. 'There was a guy in here yesterday,' she says, 'sorry, I heard you talking to Gerry. In the afternoon, he had an accent, asking if I knew Jarvis. That you, yeah?' She giggles; she has dimples in her cheeks and discoloured teeth.

'Yeah, I'm Jarvis. What did he look like? What did he want?'

'Just said you were an old friend. Sort of clean-shaven with a little beard thing in the middle, crew cut, squashed nose, slightly tanned, big fellow, broad.' And she indicates with her hands spreading apart just how broad he was. 'Had a black-and-white photograph. I recognised you straight away. Said I'd seen you occasionally in here but not for a while. Didn't know where you lived. Was that alright?' He could smell stale cigarette smoke on her breath. She looked sure of herself and he believed her. He had to.

'Yeah, no problem, thanks, Jules.'

'Had a tattoo on his neck, a serpent around a sword.' She slowly indicates the left side of her neck with her long spindly fingers.

'Sure it was left side?' he asks.

She stands up straight and closes her eyes for a moment, putting her hands up to both sides of her own neck and then leaves the left one in place. 'Oh, yes, left side, quite sure.'

After she retreats picking up some empties and wiping the table surface with a tea towel, Jarvis returns to the bar and seeks out Gerry. He leans forward, speaking softly. 'Do you know the two people who live on this side, three doors down, married couple, he's the ex-footballer, gave a talk here one night, she was a singer in the locals?'

'Yeah, Sam Warner. Delphie. I see them, they come in quite often, eat here on Sundays sometimes.'

'Do you have their number? I need to talk to Sam, ask him a favour?'

'Harry might have.' He retreats through to the back again. Harry comes out after a minute, a big fellow, cheery, completely bald. 'Hi, Jarvis.' He's flicking through his contact list on his phone. He reads it out for Jarvis to copy. 'Thanks, Harry.'

From his quiet corner position, he makes his call. 'Sam, it's Jarvis, from Number 15 over the road. I need a favour, can I come round? The back way?'

In their poky kitchen, Delphie is wielding a sharp knife, thudding with deliberation onto a chopping board. She's cooking a monster pot of broth, throwing everything in that she can find, florets of broccoli and cauliflower, carrots, spinach, chunks of potatoes and cubes of cooked chicken. Jarvis sits gratefully at a wooden stool explaining to his neighbours the difficulty he is in and his desperation for a hiding place from which to observe his own house. Sam is all excited by the conspiratorial nature of Jarvis's predicament, but Delphie remains rather more sceptical, thinking of the dangers that he might be bringing to their doorstep. She is asking about his security work at the old sugar refinery, a place she used to see every day when she worked down in Poplar a few decades ago.

'I was a seamstress, we used to call 'em, people brought their clothes to me and I repaired them or took them in, or whatever.' She manages to wrinkle her cheeks to break the hard edges around her mouth, and a twinkle in her eye at the memories. 'Occasionally I had a big job, like when once I created a wedding dress out of old material for a local actress, she was in *Z Cars* or something. Made twenty quid from that job.'

'Well, there's trouble brewing between the workers and management. There are picket lines, trying to stop people going into work. We've been employed to help keep the peace.'

'What's the problem, what are they beefing about?'

'The owners want to reduce costs, improve productivity.'

'Meaning they want to reduce the workforce, eh?' Sam says.

'Precisely. Redundancies. It was a peaceful non-event at the back end of the summer,' Jarvis explains, 'that attracted no one's attention; a few disgruntled workers giving out pathetic leaflets.' Sam and Delphie are both listening with care and glance across at Jarvis for encouragement from time to time. 'But now the big unions are getting involved, they're blocking so much of the traffic that uses the site. I mean, the place deals with a hell of lot of stuff. 50,000 tonnes of raw sugar are stored in the warehouse, for a start. Massive powdery piles, like sand. They move it around with CAT mobile trucks and JCB's. In its heyday they employed 5000 people, you know, but it's been running down for the last twenty years. The whole place is looking a bit neglected, to be honest, moth-eaten, a lot of rusty staircases and corrugated roof sheets missing. It needs sprucing up.'

'Its heyday was a long time ago. Nothing that a lick of paint couldn't solve, though,' chirps Delphie, picturing the grim conglomeration of buildings, tanks and towers that she remembers. 'Is it still that greeny-blue colour?'

'Yeah.'

'Hanging on to old fashioned ways, I shouldn't wonder,' murmurs Sam, 'trying to protect the workers in their jobs, while wanting the automation of new up-to-date technology. Maybe that's where management wants to go and the workforce are resisting change, as they usually do.'

'Understandably.' And Delphie scowls in sympathy while lifting a ladle of her thick concoction from the hot pot, touching the edge to her lips which peck gingerly at the steaming liquid. 'Umm.'

'So how many are working there now?' Sam asks.

'About 900, I think, and many of them are not manual workers, they're mostly engineers and chemists, and nearly half of them are women.'

'Good for them.'

'The derricks still function along the wharf. Delivery vessels come every fortnight, from exotic places like Belize, Mozambique, Fiji. So the volume of material they turn over is still phenomenal. They churn out 800 tonnes of crystallized sugar every week, in those two-pound white paper packages by the tens of thousands, delivered all over the country.'

And Delphie reaches into a cupboard behind her and like a magician brings out an old open white paper bag of Tate & Lyle cane sugar with its familiar design. 'Ta da,' she exclaims in triumph and drops it on the table.

'How long have you had that in there?' Sam asks, fingering the battered package.

'Oh, about ten years,' she chuckles.

'There would soon be an uproar if one of the prime distributors of domestic sugar in this country stopped functioning,' Sam declares. He lifts an eyebrow smoothly up his wrinkled forehead and the others nod in agreement.

Sam is a short stout man with a good head of hair, a thick greying moustache and a rounded belly. Now in his mid-fifties, he was a professional footballer, for a short while playing inside-right for Tottenham, which is how they had met, Sam and Jarvis, in the pub a year ago, cheering Spurs to victory in some cup game on the TV with a crowd of other blokes. They shared some anecdotes about the club, Sam bought him a unique tasting specialist beer he recommended, and after that they regularly bumped into each other in the neighbourhood or the pub and chatted, mostly about old times. Sam is a relaxed sort of character, easy to get along with who accepts his lot without complaint, loves nothing more than idling away his time chatting to people. He wrote his kiss-and-tell biography a few years back that was panned by the critics and sold a modest number of copies. Appeared on a couple of radio chat shows before disappearing into obscurity once more. Now he runs a general stores corner shop a block away up New North Road. He otherwise lives off the dwindling proceeds of his brief celebrity and still has a sense of humour.

Delphie, on the other hand, is a thin nervy creature with masses of bright lipstick and thick foundation to smooth her facial wrinkles, unconvincingly, who is not so easy to get along with. She has to like you first. She is older than Sam and more cynical and has had lots of different jobs over the years. She once was a seamstress in Mile End and a singer in the local clubs in Whitechapel and Bethnal Green. She can't sing properly anymore and so helps Sam in the shop with their daughter, Cynthia. She bustles around, wiping things, dishcloth and spray cleaner in hand, always on edge, perpetually seeing the downsides to everything. 'Just more washing up for me to do, while you're playing your little boys' games,' she murmurs, as Sam leads Jarvis away from the kitchen to explore the upstairs of the house.

In their one spare bedroom that faces the crescent, Sam helps his guest settle in. He pushes the single bed up against a wall. 'Give you more space. You're welcome to use it, the bathroom's just outside. We're at the back of the house, down those steps,' and he points vaguely along a corridor.

'Okay, thanks, Sam, you're a good friend. I won't forget this.' This pleases Sam who likes to think he might be involved in some sort of spy thriller.

With the nets hanging limp in front of the small sash windows and the lights off, Jarvis kneels on a cushion, balancing his arms against the sill, holding the binoculars steady. He has a perfect view of his terraced house opposite, with its black door, but not so good of the rest of the poorly lit street. A bay window would have been better, but he cannot do anything about that. He carefully scans one way and then the other as best he can, paying particular attention to the few parked cars.

Was there someone sitting out there now, watching? The black Ford is nowhere to be seen. Perhaps they use a different vehicle each day? The Americans, hopefully without an actual sighting of him, may have concluded that he is not around, he's moved on somewhere else. No doubt trying to beat an answer out of Joe. They will bide their time, of course, he knows that. Jarvis needs to be patient too. This is a game of cat and mouse.

Parked up close to the pub he notices a half empty builder's skip. He had already seen the stack of scaffolding on the outside of the house next door, going up to the roof.

'They still working on that house, roof repairs?' Jarvis murmurs.

'Oh yes. Delayed by the weather, but I think they're working inside.' Sam has a fondness for corduroy, trousers and matching waistcoat in a fawn softness, that he seems to think makes him appear cuddly. He is hovering close behind, rubbing his hands together. 'Well, what we looking for, eh?'

'Possibly a couple of heavy characters, Americans, who think they own the place, strutting their stuff, probably armed. Maybe mobile, maybe on foot. Not much to go on, really, Sam, just a hunch I have. May be nothing,' he adds hopefully.

'You want me to report back if I see anything, right?'

'Sam, don't go doing anything silly; no approaches, keep yourself to yourself, know what I mean? Stay away, it won't be for long, a couple of days, I hope.'

'Sure. We'll be your back-up,' and Sam gives him a wink, which Jarvis misses deliberately.

'Will Delphie be alright? Seemed pretty pissed off with me being here?' Jarvis can visualise Sam's wife, slumped on a couch downstairs, in a thick shapeless orange woolly, her legs bare at the knees drawn up under her, looking like thunder, smoking incessantly while watching *Coronation Street,* a glass of red wine at her elbow.

'When you mentioned that your life or Pamela's might be in danger she came round. She'll be fully supportive, don't you worry, she won't give the game away.'

Jarvis is reassured.

Sam slowly backs away. 'I'll leave you to it, then, Jarvis lad. See you in the morning, eh?'

Jarvis nods. 'Night, Sam.'

The city was increasingly awake, the routes into town filling up as the inhabitants stirred themselves for another hot dry day of graft and struggle. Many were aware of the booming explosion earlier in Subhami neighbourhood, uncertain about the extent of damage or casualty rate. Most were familiar with the sound and simply shrugged their shoulders and carried on about their business, hoping that it did not involve anybody they knew. Rahim weaved his way in and out of the traffic, dodging the potholes, the rubbish and the smelly drains, and the people who constantly rushed between the vehicles from all directions whatever signals the traffic lights might be showing. The noise was deafening although Jarvis could still hear Rahim swearing to himself from time to time. Jarvis used his fingers to lift the awning cover a fraction to experience the city life with its own noises, of bustle, of street sellers shouting and traffic police whistling, amid a medieval panoply of animals and humans jostling for space. Thrown about by the weaving of the bike, the stop-start jerkiness, combined with the strong smell of diesel and exhaust fumes, they were both feeling queasy. Joe felt stifled and pulled at the shirt around his neck to loosen it. He peeled off his tight gloves.

A little way off Market Square, they turned sharply into a yard and stopped in a shadowy passageway between high concrete and corrugated panelled warehousing. Rahim cut the engine, the crazy rattling noises stopped. The cover was folded back, the tailgate dropped. They sat up and imbibed something closer to fresh air. The place was filled with several trucks, of all sizes, and a hubbub of activity, of loading and unloading, cardboard boxes, crates of fruit and rattling bottles, and stacks of plastic drinking water in huge clingfilm wrappers. Lots of men sweating in the hot atmosphere, took no notice as Rahim pushed the two soldiers through a side door into one of the bigger buildings. They shuffled along a dingy corridor and down steps, into a windowless room at the back, not much bigger than a cupboard and stacked with more boxes. At a wooden desk, with open books like ledgers filled in by hand, sat a bald and grizzled man with profuse carpets of dark hair waving over his shoulders and down his back. He was crouched over his work, in a greasy white vest and green track suit bottoms with red stripes, and open sandals. He exchanged grumpily incomprehensible words with Rahim.

'Wait here, I get my cousin.' Rahim left, closing the door.

They only had to wait a few minutes, as a pungent mix of onions and body sweat became almost overbearing while the grumpy Iraqi, who appeared to speak no English, said nothing, studying his books with a biro in hand. Another man arrived, with similar features to Rahim, a younger version, with a florid black bushy moustache and an old scar along the line of his jaw on one side. His eyes were intensely dark, his face bristling with shiny black stubble. He appeared pleased to meet with the two British soldiers. 'Anything that helps the war against these bastard insurgents. No loyalty to the nation of Iraq, Sunnis on the make,' he emphasised, 'searching for glory.' Rahim from behind introduced Mustafa, who hugged Jarvis round the shoulders, pumped Joe's hand. The room was suddenly jammed with too many warm bodies. 'And this is Yasin,' added Rahim. The seated bald man with sweaty armpits turned his head upwards towards Jarvis and produced a crooked grimace before returning to his books.

Mustafa suggested the two soldiers were hidden in the basement during the rest of the day. 'Hasan. We can get you water, food, you sleep; we leave early next morning, five o'clock to Baghdad, by road, about five, five-and-half hours,' rotating his hands one way and the other, expressing his doubts, 'maybe more if the roadblocks take long. Hasan.' Under the plethora of moustache, he was smiling, pleased to be helping.

Rahim beckoned them to follow him. They went down a wooden staircase into a dank space under the building, huge and open, where a line of wide fridges along a far wall were humming quietly. The place was stacked with empty crates, plastic water barrels and boxes. A small amount of outside light came through a vent high along the wall at the back. The walls were concrete and the floor was concrete and some hefty wooden beams above their heads held the whole thing up. They dumped their backpacks. Mustafa found some rugs and dusty sacks for them and placed a couple of plastic buckets in a corner. *'You better use these. Don't go outside, too many prying eyes.'*

Rahim came over to man-hug them again, like they were his sons. *'Good luck, my friends.'* He adjusted his head cloth loosely and followed Mustafa back up the stairs, closing the door at the top. Jarvis stood in the centre of the dingy space looking around him, adjusting to their circumstances. *'We've been lucky,'* he murmured, settling into a corner, behind a wall of boxes and below the air vent.

Joe idly fiddled with the lid of one of the boxes while talking and discovered toiletries, towels and tissues. *'Never know when they might come in handy,'* he ventured caustically.

'Look, we had no choice. We had to get off that roof. I bet the bloody marines are on their way there in numbers as we speak, so relax, rest and start thinking about what I can say to Malone.'

'I don't know whether we'll be able to get through from down here. Will depend on where Lenny is with his van. Within half a mile or so should be okay, but more than that? Might have to get onto the roof.'

Jarvis signalled his understanding, and abruptly slumped onto a few bunched-up sacks, where he settled into a fidgety daydream. The excitement of the morning was still coursing through his veins. Every vivid second from the roadside explosion to his fateful shots was replayed in minutest detail *through his forensic mind. There was no regretting his actions. He found himself wanting Pamela desperately, beside him. He had not seen her for weeks. Carefree displays of her half-naked in a ruffled bed, tousled hair spread over the pillows, flashed before him. She was dozing, a lazy Sunday morning. He wanted to see her face but struggled to form a clear picture of her. Forgotten what she looked like, he smiled. But her soft plumpness was all real to him, her body coiled among the crumpled sheets. He could not make out whether she was frowning or if she was pleased with him. Would she sympathise with his dilemma, agree that his wilful assassination of Wozniak had been essential? He nestled himself close behind her, fitting his body around hers, searching for comfort and praise, his hands groping carefully for those warm parts euphemistically deemed private, where he had earned a free pass.*

Leaning on his folded arms, holding the binoculars loose as he stares out sleepily along the street, his eyes have started to droop. His phone buzzes. He jerks his head awake and much to his surprise and delight, it's Joe Street. As if by thinking about him he has willed him onto the phone.

'Joe?' Jarvis whispers harshly, sounding pleased. 'Where've you been?'

'Oh, here and there, you know.'

'What happened Sunday?'

'Something came up.' He sounded distant and non-committal.

'Yeah, well, been wanting to talk to you, about …'

'Listen,' Joe interrupts, 'I've met with a couple of American lawyers who want to interview you, ask some questions before the Appeal Court case in Washington.'

Jarvis pauses. Something is not right. Too direct, not like Joe. 'Are you…? Oh, alright,' sounding suspicious. He hurries on: 'I spoke to your mother, went to see her yesterday.'

'Did you see my sister, Jahinda?' He spoke the name with an ugly rasp, not the way he had learned to pronounce it in Arabic. Jarvis is stumped for a second. Although Joe had never really talked about his family, Jarvis knew that he was an only child. Just above a whisper, he mouths the name slowly: 'Jahinda?' Not only does Joe not have a sister, she certainly would not be called Jahinda. 'No, your sister was not there, Joe.'

'We're in London just now. They want to meet at your house, suggest tomorrow night. It's Baring Street, right? What's the number, Corporal?'

Joe would never address him by rank. 'Yeah, right. It's number 21,' he lies.

'Say, ten o'clock, in the evening? We'll be there.' Joe rings off. Since when do American lawyers arrange a business meeting to be at the client's house? At ten o'clock at night? On the other hand, they must know that Jarvis would suspect a ruse. They basically want him to know that they have Joe in their grasp, as a bargaining counter: to scare him, to lure him out.

Always impressed at how easily Jarvis was able to catch forty winks whenever he wanted, Joe sank himself onto a rug with a blanket by another wall, wedged against carboard boxes and was trying his luck. As he dozed off, sensations came to life in his mind, from the wallop of the roadside explosion and its fiery conflagration, to the oily smell and constant jerking in the back of Rahim's truck on their rickety journey through the city streets, to the blood that spouted from Wozniak's neck like a champagne cork popping. He could see the steely look of concentration and pleasure that consumed Jarvis's features, as he blew that awful American sergeant away. Jarvis seemed unaffected by any emotion, just cool resolve and determination, a job to be done. Put a precision rifle in his hands and he could be lethal.

Dreams about his time in Iraq flooded through him, his experiences, the friends he had made, the male camaraderie. Happy just to replay the fantasy world he found himself in, sleep, volatile and uncomfortable, gradually crept up on Joe.

Now Jahinda was nearby, a fleeting touch. Her whispery voice and gossamer lips, cajoling him to take care of himself. She had the nose of her father, long and thin with a bumpy ridge that one day, together with her sharp jaw line, would give her the look of an aristocrat, he was convinced. There's adoration in those shiny brown eyes of polished mahogany. There was fear in them too, that he might disappear, and he consoled her, caressing her with gentleness. He reassured her that he would come back so they could be together.

Under billions of stars, enveloped by the hot navy blue of night-time, they lay together on a patch of grass hidden around the corner of her father's yard, beyond a line of palm trees. She traced her finger over his face, tickling the thin hairs sprouting along his chin. Wearing no headgear or scarf, she sat up, bare flesh at her neck that looked startlingly pale in the sparse moonlight. She asked about his life in England, how many wives he had there. He tickled her waistline. Her skin was like softened caramel. She wriggled, and he shushed her several times, before pulling her down onto him affectionately. He respected her youth and innocence. He thought about how much he had come to love her, how much he wanted to make love to her, and how much he wanted to protect her.

Sometime later, the middle of the day perhaps, with his neck awkwardly crooked against a box that he'd been using as a pillow, he got up, needing a leak. He had backache and was wondering whether it had all been worthwhile. He raided one of the fridges, taking a couple of plastic bottles of drinking water. He kept one for Jarvis, who was also fidgeting awake. He paced the basement space to stretch his legs, his back. He tried to put aside thoughts of Jahinda and the possible dangers he had left her to.

Time passed, steamy, dull and humid. The air was stale, despite the vent in one wall, with a persistent whiff of drains. They both sweated freely and used the bucket, a few times. Joe sat some of the time cross-legged on the concrete floor, top stripped off, sketching faces of girls in the dust with a short strip of wood. Jarvis pressed ice-cold water bottles against his cheeks, as the damp patches in his shirt spread down his spine and under his arms. He constantly slurped down more water, sometimes splashing it over his chest and round the back of his neck.

Having tried and failed to achieve any worthwhile signal from their basement, earlier in the morning, Joe thought it best to wait until they could get to the roof, a higher position giving them a better chance of connecting with Lenny in his roving Signals van, with its British armoured carrier protection.

Essential supplies of food, weapons and machinery parts were in constant need by the hundreds of troops, engineers and support workers up at the hydroelectric base and US army camp of Haditha Dam. And it was often the boys of 3rd battalion, Kilo company who were responsible for bringing the stuff up from Al Assad Military Airbase, much further south. The convoys would take the shorter routes through Haditha city itself, often passing through unpredictable neighbourhoods, although they varied their routes all the time. Hence the positioning of the British sniper pairs at various sites around the city to offer maximum cover and protection. British radio contact however was tenuous. Troops on the ground were supplied with short-wave sets like the standard Bowman, with a variable frequency and a range of about a mile, although they had a good twenty hours continuous battery life. British command, temporarily set up with their American partners at their local base two miles outside the city close to Highway 19, relied on a mobile system using Royal Signals Corps equipment in armoured cars, to act as a link.

Jarvis paced irritably around to keep his legs moving. He needed to come up with a way to persuade Malone of the truth of this morning's events and the role he played in them. He lay again in the shadows, eyes closed, trying to imagine the conversation. Jarvis had come to realise how remote Haditha was from the outside world, with its own level of extremism and lawlessness; a place notoriously difficult for Westerners to survive undetected. He knew British Army Command would only have the barest details of the early morning explosion on Chestnut, with cursory mention of the US casualty situation. Info about subsequent shooting, probably described as a local skirmish with insurgents, would be glossed over. When, if, they got to hear of it, it would come as a complete surprise. The Americans would do everything to prevent any whiff of the truth getting out into mainstream news, but inevitably pictures would appear in the local propaganda papers or perhaps a Western reporter would pick it up.

A man they had not met before brought them food, fried chickpea patties and steaming bowls smelling of lemon and garlic, with strips of lamb cooked with onions. He laid them out onto the top of a cardboard box. 'I got drinks,' he said, taking two cans of cold coke out of side pockets of his baggy trousers. The two men clawed at the cans and the drinks tasted good. They started to wolf the food down with gratitude. Joe belched. 'I could do with a fag just now.'

'Really? I didn't know you did.'

'No, well, I was giving up at the start of this tour, but the smell of food always makes me want one. Used to smoke a pack a day.'

Shortly afterwards the same man returned for the plates and brought two small china cups of the blackest gravelly coffee Joe had ever tried. Jarvis asked about getting onto the roof to make a radio call to his base and the man promised to find out for them.

Debriefing interview, MoD, Aldwych.
December 12, 2005.

'So, let me get this clear, Collingwood. You took it upon yourself, without reference to your superiors, to your line of command, to shoot an officer of the US marine corps, during a combined operation between allied forces. Shoot to kill?' Malone had taken on a bleak expression, mixed with a disdain for the junior soldier in front of him. He had started to suck on his lips at one corner of his mouth on completion of his sentences, while waiting for an answer. At the same time, his head would rotate a little anticlockwise, as a pale eyebrow would be cocked in anticipation. This was a new habit that Jarvis had not seen before which he found disconcerting. He would probably have laughed in any other circumstance. 'Was this some warped kind of loyalty on your part?'

'Sergeant Wosniak had an uncontrollable anger that knew no bounds. He also seemed to be taking instructions over his radio. He would have carried on with his senseless slaughter if I had not stopped him.'

'So, you were doing us all a favour, pronouncing on the intention of this man, who in all good faith was carrying out his duty as a full serving officer of the US army. You decided to assassinate him, in effect.'

'These were war crimes. The American military cannot possibly suppress the truth. The victims were women, old men and children. If there are any photos in the public domain it will be hard to explain the multiple wounds, point-blank range in some cases, and the blast damage from grenades. We had no instant communication with the marines, it would have taken us ages to get in touch with yourself or Major Shawcross. By which time, he would have committed further slaughter. What could you have done, from where you were at US base, two miles away?'

'Nevertheless, this was an extraordinary decision, Corporal.'

'Sir. There was no other way.'

Midlogue

**Haditha, Iraq
November 19, 2005**

Later Saturday morning

Bundled away from further danger, slouched against a stone wall, Bob Wosniak, with fear in his eyes, struggled to breathe and bled out his last beside Tom Flynn and Ed Kingfisher, his two best mates in the Company. They had all joined up together, trained at army college together, served together in Iraq from the outset. They had eaten, washed and fought together, sweated for each other: they were like brothers. They had special names for each other, Woz, Thomas The Tank, Steady Eddie, had devised their survival plans together, playing camp versions of baseball and macho games of chariot racing in togas. Back home in the mid-West they had chased the same girls. Now within seconds of the hit to his neck, Wosniak was dying in their company, fighting the good fight.

There was no ceremony, just undignified human mess, his lifeblood emptying out over foreign ground, soiling his mates' uniforms, splashing their faces. Tom and Ed were frantic, horrified; they could not accept what was happening. After all their times together, this was not what they expected. The three of them were invincible, nothing could take them down. Together they were strong, they always won against any opposition. They screamed that Woz should live. They ripped his helmet off, pressed down on his wound, they thumped his chest, slapped his face. But Wosniak's larynx was shot, his carotid ripped, he was slumped motionless, the colour drained out of his face. There was no response. His eyes lost their sparkle: they stared at the sky as his head flopped to one side.

Not long after the shooting of Sergeant Wosniak and less than twenty minutes since the original roadside bomb explosion that blew one of their Humvees apart, reinforcements arrived in a flurry of dust and rumbling noise, as half a dozen more Humvees and a Stryker personnel carrier crowded along Chesnut. Dozens of marines discharged from the trucks and dispersed themselves around the scene, to lock down the site. Roadblocks were set up at either ends of the route, watching crowds were pushed back and cordoned off. Specialists were scanning over the ground and roadway with their detectors to make sure they were clear of any further danger. Smoke was still spilling out of some of the windows of the nearby houses and a fire was raging on the ground floor of one, with flames and blackening smoke licking the outside of the brickwork close to a burnt-out air-conditioner unit. Groups of troopers spread out to ensure clearance and safety, while confused by the extent of the damage inside. Medics attended to the wounded, as body bags and stretchers were placed in readiness. Several marines were shouting at the meandering goats further down the road.

Grief stricken survivors and inhabitants were emerging with trepidation from their hiding places and some darted hysterically from body to body, looking for their loved ones. There were shrieks and screams and much crying, figures bent over the dead and wounded, wanting to touch and comfort them. The marines tried half-heartedly to keep them off, while the clear-up team were taking names and marking them with tags.

Two Black Hawks landed like giant spiders thirty yards apart amid a whirlwind of dust and ear-thrashing noise, the very air vibrating all around. Everyone on the ground took protective attitudes with their hands over their eyes, some pulling their shirts over their faces, until the blades slowed to a halt. The blazing parts of the damaged Humvee were sprayed with anti-fire foam, which slowly dampened the flames, although for a while the choking smoke that continued to swirl skywards seemed thicker than before. Engineers started to pull the wreckage off the road using chains attached to one of the Humvees, to be recovered later in the day, to be examined by US experts in forensic detail. The body bags of Wosniak and the Humvee driver were loaded onto one chopper and the two wounded marines on stretchers with drips in place and medics assisting at their sides were slid onto the landing floor of the other. And soon the blades started their noisy revolutions again and amid more clouds of dust, they ascended one after the other to sprint up and away westwards to return to the busy US Military airbase at Al Assad, twelve miles away. The whirring sounds of their engines gradually faded away as they shrank down to two tiny black spots in the huge sky and finally disappeared.

A pair in white uniform and US helmets, official recorders, were taking photographs, of the crater in the road, of the damaged Humvee, of the wounded marines, of the body parts, of the Iraqi dead. Numbered markers were placed by each body and at various points in the scenario, where there were bloodstains or bullet casings. They started with the men in the road close to the Opel, their bodies bagged without labels and laid out in a row. Then more bodies were lifted out from the shot-up houses and the bags placed in a row by the road, a marine at either end: the zips were zipped and tags tied to a convenient toe. A personnel carrier arrived, weaving its way through the parked vehicles to the centre of activity. The first bags were hauled up one by one to slide into the back, but the floor space was soon covered. The next few bags were laid on top and then a third layer on top of them. A second Stryker arrived to complete the task: twenty-four bags counted in all. To be transported to the morgue downtown at the main hospital for official certification.

Flynn and Kingfisher were joined by Philip Pansecker, and a couple of other loyal troopers, armed and furious, to go in search of the sniper that took out their leader, their friend Woz. All physically strong, built to last, with crewcuts, tattoos and overnight stubble, they were sweating heavily in the heat. Tom had a shrewd idea who was responsible. He was once an amateur boxer, a bull-necked tough guy with wide-set blue eyes and a flattened nose dominating his broad face. Using a pair of binoculars, he focused on the buildings up on the ridge by the junction of Chestnut and West. The dull two-storey Alfrasheed Bank, with the national flag of Iraq fluttering from its roof, dominated the skyline. The adjacent stretch of scrubland was where he knew the British paratrooper Collingwood was positioned with his spotter. And that's where Tom was sure the shots came from.

Ed, darker, a bit taller and thinner than Tom but just as well-built, agreed that it has to be the work of the fucking Brits. That fucker, Collingwood, what was he trying to do, sabotage the US doing its job? Collateral damage was the cost of marine business, what did he expect?

'The Brits always fuck things up, and get in the way, with their bumbling incompetence and upper crust ways.' Tom was seething and the others, crouching together behind the cover of the houses they had just ransacked, nodded their heads, their helmets knocking together.

'Maybes he confused by the smoke? Couldn't see goddamn clear,' Phil drawled slowly. 'No fucking excuse, no way.'

'This was one appalling act of assassination,' Tom insisted, sneering and snarling. He wiped the back of his hand across his mouth, licked his dry and cracked lips. 'A deliberate act and we intend to make him pay with his life.'

'The Brits are supposed to be working with the US, not murdering us,' said Ed. 'Fuck's sake.'

'All agreed, rah?' Tom urged.

'Hell, yeah,' they responded as one.

Among all the activity and the noise of the helicopters and the smoke still swirling around, leaving one of the marines behind with the body of Wosniak to ensure it was handled properly, four of them, Tom in the lead, with Ed, Phil and another called Shorty, piled into a Humvee. Pansecker took the driver's seat, and turned it around onto the road, heading back along Chestnut the way they had come. They turned past the square block of the bank into Route West and parked up a hundred yards further on, at the edge of the rough ground there, under the few sparse trees that lined the road. They set off on foot into the scrubland, armed, alert and hellbent on revenge.

Crossing a rutted track, they scampered over sandy ground in a line into the dim shade of palms and pine trees, where it was a little cooler. Mangy-looking tufted grass was interspersed with wild oak and hawthorn bushes. They had to avoid various dumps of domestic rubbish, mixed with human waste, a fetid mush of discarded food, plastic bottles and cardboard snack boxes, where flies and rats congregated. Assault rifles loaded, semi-automatic pistols easily accessible, the four marines spread out twenty yards apart. They darted five yards half left, stopped and crouched, using whatever cover they could, before darting five yards half right, always going forward with caution.

They expected the snipers' position to be at the edge of the scrub, where the ground fell away to give good views over the city and across the river valley. The marines should be able to surprise them from behind. Tom signalled with his hands for everyone to slow down, to crouch low and keep quiet. They knew the snipers were expert at deception and disguise, using natural materials from their surroundings to blend in, so finding them hidden under their camouflage would be tricky. They did not want to stumble over them, literally.

Slowly they advanced, their weapons at the ready.

Ed was thinking he would like to shoot the two buggers at first sight, tell the bosses later it was self-defence. Get up close, point-blank, single shots through the skull. No questions asked. Teach them a lesson. Revenge for Woz's killing. And deal with the issue of them being witnesses to Kilo Company activity, at the same time. In his mind he can see what an insane issue that's going to turn out to be for them back at US base. So, kill the Brits clean, no questions. Both problems solved in one. Period.

After twenty minutes of fruitless creeping crab-like amongst the undergrowth, without success, the troopers stopped and began to relax, to breathe easy and slump in anti-climax. They had found only bare sandy ground, apparently undisturbed. There were no signs of human existence, army personnel or otherwise. Perhaps the two Brits had packed up and left after the shooting, covering their tracks, so everything looked normal. Perhaps they had never been there in the first place, but had moved away to some other nearby spot, with better vantage points.

The marines drifted away for leaks, chewing chocolate. Pansecker pulled his helmet off and smoked a cigarette while perching on a fallen tree trunk. Tom paced around chewing gum and looked repeatedly towards the ramshackle buildings over by the corner of Chestnut and West, on a ridge of land eighty yards away. His attention was distracted by the sound of a noisy motorcycle engine. A dusty three-wheel truck driven by an Arab in orange and white headgear, in apparent haste, turned onto the track at the back of those buildings, beyond the far edge of the scrub. It twisted up into a walled compound in front of a garage where they could make out several rusted colourful signs in Arabic, along with Castrol and Esso, fixed over the entrance. Tom was intrigued. If the two British snipers were looking for somewhere to hide, those nearby buildings would be ideal, close by the scrub, with good views and protection to remain unseen on the roof above the garage.

In a coordinated trot the four marines set off towards the buildings, keeping close, pushing their way through the bushes and wispy grasses. As their cover faded away, they paused and advanced cautiously to check the driveway ahead. Through a gap in the brickwork was a wide opening leading up to a garage, where a young mechanic in jeans was seen at work. Old trucks and bikes were parked about the place, cycles leaning against the walls, and in the driveway, its nose driven into the shadows of the building, was a red Dayun truck. Tom caught sight of the portly Arab in white robes pottering about inside.

Kingfisher and Shorter stood either side of the driveway, keeping watch, leaning into the shade of the crumbling wall, looking up at the dilapidated buildings behind them. Pansecker (Cocksucker to the others) and Flynn, the one tall with a loping stride, the other broad with more of a lumber, scampered up the slope of broken concrete where the dusty Dayun truck partially blocked the open entrance of the garage. The sharp contrast from the bright glare outside to the darkness within took them a while to adjust to. Tom pulled at the tarpaulin sheet crumpled across the back of the truck, confirming there was no one hidden there. He picked up a glove, loose on the floor, green canvas, fingerless, the left hand: the sort gunners used to help their grip. Crumpled and sweaty.

They sidled past the truck, their rubbery footsteps and clinking equipment alerting Rahim. Taking up stationary positions in the middle of the floor, legs apart and looking threatening, Tom shouted a challenge to the two figures half-hidden in the shadows at the back.

'US Army. Stop right there. Hands above your heads, turn around, towards us, slowly. So we can see your hands. Above your heads.' Rahim the older man, with his grizzled face and clipped moustache, turned towards the American soldiers, attempting an innocent expression of cooperation. Ahmed, a mere teenager, turned out of fear, not really understanding the language. Rahim muttered reassurances to him in Arabic. Their arms were half raised. Tommy advanced a step. Rahim asked if he could be of any help.

'Sure, you can help. You speak English, yeah? You own this place, you work here?'

'Yes, I own this garage. This is my work.'

'And the house?' nodding towards the open doorway in the wall.

'Yes, and the house, I live here.'

'The British soldiers, the snipers, they been on your roof?'

Rahim's sun-drenched face, grown old through hard work and the daily struggle, managed a look of innocent surprise, as he shook his head and turned his palms upwards. 'British, no.'

'You seen them, two of 'em, with long rifles, in camouflage? Shooting?'

'British, oh no.'

Ahmed on the other hand looked uncertain, shifty, worried. Tom, whose face was infused pink with all his running about and excitement, stepped closer and pushed the barrel of his automatic into the boy's chest, stabbing him, which clearly hurt. 'You, you seen the Brits?'

Something about Ahmed, his stammering, his wincing expression and nervy eye movements made Tom press him harder. He stepped up and grabbed the boy's face in his gloved hand, squeezing his jaw in his rough grip. He stared straight into the frightened eyes and aggressively shouted: 'You sure, you not have two Brits up on your roof?' Ahmed winced and screwed up his eyes, as he tried to shake his head.

Rahim stepped in. 'What makes you think we have British soldiers here?'

Releasing Ahmed, Tom lifted the used glove he held slowly in front of Rahim's face. 'This an army glove. We see the shooting. We don't trust you Shiites,' he added contemptuously. 'Come on, mister, show me up to the roof.' Tom grabbed Rahim by his collar. 'Up those stairs, yeah?'

They made their way over to one corner, where a stream of sunlight was spilling down stone steps from above and started climbing. Rahim in front, Tom pressing his rifle into his back, Ahmed next and Phil following up behind, pushing Ahmed forward. At the top a door led outside onto a flat concrete slab and they all stumbled out into the bright stifling heat. Sweat ran freely from Tom's armpits and down his back as he walked around the space, that was adjacent to the house, the size of the garage below, barely enough to take his Dodge pick-up back home. A parapet three-foot high on three sides offered shielding. Linen and sheets and men's robes hung drying in the sun across several lines, and scattered around were bits of broken furniture, empty fruit boxes, washing buckets and other junk.

Phil kicked at a pile of muslin cloth and a decrepit mattress in one corner. An old metal bed frame was turned on its side against one wall. There were no signs of recent shooting, no gunpowder marks or old cartridges. At the front wall, Tom noticed some wooden stakes nailed crudely into the bricks, used for hanging something. 'We use for washing,' Rahim explained, without being asked. Tom peered out over the parapet, taking in the views, and watched the continued mayhem way down on Chestnut, four hundred yards away. Black smoke was still spiralling up from the backend of the broken Humvee and occasional flames burst from the wreckage. The crater in the road from his position looked pissing pathetic. He saw marines running about, pressing inhabitants back; some in plastic outfits heaving body bags to the side of the road. Two monster Black Hawks were lifting off near the scene, whipping up clouds of gritty sand and dust in all directions: getting his stricken mates off to the medics.

He noticed the gaps at intervals in the parapet, perfect slits in the brickwork for snipers to point their rifles, with a good field of view, while hiding behind the wall. Tom needed no explanation and understood what he wanted to see. He was convinced. 'You see that, you see the explosion,' he shouted, pointing down to the scene. 'A bomb planted by you people in the road. Someone triggered that for maximum effect. Killing my fellow troopers.' He was turning red in the face and a little short of breath with his ranting. 'Who did that, you know?'

While Phil kept his eye on Rahim and the young lad, Tom went searching through the few rooms of the house. Meagre, shadowy and humid, there was precious little there for a family: a few sticks of cheap furniture, clothes in heaps, faded rugs on the concrete floors. A few trinkets, pictures and magazines; no television. A room with a table and some wooden chairs, a small larder for storage with not much on its shelves, that stank of sour milk. In the cramped kitchen, Rahim's mother, the old lady shrouded in black, and shrinking herself into her granny's voluminous robes, a slim girl, hoping not to be noticed. At the metal sink at the only window, signs of meal preparation, with rice and chopped onions and cucumber, a small kitchen knife left on the board.

Tom called the girl over to him. She wore no headgear and her black hair was swept off her face, held in a cluster behind her neck, the long tail trailing down her back. She was wearing a green cotton top over loose trousers, with her chador held around her neck and pulled closely at the front. 'What's upstairs? Show me.'

He pushed her ahead of him, through to a narrow wooden staircase. Jahinda was terrified and stumbled on the stairs, Tom pressing closely behind her, his automatic prodding her in the buttocks. A sparse back bedroom, where two mattresses covered in dull stoles were flopped on the wooden floor in opposite corners. Tom kept asking her questions about helping the British soldiers, but got nothing back; Jahinda just looked vacant. He kicked his way around the enclosed space, but there were no cupboards to hide in or hidden doors to sneak behind. Through an arch into another room space there was a bigger mattress in the middle of the floor, with a colourful spread. In a wooden frame a photo of a handsome young woman in her jihad sat on an old chest of drawers.

Tom dragged Jahinda around with him. He towered over her, twice her width at his shoulders and with his curved visor pushed up over the front of his rounded helmet, he looked like an alien to her. He turned her round to face him, a doll in his rough hands, and tried a more consoling voice. 'We want to help them, little lady, they're on our side. Where did they go? The two of them,

British soldiers, where are they?' He glowered into her eyes for a moment, one gloved hand pulling at her top, the other gripping the automatic across his bulging chest. She was trembling and tried to avoid his angry gaze, fixing her attention for a moment on the radio gadget pinned to the front of his uniform, its wiry aerial flicking about from side to side.

Thomas The Tank filled the small space. He was losing patience and pulled her closer lifting her off her feet across his ample stomach. His armpits stank. The heat of his breath wafted across her cheek, as his thick lips brushed against some loose strands of her hair to whisper into her ear.

'Where are they, little girl, the Brits?' he demanded slowly through clenched teeth. But she shook her head a little, scared of what he might do, but determined not to let her father down. 'I don't know,' she croaked.

He let the automatic hang freely from his neck and reached for the hunting knife in its brown leather sheath at his waist, which he brought up close to the front of her face. Her wide eyes crossed to focus on the shiny steel and serrated blade. He placed its point under her nostrils. She held her breath. 'Do you want me to use this knife? Slice your pretty little nose open?' He shouted into her face: 'Do you?'

His spittle sprayed over her forehead and she blinked.

'You must tell me where the British soldiers have gone. I mean them no harm; we need to find them.' Jahinda whimpered. 'Or I might just slice your throat and watch you bleed to death. Slowly. Is that what you want?' He poked his face viciously into hers again, but her darkened lids had closed and some moisture was squeezed out from between them. 'Where did your father take the two men, um? I know they were here, I know where they were shooting from. They killed one of my men and I want them to face justice.' His anger rose inside him uncontrollably like wind belching from his gullet. He stamped his foot. 'Where did they go?' he screamed.

Tom grabbed her by the neck with one large hand; he wanted to squeeze the life out of her. He pressed the sharp cutting edge of his knife to her flesh along the line of her jaw. She flinched and yelped, as a pin-point bubble of carmine blood welled up. 'One last chance, you little tart.'

She shook her head and said: 'They were here but I do not know where they are now.' Tears were bobbling over her cheeks. The sharp blade was pressed onto her skin. She yelped again, 'I don't know, I did not see anything.' The fist of his free hand wedged into the small of her back. He pressed her body into his, and even through the thickness of his uniform, he could sense her soft outline. Jahinda's complexion was clear and coaxing and Tom had a sudden urge to kiss her lips.

Downstairs Phil was holding Rahim back, stopping him from running up to the bedrooms, as they heard Jahinda's cry. Phil called up, 'What's happening, Tom?'

Tom let Jahinda go, stepped back and slammed his knife into the wooden top of the chest. It remained wobbling upright. He shouted to Phil to bring Rahim up. When he appeared, bundled forwards, Phil gripping him around the neck and using his heavy boots to kick Rahim's shins, Tom lashed out without warning, punching the older man across his face with his gloved fists twice, three times, hitting him hard. Rahim grunted loudly and stumbled to his knees. Tom hovered over him like a man possessed, his fists still clenched. He looked across at the girl. 'Tell me where, or he gets more.'

She looked despairing and tearful. Tom turned to her father and smashed his fists into his face again, first the right and then the left. He was putting all his effort into it, his knuckles stinging, even within the gloves. Jahinda called out to stop, no more. Her father slumped against the wall, dazed, his bloodied face painful. A cut above his eyebrow had started to bleed, trickling down one cheek, spreading through his stubbly moustache. A few drops stained his white robe.

Tom shouted over his shoulder to Phil to get Rahim out of there, while he removed his gloves, unclipped his webbing belt. His pack and automatic dropped to the floor, his helmet followed. He stepped over to Jahinda, grabbing her shoulders, her loose clothing. He shuffled her against the low mattress, as she tried to resist, tried to push him away with her small hands. But he was a brute of a man, while she was a mere wisp. She tried to dart away. He yanked at her clothes which came away, her top ripping. She looked horrified, and started to scream, trying desperately to get her arms back up to cover herself. Tom hit her across the mouth with the back of his hand, her head jerked away, jet-black hair loosened from its ties falling freely over her bare shoulders. Aroused now, he tossed her backwards onto the mattress, a sense of urgency pounding through him at the sight of her tiny nipples.

The Humvee, with no mounted machine-gun up front, bumped along the hilly track, no wider than the truck itself. They were exploring the unfamiliar terrain west of Haditha, rocky, dusty and mostly bare, shimmering in the morning heat. A sparse wooded area lay ahead, spreading down into a dry steep-sided and deserted valley. Meadowland and scattered farmsteads looked down upon them from either side and Ed was warning Tom not to go too far, as the track might get so narrow he couldn't turn the Humvee around.

Shorter, who had said little so far, was poring over a map at the back and declared that they were in the Valley of Guadalahasha and a brisk climb on foot over the ridge to their left would bring them up to flatlands above and give them a pretty good view of the surrounding countryside.

The others ignored him. Ed stared through the flat windscreen, scanning the distance, sometimes bringing up a pair of binoculars to his eyes. 'If those two sons of bitches are hidden up ahead somewhere, they might be watching us. They might have us in their sights right now.' He casually wondered how bullet-proof the glass was. 'They could blow us out one by one.'

'Ed, shut the fuck up with that talk. We need to find those skunks.'

Phil moved the Humvee to a slightly wider part in the track and manoeuvred it awkwardly into a multi-point turn, backing it up towards the woods. Through the back doors, Tom dragged a dazed Rahim out by the scruff of his neck. He had a swollen face, his right eye closed, and a dried stream of blood adhered to the skin, forehead to neck. His broken nose was hurting. His ribs too had taken a beating and breathing in was painful. He had lost his headdress and one of his slippers. He clutched at his side groaning while scrabbling in the dirt. He was only partly aware of what was happening, being half dragged and half pushed across the ground, with Tommy shouting at him to walk. He stumbled painfully catching his bare toes against the sharp stony ground.

'Okay, Mr Shiite, whad ya think they did after you dropped them off? Was it here?'

Rahim stared unseeing about him, pretending to remember what he did. He nodded: 'Yes, here, here, somewhere.'

'Okay, so where did they go from here?'

'I don't know, I turned around. Left them straight away. I come home. I don't know.'

'So where do you think they might have gone? You must have brought them here for a reason. Through the woods, yeah?'

'As far away as possible, away from Haditha. To hide in the woods. There may be water down there. There are farms. A plantation on the other side, dates to eat.' He shrugged painfully, sinking to the ground. 'Maybe they watch you now, from somewhere? That big blond one is good shot.'

'Okay, shut the fuck. We know what that son of a bitch can do.'

Tom edged them towards the relative protection of the trees, keeping himself behind Rahim's body where he could. The others followed behind them. It was heavy going. He soon dropped Rahim in the dry dust, and darted over towards the nearest collection of pines, offering some cover. He crouched low among the scratchy grass and scrub, thinking no one could see him. As he held his automatic in both hands at the ready, he reassured himself that he would defy those two Brits and blow their fucking heads off.

As the four marines took up positions behind different trunks several feet apart, they were all wondering what next.

Over the next hour they slowly searched through the woods ahead of them, much as they had done at the scrubland area in town, which turned out to be a waste of time. They were all disenchanted and tired: the bloody Brits had somehow got away and for the moment there was nothing they could do about that. 'Fucking waste of time,' Ed proclaimed, not for the first time. And Tom gave him a glare, tempted to smack him hard around the head.

Tom continued to lead his increasingly disgruntled band of three through the bushes, from tree to tree, testing the undergrowth with their boots or the tip of their gun barrels, for what they were hoping would be two soldiers lying low. By the time they reached the far end of the wood, giving way to vast open views of sandy terrain back towards Haditha and the long twinkling line of the Euphrates river miles away, they were hungry, thirsty, sweating and fed up. Tom had been chewing madly and spat his tasteless gum out. He kicked at the ground, looked way into the distance towards the ridge up to their left and wondered if that nasty piece of shit, Collingwood, had a concealed position up there and was laughing at them at that moment. He slipped back into the protection of the woods. Sinking onto his haunches, he shared the water bottle being passed around. They all took leaks against the trees.

Shorter now had the binoculars. 'I can see Haditha dam in the misty distance,' he mumbled.

Ed caught a tiny glittering reflection of sunlight off the vast concrete face of what he knew was an enormous structure and claimed he didn't need no frigging binoculars.

'There's the golden roof of Rifai mosque and its minaret,' Shorter continued, untroubled, pointing down to the city.

Tom passed wind. 'Excuse me, my friends.'

'What now?'

They looked back at him with blank expressions, and Tom sensed they none of them had the appetite to proceed any further, either up over the ridge fully exposed or down to the bare valley beyond, where there were several farm buildings. They might try with the Humvee, although the sides were all too steep and there was no natural track to follow. Tom reached for a fresh strip of gum. 'I reckon that Eye-raki A-rab has been telling us fibs. Taken us on a wild chase. Those Brits are not up here, they probably took another direction. Down south to Base HQ maybe, hitched a ride, I don't know.'

The others easily assented, nodding weakly. 'We might catch 'em there, boss.'

By the time they returned to their Humvee, Rahim had taken himself off to a grassy patch on the side of the track and was lying in the sunshine, half dozing, desperate for his daughter, wanting to return to her, to help her. Pansecker marched over to him, picked him up roughly and held him while Tom punched him across his jaw and then kicked him hard in the chest when he flopped to the ground. The feeble groan he gave off was one of sheer exhaustion.

'You fucking liar, they're not here, are they? You didn't bring them here, did you? You cheated us.' Tom was short of breath and quite red faced with his exertions. He took a long deep breath, as if finding his courage, as he reached for his SIG Sauer, unbuckling it from its leather holster. 'We have no further use for you, you know. Unless you can think of the truth to tell us. Eh?' Rahim was on his knees and Tom pulled at his hair, wrenching his head backwards to stare into the puffy face. Rahim, his eyes closed, spat out some blood.

Tom checked the magazine, pushed the catch and without compunction fired a bullet into Rahim's skull. A splurge of reddish tissue and a streak of hot blood exploded from among the waves of grey hair at the back, producing a lumpy crimson patch to mix with the dirt behind him. An appalling charcoaled hole had appeared where his left eye used to be. The body crashed backwards awkwardly in a huddle.

The marines walked away, and Tom replaced his pistol.

'Let's move on, boys.'

Four Years Later (Part 2)

**London
November 10 to
November 12, 2009**

Chapter 5
Tuesday November 10

After an uncomfortable and restless night on Sam's narrow spare bed that was too short, Jarvis is up around six for a cold shower to sharpen up. He dresses in his working clothes and surveys the road outside to check if anything has changed overnight. Downstairs he makes a strong coffee, trying not to clatter too much, and munches a handful of cereal flakes. On his way out he takes an apple from the bowl on the kitchen table.

As he emerges through Sam's back gate, which locks itself on its Yale, a number 141 bus happens to be slowing to a halt at the stop. It takes him all the way down to Aldgate East via Haggerston. From there, he makes his way to the familiar scene at Silvertown using DLR. A few weeks into the dispute and all the road entrances to the refinery are seriously picketed, with crowds four or five people deep, shouting abusive language and throwing stuff, their purpose being to prevent anyone from going inside to work. Many of the determined workforce were being picked up elsewhere and bussed in by contracted coach companies, the demonstrators shouting even more vitriol at the drivers and the scabs inside for disloyalty to their brothers and sisters. They bash their banners on the sides of the buses, throwing eggs and tomatoes at the windscreens.

It would seem the demonstrators have had instructions to be more vociferous, more pushy, to get stuck in. They look as if they are ready for trouble and are prepared to cause it if necessary. The police have responded to the raised level of incitement with reinforcements arriving all the time, their white vans with crowd guards parked up at the western approach to Factory Road, with dozens of uniformed men and women behind shields with several dog-handlers clustered in front. In a massed gathering nearby, London's finest journalists, reporters and photographers from the full spectrum of media opinion, are assembled. Never ones to let a good punch-up go unrecorded, the hacks have pitched up early in numbers, with their flasks of coffee and slices of fruitcake, and are gabbing cheerfully with several police, stamping their feet for circulation. Like armies of old, the two sides are massing their ranks to prepare for battle.

It's well after eight by the time Jarvis arrives and a queue of cars lines up along the road at the staff entrance, prevented from driving in. A long way further up at the deliveries entrance, a line of four HGV's are queueing back into the road, their engines switched off, the drivers leaning against their vehicles, smoking, nattering, not too bothered. He pushes his way through the early gathering of protestors, who cheer every slogan chanted and jeer at every trapped driver.

Dark green uniform jacket and cap in place, Jarvis crowds together with a half dozen other men out in the open forecourt to listen to his brother fret about the risks of failing the contract. 'It would all have died down if the grievance had been dealt with properly in the first place.' Jonathan, looking out of place in a black track suit, trainers and baseball cap, has come down in the Range Rover to see for himself the extent of the situation. He's pacing around on the crumbling tarmac in front of the main factory building, inside the gates, a safe distance from the jeering protestors outside, like a football manager berating his team four-nil down at half-time. 'Now we have the police and the world's press gathering at one end of the road, and the mass of our brother workers in the middle,' he raves at his senior team. 'There's going to be a bloody battle, if we don't keep a lid on this. And the television channels will record it all, for the six o'clock news.'

Jonathan is walking up and down, a few steps this way, a few that. He's agitated and the tight control he normally keeps over his temper is beginning to loosen. He keeps pursing his lips and screwing his eyes up as he gazes at whoever is trying to answer his rhetorical questions, to explain the current impasse. With his voice rising in desperation, he's looking for a quick fix and will embrace anything with the remotest chance of success. He's yet to hear of anything and his fingers are restless, wanting but managing to resist the urge for a cigarette.

'A few days ago, we had five miserable blokes objecting to the new working arrangements. Now we've got a fucking demonstration. And people are coming in from all over the city to join in. How did that 'appen? And where's management when you want them?'

The protestors have started rattling the twin gates, already battered from years of use, but solid enough to hold back the mob outside. Built with corrugated metal in vertical strips, they open inwards, operated by a man with a switch, who sits in a small windowed concrete turret to one side, watching the CCTV screens with views of both sides. The only problem is the time they take to close, the motors cranking into action with agonising delay – it would be easy for a determined group to rush in from outside before they had fully closed, after an HGV for example had passed through.

Once firmly closed, the men inside feel protected. There are coils of barbed wire over the adjacent brick walls, but even so, Jarvis recognises the weak spots of the site, especially the other two entrances, with manually operated barriers. The meagre number of *Security First* staff have been allocated rotas, to cover the three entrances as best they can, and Jonathan confirms that a further half dozen new recruits are on their way later this morning.

Jonathan is under contract to deliver, and the strain is showing. Before he leaves his trusted troops to get on with the job, he confides in Jarvis that a dawn phone call this morning from the irate chief operating officer of the owner conglomerate made it clear that failure to comply with the contract would result in loss of said contract without payment: it was pay on performance.

Jarvis is wondering how Jonathan's little outfit won this contract in the first place, but his brother is nothing if not ambitious. Promising beyond his means, most probably, thinking that providing security to a long-forgotten factory tucked away by the waterfront in East London that employed less than a thousand workers could not possibly be anything but a doddle. What he didn't appreciate at the beginning was that Tate & Lyle had new owners, not the indifferent old guard who had allowed lax and slovenly practices to embed among the workforce which guaranteed no progress in productivity and wafer thin profits, but a shiny new private equity group who wanted their money to work for them, expecting a handsome return, who were not prepared to make exceptions.

Someone mutters urgently into Jarvis's ear that there are serious scuffles breaking out at the car park, and he calls for half a dozen men to follow him. They make their way through some of the long buildings and warehouses, and across turning yards, wishing they had a faster means of transport, like golf buggies, to cover the distances more effectively. A large gathering of angry sounding protestors surrounds the man on barrier duty and a small car at the entrance off Factory Road.

Workers are being pushed and shoved, and a few fists have already been thrown. Two manual workers have taken a few blows, one holding a hanky over his nose, the other with a cut mouth is being restrained by a couple of mates. A few security men are already lost among the confusion, workers and pickets mixing in the scrum. Hard to tell which are which sometimes. A few helmeted police in uniform have arrived and are wading in from one side. In the middle of the melee is a staff car, stopped short of the barrier and surrounded by a shouting gang of protestors, leaning over the bonnet and rocking the car from side to side with the terrified driver inside.

The television crews have distributed themselves among both sides and the inevitable conflict will be caught nicely on camera for the midday programmes. Standing recalcitrant at the barrier between the two sides, looking determined in his bright yellow hi-vis jerkin, over a thick jacket and jeans, solid as a rock with his square jaw and white hardhat, that had *Security First* printed around the rim, is Jack Appleton. Fearless and self-confident, he knows that all his men have been trained properly in crowd control, they know the ropes and understand the sensitivity of the situation. They are not here to take sides but to allow normal working activity to proceed and to protect those that feel threatened. With eyes narrowed and lower lip pouting, Jack confronts the thugs, with a deep throated bellow. He calls for order. His arms are crossed behind his back, a shortened truncheon swinging from a loop-tie around a wrist, which he would use without hesitation if he had to. He has already pleaded that they have everything under control and that there is no need for the police to pile in and get shirty; he is sure the pickets will play by the rules when they see what they're up against, and will let the workers through.

Jarvis organises his men into a line and orders them forwards, pushing everyone back towards the road, around the trapped car. They hold on, arms linked to form a strong human barrier across the entrance. The protestors begin to succumb, resorting to vicious, stupid and ruder shouts of abuse, at the workers, the security and the police, as they retreat. Jarvis is spat at and takes a blow across the face. He shows restraint, tempted as he is to respond with equal force. Instead he makes a mental note of the offending thug and promises to himself to get his own back at some point.

The barrier boom is raised, and the driver moves forward into the car park. The security men are sweaty but pleased after their effort. As the boom is lowered with a judder and order seems to be restored, at least until the next car arrives, the disgruntled demonstrators form smaller groups across the road, discussing their next move. Jack, not a hair out of place or bead of sweat anywhere, looks pleased, standing aside tall and commanding like a supervising general, a hint of a smirk wavering across his face.

Around midday, there is a lull in proceedings, with the mobs outside backing off mostly to the other side of the road, to watch from a distance. The police have drifted away as well, leaving two pairs of uniforms on foot to patrol up and down Factory Road all morning, while the rest are pulled back to the junction at the west end, under the DLR viaduct and close to a roundabout. The press are also gathered around their vans, the ITN crew and one from Sky News.

Jarvis slopes off with Jack to the canteen inside the main building for a cheese roll and a mug of tea. They sit for a while chatting. Jack moans about his knee problem, a cartilage causing him pain. Says he twisted it playing football with his grandson in the garden over the weekend. Jack is mid-fifties, one of the original founders of *Security First* with Jonathan. He has a designer beard turning grey that hides the deep creases in his jowls and a bit of a paunch from the beer. He's a touch on the tubby side, the result of several years of neglect after a sporty youth. How effective Jack might be in a confrontation situation that required quick reactions and speed of foot is a moot point.

Jack explains why the dispute has escalated this week. His voice sounds sceptical, complaining, a little superior. 'Management were prodded into action because of declining activity and disappointing sales. They introduced two lines of strategy: one was to improve efficiency, the other, to reduce waste.' He clearly has a grasp of the current situation. 'The ante was upped last week when the shop stewards were told by e-mail that at least another sixty jobs would be going by the end of the month. To add to the endless stream of jobs that have been lost over the last ten years. The ballot was hastily convened and the result: an unhelpful split between strike action and continuing discussions. But the unions are gaining the argument and the workers are worried about their security. So more of them are prepared to stand up to management. Plus, they decided to bus in a whole lot more workers from other sites, to swell the numbers. Rent-a-mob thugs, who are looking for confrontation and will use a bit of muscle, no doubt.'

During the afternoon, Jarvis watches as a vanload of fresh men in donkey jackets and big boots arrive, with a further police vehicle trailing close behind. They distribute themselves among their peers, the numbers on both sides growing relentlessly. From where the police congregate, they can observe activity the full length of Factory Road. In fact, one officer is positioned lying flat on the roof of a van with a pair of binoculars, keeping his eye on the protestors four hundred yards up the road. Jarvis can see that tensions are rising, the protestors agitation inflamed by the heavy police presence.

Jack and Jarvis do some patrolling of their own, to try calming the demonstrators, calling for them to retreat across the road, keep back from the entrances, stop obstructing the vehicles or they may get hurt. After several VIP cars have arrived and entered, apparently for a full board meeting in the main offices, a smart black Jaguar with a personal number plate weaves its way through the milling crowd, towards the big blue gates. This is the chief executive, arriving in chauffeur-driven style. The windows are neatly darkened to comfortably protect the occupant from the realities of the world outside.

Jarvis joins the cordon of his colleagues, all solid muscle, linking arms, stretched in a line across the front of the gates. Tomatoes splatter the windows of the limousine and splash drops over the security men. A roar of ironic cheering goes up when a couple of Tate & Lyle bags of sugar are thrown and split open on impact, spilling white powdery crystals across the windscreen that mix horribly with the remains of the smashed fruit. Jarvis's men break into two lines, moving each side of the advancing car to force back the pushing protestors who have rushed forward to get close. They thump the sides and bang on the roof with their hands and placards, offering much advice to the men inside with nasty hand gestures. The shouting gets so loud Jarvis cannot hear himself speak but eventually the electric gates swing back and allow enough width for the car to pass. Then the gates judder and shake before starting to reverse back together.

The security team relax but still must barge their way back inside the factory through a pedestrian side gate. Eventually they all slip through into safety behind their defences, to review the damage. A few bruises, splashes of sugar and tomato, and one man has a bit of a nosebleed.

Ten minutes later, the same scenario looks as if it will be repeated when another black limousine, a luxury Chrysler which Jarvis knows to be the chairman's car, winds its way through the crowds around the main entrance to wait patiently at the blue gates. For some unknown reason, the senior man decides to open his back door and step outside the car, to remonstrate with the protestors; even stepping up onto the running board to help get his voice heard. With swept-back silvery hair catching the light, he calls for them to disburse, to stop causing such unwelcome disturbance and allow dedicated workers in to do their jobs, so they can collect their much-deserved wages, surely a creditable desire in this time of austerity. You are not helping your cause by being bloody-minded, he boomed with a surprisingly strong voice, so go home, allow your leaders to come to the negotiating table. Or words to that effect. Which seems to do the exact opposite of what he misguidedly expects. The mob around his car surge forward, incensed at his audacity and his cheek. They smell an opportunity and crowd menacingly around him in his camel-haired coat and polished brogues. He is pelted with vegetables and abuse and manhandled. And then his driver, thinking he sees movement in the gates, a chink of space opening through which he will be able to dart to safety before his car or his passenger get damaged, starts to move the car forward. The chairman stumbles and a few thugs set upon him.

Among the mob around Jarvis is one particularly aggressive man that he has had his eye on, the very same thug who had hit him across the mouth a few hours earlier. This short thick-set specimen of hired aggro has studs in his nose and eyebrows, is shaven headed with barbed wire tattoos around his neck and armfuls of black and blue inkwork down to his wrists. He has purple swollen lips and his eyes seem unusually wide apart, set in a granite-like face that is speckled with dark bristles. Built like a wrestler, he gesticulates and salivates like the badly behaved bulldog that he reminds Jarvis of. In a dirty leather jerkin that has spiky studs all over it and heavy Dr Martens, he will be foul-mouthed and unreasonable, a formidable opponent for anybody, but when Jarvis notices the short blade in his right fist, he knows he has to get him down. A blow to his testicles would be a good start.

The angry bulldog, screwing up his little eyes, is pushing his way between two other blokes in front of him with a look of hatred. In a forward crouch he is but two strides away from the well-dressed and besieged elderly chairman. He is about to spring forward, hell-bent on causing injury, intent on sinking his blade into the chairman's side.

Reacting instinctively, barging against some other bystanders,

Jarvis throws himself in the way, just as the knife is swung backwards to prepare for its hurtful arc. Jarvis grabs at the thug's jerkin, barging into him, knocking him off-balance and swinging his right arm to get around his neck. They both go down onto the asphalted roadway, landing painfully on their knees. The man wriggles and lashes out, fighting ferociously and with speed. The body blow he delivers is forceful enough to knock the breath out of Jarvis. Gasping, his attempt to jerk his knee up into the man's groin is foiled. But he pins the thug down with his other knee, using his full weight and strength to hold him there. The man screams at him, spits up at him and swipes at him with his right arm, tries to push him off with his other fist wedged under Jarvis's jaw. Jarvis slams him across his mouth with a swiping right fist that shakes the man's teeth, producing bright blood at the corners. Some of it spatters across Jarvis's face as the ugly man spits again.

Jarvis knees his opponent's groin properly, hard and well placed. The bulldog goes quiet, screwing up his face, wanting to double up and be sick. He reaches for his wounded manhood, but Jarvis turns him sideways and forces his right arm back in a vicious brace. There is the sound of a nasty crack and the bulldog now has two good reasons to scream. Unable to hold onto the knife any longer, he drops it to the ground.

The surrounding crowd has moved back to give the two squabbling men room to manoeuvre. When the attention switched away from him, the chairman recovered his balance if not his dignity, and is standing open-mouthed at the fighting spectacle on the ground nearby.

A policeman with perfect timing kindly steps forward to retrieve the blade from the pathway, calling for a halt. Bulldog man, screaming that that bastard has broken his bleeding arm, is yanked to his feet, cuffed and dragged off between two hefty men in uniform, towards the back of a big white VW transporter van in characteristic Battenburg blue and yellow chequered side décor.

Right in front of Jarvis stand a couple of modern men of indeterminate age with ruffled hair and designer stubble. One of them has a chunky camera balanced on his shoulder, daylight reflecting off an impressive glass lens, pointed straight at him; the other in shirt and tie with a fluffy microphone held aloft in one hand, his other hand casually tucked in the outside pocket of his padded Barbour. 'Wow, mate, that was something. Have you recovered?' asks Mr Microphone. 'Can we have a word, do you mind, to camera, alright?' And before Jarvis can mount a refusal without sounding petulant, the yellow fluff ball is poked under his chin. The TV journalist, politely fawning in a well-spoken manner, is happy to make fatuous comments about Jarvis's heroics, his special skills, does he have a medal for armed combat, is he part of the team trying to keep order? 'You do realise you probably saved that man's life?'

By this time, the chairman has long made his getaway, through the main gates with his chauffeur, recognising the right moment to withdraw from the scene of his own making.

This is live national television, Sky, ITN and Channel Four all waiting their turn, and this is apparently a well-known face from the box, although Jarvis is quite unable, even when describing the incident in detail to Pamela a few days later, to put a name to the face. They all looked blurred and different in the chaos of the moment. 'John Snow? Anastasia Bellingham? Johnny Fry?' Pamela is determined to guess, but Jarvis keeps shaking his head. All he can recall of the interview later was that the fellow was a man and he wore floppy green Wellington boots. Quite what he was asked or what he said in reply is a mess of rowdy noise in his memory, all the time conscious of the revolting sticky streaks of the bulldog's blood across his face, that he consciously kept wiping with his fingertips. He recalls a young lady from the TV team handing him a handkerchief to use. He realised then that he had a cut himself across the back of his knuckles, which added to the mess, and he backed away wiping the white cotton across his face and tightly pressing it onto his hand, to the sycophantic mumblings of the unknown friend from the television.

There are quiet cheers and congratulations for him from some of his security mates nearest to the scene, who grip him across his shoulders, and the cameras soon move on to other people. He stumbles away somewhat unsteadily back inside the grounds of the factory, heading towards the office block, where there is a toilet he can clean up in. He finds a seat. Someone presents him with a cup of tea, which is surprisingly welcome, as his mouth has become parched dry. It is then that he becomes aware of the stinging along his leg and his fingers discover the cut edges of his jeans which are soaked with a deep red wetness, that is trickling inside and has reached his sock and upper rim of his ankle boot. A knife wound, that thug with his kitchen knife. He's sure the blood makes it look worse than it is, it can't be serious, it just stings like hell. He finds another sore cut higher up near his waist, oozing freely, his shirt caked with blood. He presses hard against them both using the cut clothes as swabs. At this point the sensible girl with the tea is looking quite pale but she's on her mobile, calling for company medical aid. Jarvis's hands are caked with the warmness of his own sticky blood, and all he can think about suddenly is the swift and deep cut he inflicted on his friend Joe all those years ago. *His* blood had welled up then and soiled Jarvis's army shirt and covered his hands as he tried to stem the flow with pressure using Joe's own shirt sleeves.

In the early hours before Sunday dawned, Mustafa appeared dressed in jeans and leather lace-up boots, with a discarded US combat jacket, to wake the two British soldiers. Several other swarthy Iraqis hovered behind him. Slumped asleep, Joe had lain groaning for some of the night, and Jarvis had had a bad time, nodding off while trying to keep an eye on his partner. The tourniquet had been successful, and Jarvis loosened it a bit, not wanting to compromise the circulation to the rest of Joe's arm. He woke him and Joe gulped at the water offered. The wound was a clean cut, blackened with dried blood. Joe's sleeve was stuck to the area under the bandage which was equally caked and stiffened. Best left in position. He struggled to get him to his feet and they made their way up to ground level, Jarvis gripping Joe under his good arm. The blood puddles staining the concrete floor where Joe had lain, Jarvis had already covered with a rug, hoping that they would not be discovered until they were far away.

When Mustafa asked directly what had happened, Jarvis mumbled something about a fall, not to worry. They stumbled out into the crisp air, where the morning was still dark and chilly. A couple of the Iraqis carried their backpacks and they were led across the courtyard to the back ramp of an old Ashok Leyland truck. They settled up at the front, where wooden slats separated them from the driver's cab. Then dozens of plastic bags of fertilizer and dates and potatoes were piled all around them both, before a wooden pen was erected across the rest of the floor space. From across the yard, a gathering of bleating goats and a few sheep were herded up the ramp into the pen, where they stamped and butted against each other, sounding scared and defaecating freely where they stood. The rear gate was closed, as everyone else readied themselves. Mustafa shouted a few muffled instructions, truck doors slammed, engines started up. There appeared to be several trucks that would move out in a column, with the Ashok third in line. Joe for all his apparent drowsiness sensed they were in for a rough journey.

The trucks manoeuvred out of the yard in a juddering line and turned away from the city centre, heading south. Joe was restless, feeling every jolt over the rough roads pulling at his arm and he kept sucking his breath in between clenched teeth, holding it close. He dared not touch the wound itself, it felt swollen and numb, but stinging at the same time. He was imagining that something more than muscle had been damaged. Because he was scared and confused, his anger made him want to cry. Encouraged to lie still, to close his eyes and relax, told that the time would pass and they would find themselves in Baghdad before he knew it, Joe resented being patronised and treated as a child.

Jarvis was pressed in his corner against his backpack, one hand on his gun holster. Every bump and knock juddered through the truck, devoid of any useful suspension. He took some comfort in being on the move, leaving

Haditha behind them, heading towards Baghdad, their only escape route. Mustafa seemed confident that there would not be any US roadblocks on the main highways.

'Let's hope no one is searching for two renegade soldiers trying to reach the capital,' Jarvis murmured to no one in particular.

The top US brass would be wanting to quash any potential fuss arising from the Haditha roadside bomb and subsequent slaughtering of civilians, and certainly would not want any newspaper reporting until at least they had carried out an investigation. If they were aware of the role played by the British pair, Jarvis was sure they would want them silenced. The sooner they reached relative safety at British HQ without being discovered the better - after that, all they would need was a quick chopper ride down to Basra.

He tried to occupy his mind with plans, reflecting on his difficult conversation that he had had with Malone last evening. It had been a bit of a shock for him as he presented their dilemma, but Jarvis thought the captain got the gist of it in the end.

The lorry convoy gradually cleared the rambling outskirts of the city, the streets deserted, while a creamy moon stared benevolently over them from a vacant sky. The line of trucks rattled on Route South through Al Haqlaniyah, and then turned onto Highway 12, when it started to move at a fair clip through the greyish desert landscape. After an hour or so the change from dull night to a glowing sky was a sudden transformation. The beautiful orange streaky sunrise promised another relentlessly hot day.

Jarvis wondered what they would do if the convoy were ambushed. Mustafa had reassured him earlier that they were travelling with armed escort, a coalition armoured truck with Iraqi government soldiers on board riding shotgun at either end of the convoy. He had his doubts they would be any good at fending off rocket attacks from a determined bunch of al-Qaeda insurgents, but decided not to worry about something he could not control.

Joe was constantly stirred from sleep by the restlessness of the goats, bleating feebly so close. The sudden brightness of the light glancing through the slats and between the stuffed sacks played shockingly over his troubled eyelids. Despite the stinging of his upper arm, he drifted off to where he would rather be, staring into Jahinda's brown eyes, while her fingers trace a pattern over his face. He was anxious for her safety but kept entertaining happy thoughts of returning to Haditha, taking a year out, when the bloody conflict was over, when he might travel and take her away with him. He was not planning to stay with the British Army, that was for sure. He hated the formality, the foot stamping, the saluting and the early morning discipline, the staff sergeant shouting orders into his ears, the lack of sleep, the awful food, Christ it was all so tiresome.

And for want of having anybody close to him he might hold, to comfort him from the unimaginable humiliation of Jarvis's knife attack, he tried to hug his backpack with his one good arm, his eyes closed, letting the rhythmic movements of the lorry and the warm air lull him further into dreamy visions of romance.

Joe stirred from his reverie. 'So was the Captain convinced, do you think?'

Jarvis was surprised by the question, out of the blue, thinking Joe was still asleep. They had to shout out to make themselves heard over the rumbling noise of the convoy. 'Not at first. He needs time to talk to the right people and to get some reportage on Chestnut. Getting him to step out of line is a major thing: not his style. Anyway, we'll find out when we get to BAHQ.'

'Well, I said it was suicide,' Joe moaned unhelpfully.

A burning orange sun dominated the clear skies, and a distant haze shimmied over the vastness of the desert sands, making the horizon look as if it was on fire. Jarvis pulled a piece of coloured cloth, a scarf he had found, over his head, but still the heat of the sun burnt through his cropped hair to roast his scalp.

Joe remained fidgety, groaning as he shifted position, from one buttock to another. 'Do you think Rahim and Jahinda will be alright?' he asked during a roadside comfort break. Their short convoy had stopped for water and stretching the legs after more than two hours of tedious vibrating and noisy movement. They had rumbled down the Euphrates valley, through vast stretches of rock and scrub vegetation into flatter but no less dry and dusty terrain. There had not been any rain in these parts for months, not since last April. The wadis were mostly dry and the wading birds looked miserable. Nearby a cluster of farm buildings lay neglected among the surrounding fallow wheat fields, close to where they merged with the encroaching arid stone and sandy terrain of the western deserts.

The two soldiers struggled up and Jarvis had to help Joe over the side of the truck, avoiding the bleating animals. Joe squealed and Jarvis grabbed him tight around the waist in a brotherly fashion, his way of offering something of an apology for all his discomfort.

Their eyes were dazzled by reflective spangles of sunlight that bounced off the surface of the sand. 'The US marines can be a bit rough when they get excited.'

'You bet. But they'll probably find our original hideout in the scrub, abandoned, and return to their team. There was enough to be getting on with on Chestnut.' Joe did not think Jarvis sounded particularly convinced.

Jarvis, desperate to avoid the subject, told Joe to stay put, as he walked away from their truck, over the surrounding scrub and climbed a ridge of sand and rock. Joe lent against a wooden telephone post, gulping at a warm water bottle, and watched Jarvis disappear for a while. He heard two gunshots. A minute later Jarvis casually returned, sliding down the sandy bank back to their truck. His holstered Glock was hidden from view, covered under his floppy shirt tails.

Jarvis looked Joe in the eye: 'I shot two insurgents, remember.'

Back in the truck, climbing stiffly into their positions over the side railings, they settled once more behind their protective barrage of fertilizer bags and sacks of dates.

'Do you think they'll have an investigation? Surely the brass will ask questions. Those dead Iraqis, women we saw, an old man, there would have been children in those houses. They weren't armed, they weren't even fighting.'

'There will be an inquiry,' Jarvis said quietly, 'have to be. If word gets out. If the press get some pictures, accusations will fly. They will have to deal with it.'

'So they will report that Wozniak was taken out by a British bullet, not an Iraqi insurgent.'

'I'm counting on being thousands of miles away by then.'

In a waiting area of the A&E department at Mile End Hospital, the day-time TV news is running soundlessly on a screen on the far wall, when Jarvis catches the familiar sight of the factory down by the Thames and the Tate & Lyle logo flying hugely over the scene. There are crowds cheering, jostling around the gates with their placards, as a black saloon crawls into view. The security team in their green uniform jackets and caps are in a line across the gates. And then chaos as the cameraman is obviously jostled out of place and off balance: pictures of shoes and boots on the ground, and then suddenly the clear blue sky. And across the bottom of the screen, FIGHTING INCIDENT AT PICKET LINE is the headline, white on red, moving right to left. The editing switches to the silver-haired chairman of the company in his camel wool coat appearing among the protestors, and then stepping up onto the running board to address them. Jarvis recalls his gravelly voice and the murmuring derision of the crowd around him. He is holding both his hands up as he makes his appeal. The crowds surge forward and swamp the man, he totters over and disappears from view, as those nearest him set upon him. Among the scuffling chaos, Jarvis's blond head suddenly appears across from one side. His cap has been lost and he's barging into a hefty-looking thug with shaven scalp and tattoos, bringing him down to the ground.

The screen shot switches suddenly to his blood-smeared face, his name hovering in big capital letters underneath. A fluffy microphone is thrust under his chin by an arm, and Jarvis looks startled, his jacket and shirt dishevelled and his nose bleeding. He keeps wiping his fingers across his face, pinching his nose, smearing more streaks of blood as a silent interview proceeds. He cannot remember what he was asked or what he said, something about instinct and training, the need for quick reactions. The footage continues with two beefy police officers handcuffing the tattooed thug and escorting him away. He is shouting silently at everyone and looks drunk. The camera catches the interviewer smiling at

Jarvis, trying to shake his hand, presumably congratulating him on his act of bravery as the title HERO OF FACTORY ROAD follows across the bottom of the screen.

A nurse calls his name. In a tiny curtained-off area, with his coat off and trousers discarded on the chair, his side and leg are examined, and the quiet-spoken Asian doctor advises cleansing, stitching under local anaesthetic, and injections of anti-tetanus and antibiotics. Forty-five minutes later, when finished, Doctor Singh reassures Jarvis that the injuries are not too serious, happily not deeply penetrating wounds, but nasty cuts, nevertheless. He is advised to see his GP for the stitches to be removed in about ten days. With wounds covered and dressed, it's early evening by the time Jarvis is ready to leave. Someone he does not know has volunteered to drive him home to Hoxton, kindly dropping him off at the end of Baring Street. He is almost beyond caring whether there is anyone in a little black car to spot him or not, as he stiffly hobbles along key in hand to Sam's door in the brick wall by the bus stop.

Pamela, who also happened to be watching Sky News at the same time only a few miles away in her mother's front lounge, recognised the pain on her husband's face, and seeing the blood smears on his hands realised that he had been hurt. She immediately tried to call him, was blocked, and left several messages of affection and worry at regular intervals.

Jarvis reads her messages in private when he returns to his room and sends his own message of affection and reassurance.

'My wife, she die with our next baby, they both died, a few years back,' Rahim recalled quietly one evening, as they shared a cool bottle of Indian beer from his fridge downstairs, sitting on the rooftop hideaway, under a warm panoply of bright stars. 'I try to bring up Jahinda as best I can, but I have to work. She is getting restless, asking questions. You have children, Corporal?'

'No, no.' Rahim liked to address him by his rank: more respectful, he

would say. 'I have only been married a couple of years, Rahim, children can wait.' Jarvis barely managed a twitch of his mouth. 'Sorry to hear about your wife, Jahinda's mother,' he added.

'Always asking things that girls ask, about this and that, wanting things that girls want, wanting to go out. I tell her, not in Haditha. You go out in the market here and you be set on in no time, men making propositions, you not come back, believe me. She listens but I cannot stop her for ever.' Rahim looks defeated for a moment. 'I hope this war is over soon, it destroys us, all of us, making everyone suspicious, nobody trusts people anymore. Haditha used to be lovely place, quiet but a farmer could grow things, you could bring up children in the street, it was safe. The dates were good.' He chuckled to himself, his face creased up in deep lines.

Jarvis recalls his day's activities briefly and with little detail. Sam has been listening with amazement. 'It was quite an interesting morning, actually,' Jarvis says with a sarcastic laugh. He is slumped in the kitchen with a ham and cheese toasted sandwich and Sam, while eating his supper, explains that Delph and he saw it on the news earlier.

'My God, Jarvis, you were the hero.' Sam is pleased to be associated with such a man, but he looks anxious. 'Were you hurt?'

'I took the knife across my leg, my side.' His hand hovers over his left side, as if still sore to touch. He has changed trousers, so there is nothing to see. 'I needed some stitches. Went to Mile End Hospital, casualty. It wasn't too bad in the end. Somebody drove me back.'

'My God,' Sam exclaims again, 'you could have been seriously hurt. You could have been killed.'

'Don't exaggerate, it's just a flesh wound. We stopped the madman, anyway. Not that that will end the union trouble.'

'At least you saved that executive's bacon, he could have taken a nasty knife wound. Let me look.' Sam is bending forward and reaching for Jarvis's shirt, as if he is going to start prodding him for damage.

Keen to get back up to his watching station to see what might be happening on the street, Jarvis is not looking for a prolonged conversation or bodily examination. 'It's been dressed, you can't see anything. It's sore at the moment.'

'I find it incredible,' Sam mused, 'that these people would believe that a violent assault on the boss was the answer to industrial relations.' Sam had been relatively well schooled, which was a bit unusual in his day for a professional sportsman. He even had an 'A' level in something, Jarvis could not remember what. Geography, probably.

'These people were incensed. Jealousy, dogma, anger.' Jarvis touches the side of his sore nose, which felt bruised. 'Anyway, the big guy I had to tackle was hired to make trouble, it didn't have to make sense to him.'

Through the open door to their little sitting room, Delphie is seen working on some material across her lap, repairing the hem of a dress. She listens to all the talk, her spectacles slipping along the bridge of her nose, while a cigarette sits emitting a wavy line of ashen smoke that bridles up towards the stained ceiling. She murmurs her support for the working man. 'These people have a right surly to protest and to let management understand how strongly they feel about it. It's part of the divide in this country, it infuriates me. The wealthy bosses get wealthier and their workers get peanuts. Being forced to take pay-cuts and redundancies. There's a disconnect. It's going to get worse.'

And Jarvis finds himself agreeing with her.

'Yes, but a violent knife attack, that makes no sense,' Sam says with some force. 'I think you deserve a medal. Delphie, what do you say?'

'Absolutely. Very brave. Your soldier's training did you proud.' Delphie has interrupted her delicate work and is looking with something close to admiration, albeit reluctantly, acknowledging that Jarvis is not just a big bully like all the rest but can do something worthwhile. 'The hero at the gates, definitely.

Protecting members of the elite from potentially vicious attacks on their lives. Definitely. Well done, Jarvis.'

'I must get back up to my station.' He smiles thankfully at his friends.

'Nothing's been going on in the street that I've noticed, by the way. I've been watching, discreet. Walked up and down in my overcoat and woolly hat and had an umbrella up at midday when there was some drizzle. Didn't see that Ford you mentioned.'

'Be careful, Sam. Don't want you getting involved, really.'

Joe's earlier gloomy predictions were turning out about right, the convoy journey stuffed in the Leyland with livestock was damned uncomfortable and tedious. The sun had become relentless, the animals increasingly restless and noisy, with their bleating and clacking feet and constant defaecation. The road was mostly clear, and the line of trucks made good progress, without any roadblocks, but the noisy vibration of the engine and driveshaft under them and constant rattling of the metal side panels were maddening, and sleep of any kind was impossible.

Jarvis could still hear the shocked voice of his captain in his headset. 'You shot their Sergeant?' The surprised indignation of Malone's crisp tones had been palpable. 'Dead?'

'Yes, sir, it was all I could do. I could not communicate with them. It was the only way to stop him. He was going ballistic with anger. They lost one marine in the bomb and two injured, but his response was crazy. Murderous.' Jarvis had tried to find the effective words. 'And illegal,' he had added.

His head was wobbling from side to side, against the webbed fabric of his backpack. A rough sack bulging with dates was juddering unforgivingly against his face. His mouth was dry, his lips cracked but he could not be bothered to reach for the suction of his horribly warm water. His mind kept recalling Malone's disbelief. 'The US marines are likely to send a hunting party after us and they will not stop till they get us, you know what they're like.'

'I know nothing of the sort, Collingwood.' Malone's indignant reprimand.

Was it for effect? He knew Malone, he was a good commanding officer, practical, steady. Or so he thought.

'They will want both Street and myself neutralised, dead or captured, either way silenced, I promise you.' Whether Malone was sympathetic or not he could not really tell.

He tried to stretch his cramped legs, pushing against other sacks of whatever else is stacked around them. His backside was sore. 'God, Malone better pull his finger out, otherwise we really are fucked,' Jarvis mused.

Joe had his eyes closed, as he drifted in and out of dreamy thoughts of holding Jahinda's hand and kissing her girlish lips. He had rarely heard Jarvis swear like that before and pretended not to have heard. He did not want to interrupt the spinning of his imaginary carousel of romantic pictures, however fanciful. As mile after mile added further distance between them, Joe relied on memory to tell its own tale. He viewed them almost as not themselves, but as two other people, and he was watching them as if on a screen.

Jahinda sitting cross-legged beside a young lad, smiling in the darkness, with a distant moon as their only lighting, as she traced the patterns of his veins along the backs of his hands, caressing the pads of thickened skin on his fingers. Jahinda busying herself with her granny in their tiny kitchen, chopping cucumber and peppers, draining rice, humming to herself.

Jahinda at the side door late into an evening, whispering her nightly goodbye into the young man's impressionable ear, as they held hands. Jahinda once pressing her dry lips to his for a fleeting moment, before answering her father's call from within the house and quietly closing the door on him. And once, with a mind made lucid by their intimacy, as they lay together in the grassy fields outside under a clear night sky, Jahinda asking him about his friends, and with a hint of a smile in one corner of her mouth, about all the women he has made love with before coming out to Iraq. His head rested across her chest, the rhythmic thumping of her heart so close beneath, as he teased her with his counting on his fingers imaginary lovers that he could barely remember. Watching her sparkling eyes widen with innocence and surprise, a hand comes to rest across the soft mounds of her young breasts, with layers of cotton and silk between them, and she does not complain or push him away.

And the young man imagines a time after they are married in her father's home and she is able to reveal all of herself to him, in a large bed under clean sheets; and the two of them can frolic together with complete freedom, without any shyness, somewhere far from the heat and repression of her homelands.

After a few minutes, Joe murmured sleepily: 'When we get to Baghdad, you mean?'

Irritably: 'Yes, in Baghdad.'

After several more uneventful hours, traveling south on the tarmacked Highway 12, with its aluminium towers every hundred yards carrying power lines running alongside, they finally came close to the International Airport, about to enter the Presidential region in Radwaniyah. Their line of six trucks was at a standstill waiting their turn at a coalition roadblock. A growing queue of cars and vans were joining at the back.

A short distance from the road was a massive fenced-off area of earthy land enclosures for dozens of ostriches, their weird long necks bobbing up and down, pecking at seed on the ground and squawking argumentatively at each other. They seemed to be chained and their wings clipped, and Jarvis assumed they were used for meat.

Mustafa on foot talked discretely to Jarvis through the side of the truck and their barrier of bags. He advised absolute quiet and they remain well hidden. They would be arriving into the south-west corner of Baghdad shortly, and the US/UK military base camp was close by. Jarvis thanked Mustafa sincerely for his hospitality.

'Worth your weight in gold, mate,' he murmured.

Dozens of young Iraqi soldiers in their untidy camouflage kit with floppy baseball caps were sitting around on damaged walls, with barely an AK-47 between them. There were twisted metal road signs scattered over the dry earth and groups of dirty woolly sheep with droopy brown ears munching forlornly at the last remaining patches of brush grass. Some way off was a burnt-out Russian tank and an upturned armoured vehicle, blackened and charred, tyres melted.

It was after eleven o'clock and the wait had been at least an hour in seething temperatures. Their trucks had moved forward and were being checked, driver's cabs inspected, the backs opened up. The men in charge were mostly tough-looking Americans, while the armed support of Iraqi soldiers stood around leisurely joking and drinking coffee out of paper mugs, their automatics shouldered. The inspection was mostly cursory, although marines climbed aboard two or three trucks and rifled through the contents, demanding boxes were opened.

Using an Iraqi interpreter, they questioned their driver about destination and contents. Joe and Jarvis remained motionless under their sacks, not daring to breathe. Once the marines had seen the messy and bedraggled collection of nervous goats and sheep in the open pen in the back of the Ashok, and smelt the piles of dung, they seemed to lose interest.

'What's in the bags at the back?' one marine asked.

Jarvis heard the muffled droning of the driver explaining. The marines were satisfied and they moved onto the next. Their truck was waved through, following the others in slow single file.

The convoy moved on and soon they were turning onto Highway 1 eastwards towards Baghdad. Their driver had his instructions and the Ashok peeled off from the line, taking the airport road. Jarvis roused himself and got up to lean over to knock on the glass at the back of the driver's cabin. The truck pulled up on the side of the road. Jarvis got Joe up and together they climbed out over the side railings as before. He left their weapons, their sidearms, his sheathed knife and precision rifle in the backpacks in their hiding place. Jarvis had retrieved his beret, tidied his clothes as best he could, tucking his dirty shirt into his waist, and using the big wing mirror on the truck to smooth his hair down with wetted fingers, before placing his beret in position. They climbed up into the cabin with the driver, Joe in the middle, and indicated that he should drive on.

They followed the uninterrupted low concrete wall around the perimeter for half a mile to the next corner, turned left and then along the wall for another half mile north, until they encountered an entrance, complete with twin towers and marksmen, a heavy barrier and a small platoon of US marines armed with machine guns. There were concrete blocks spaced across the road, and a tricky chicane for an Ashok to wend through.

'Make it look convincing, Joe,' Jarvis muttered.

At the barrier, the driver called out to the nearest officer, in broken English, that he had a couple of British soldiers seeking refuge within. Armed to the teeth a crowd of Americans surrounded the truck and could clearly see the two bedraggled British soldiers sitting quietly in the front. One indicated for them to climb down. Jarvis opened the door and jumped down onto the concreted path.

'Corporal Collingwood,' Jarvis called out, straight-backed, saluting the apparent commanding officer. 'Serving British Army soldiers with First Battalion Special Forces, escaping insurgent trouble in Haditha. I have a wounded soldier with me, Private Street, in need of attention.' Jarvis was hanging everything on the fact that US command would not have communicated yet with their mates about searching for two runaway Brits, concerned at senior level for keeping the already traumatic scenes in Haditha to themselves. Or if they have been alerted, they knew to first refer to British command for clarification.

At which, Joe staggered down gripping his bandaged arm and grimacing suitably. The two of them stepped forward together. 'We have packs in the truck, in the back, with our arms.' Two marines boarded the Ashok over the railings and rummaged around among the sacks, before throwing the backpacks over the sides to waiting colleagues. Jarvis turned to call out his thanks to the driver, who was eager to be on his way. They were both pleased to see the last of the Ashok, to be sure. The smell of dates would be forever associated for both of them with the pungency of fresh goat droppings.

With two armed marines behind them, and two in front, the commander led them up the pathway to a waiting open Jeep. Their backpacks were carried by two other soldiers who tramped the full distance to the camp HQ. They were driven away by mystified marines towards the British section, that occupied a flat rectangle of land the size of a football field, with row upon row of easy-build huts in long parallel lines. Under a neat collection of flagpoles with the Union Jack, the Stars and Stripes, and the national Iraqi emblem all hanging limply in the intense heat, they dismounted in front of a squat building that stood in for British Army Command, Baghdad.

Jarvis breezily thanked their handlers. They picked up their packs and stepped gingerly between a couple of impeccably kitted out armed soldiers in white webbing and peaked caps, towards swing doors. They must have looked a dreadful sight, with their whiskered unwashed faces, dishevelled greasy hair, in mucky-looking mufti, wreaking of body odour, goats and ripe dates.

Later that evening, desperate for a sleep, as Jarvis crouches on the floor below the windowsill in his room, his head lolling on his forearms, a black MPV cruises along the crescent of Baring Street. Jarvis's eyes come to life. He checks the time: nine-thirty, a half hour earlier than agreed. Trying to be clever. The Chevrolet moves slowly, yellowy lamplight catching intermittently along its shiny roof. It pulls over into a space before Jarvis's front door. The engine is switched off, the lights go out. Two bare-headed men step out of the side door, looking confident, in command. They pull their dark raincoats around them against the cold at the same time. He notices the left-hand drive and through his binoculars the diplomatic plates: 274D102 - allowed to go anywhere, park anywhere and bullet-proof to boot. They must have access to all the support and tech that they want, even if they are under the radar in this country. They'll be armed, too, although he still believes they will be looking for a quiet extermination.

Through the darkened glass he can pick out the outline of the driver. The first man, the shorter of the two, waits on the pavement punching a gloved fist casually into his other palm, looking at the row of terraced houses in front of him, with his back to the car and to Jarvis. The other one stands not far away looking around. Both men are heavily built, like baseball players, broad shoulders, solid legs, their trousers stopping just short of the same black lace-up jackboots. There is something stereotypically American about them, the way their arms hang, their bodies move, the way they assume control. Jarvis just knows they are ex-marine. The shorter man turns to look along the housing on his other side, staring straight at number 59, towards Sam's house. Although it has been four years since Jarvis last saw it, when it was helmeted and dusty and red-cheeked, and the man was yelling commands in the heat of the action on Route Chestnut, he recognises that face instantly. He catches sight of a tattoo on his neck, above his collar, left side. Tom Flynn, Wosniak's second-in-command. A little bit heavier, a bit thicker maybe around the jowls, with possibly a goatee, although difficult to be sure in the shadowy darkness. But definitely Thomas The Tank Flynn.

All the evidence he might need to convince himself that his life really is in jeopardy is there before him: Tom Flynn, in London looking for revenge, no mercy. His fair complexion and flattened nose are unmistakable. Jarvis can almost smell the cordite and the burning fuel, hear the noise of the screaming marine and the whipping helicopter blades of the Hawks, as the thick smoke swirled around in the breeze. He can invoke the taste of bitterness in his throat.

He wishes he had his sniper rifle in his hands instead of just a pair of binoculars.

He's not sure about the other man, who looks tall and lean. He guesses the driver is John Shorty Shorter. For a second, Flynn seems to be looking straight up at his window and Jarvis shrinks back a little away from the nets, making sure they stay undisturbed.

He sees no sign of Joe. He imagines him in the back of the vehicle, trussed up and subdued, of no risk. Ready to be dragged out, perhaps, and used as a negotiating ploy. He remembers him in the back of that truck with the goats, the smell and the insufferable heat. And the nasty cut across his arm he had inflicted. Poor Joe, he had complained noisily, shifting restlessly when he should have been lying curled up, hidden and quiet. Jarvis had had to throw cold water from a plastic bottle over his face to wake him up, so he could tell him to shut up moaning. That was harsh. He had had to convince Mike Malone, otherwise they would never have been flown out, he's sure of that. Poor Joe.

The two Americans have set off along the pavement walking slowly in opposite directions, Tommy up and other man down the street, searching for the house numbers. The front doors of these houses are a mere step from the pavement, no front gardens to tend to, just narrow concreted strips, where a bicycle or a motor bike might be chained, among a pot plant or two, behind iron railings. There is nobody else about, everyone behind their closed doors; there are no dogs barking or walking the street. This is how it always is. You might not see the residents from one week to another, they are not to be found playing outside, especially with autumn setting in, temperatures dropping and the days getting shorter. Hardly any lights are on behind the closed windows, all is quiet, as if the place had been deserted. Except up at the end, where a few customers come and go from *The Baring*, and voices and muffled music can sometimes be picked up drifting along the street.

Once he realises the sequence of numbers is working up from the bottom, the second man quickly turns around to join Tom and they move on up together, looking for number 21. But the terrace numbers end at 20 and then there is a gate into a garden behind a brick wall with iron railings along the top and more railings around the miserable-looking yellow block on the corner, going round into Wilton Square. They plod back towards their car, watching the numbers decrease back to ten, nine, eight. They're back at the bottom of the street and they swivel their heads this way and that, looking lost. Then they cross over the road to Sam and Delphie's side, but here the numbers move from 62 to 61, to 60 as they pass further up the road, moving below Jarvis hidden behind his net curtain, and then it's 58, 57, 56 and they're back at the pub on the corner. Where is 21, they must be thinking, or has that little shit given us the wrong number? Has Collingwood played a game with us? Fuck the man, Tom will be thinking.

They cross back to the MPV and have a conflab, the three of them. The driver is pointing towards Jarvis's black front door, his arm out of the open window. He seems to know - one of them must have seen Pamela rushing from the house to the back of the cab yesterday evening. Flynn and his mate return to the front of number 15. The wrought iron gate is gingerly pushed inwards, and Flynn side-steps a conifer bush in a wide pot to peer in through the ground floor window. Then he looks up at the first floor. He takes something from his pocket and looks at it in his gloved hand: it's dark and cylindrical. He fiddles with something, pulling on the end of it. Then he steps up to the door and pushes whatever it is through the letter box. They both stand back on the pavement and wait. The minutes tick away, five or more, while the two of them walk up and down a few yards watching his front door. They seem to expect the door to be opened and Jarvis can only conclude that it's a stink bomb or something like, that they have thrown into his house.

Tom steps forward and prods at the bell button but hears nothing. He waits, his hands in his coat pockets. Gripping a small Glock or Ruger, no doubt. There is no answer; the black door remains shut.

As he watches the two ex-marines prowling like tigers, it has become clearer to Jarvis, in case he was in some doubt before, what he is really up against. He is going to have to be clever and resourceful to escape these vengeful killers. Their body language mimics anger and brutal desire. They will show no mercy.

He was right to move Pamela out in the first place. Definitely. At least she is safe at her mother's. He's convinced that Joe is captive, probably hurt, tortured, maybe dead already.

As he watches the MPV finally cruise out of the crescent of Baring Street, he decides to ring Joe's mum to find out if she has heard from him.

'Hi, Doris, just phoned for an update.'

'I've heard nothing, Corporal Jarvis, sir, not a peep. I'm worried now, don't mind telling you.'

He listens to her for a while and does his best to reassure her that he will find Joe. But in his own mind, he is sure that Joe has bought it.

Debriefing interview, MoD, Aldwych.
December 12, 2005.

Not wanting to sound denigrating, Malone takes his time framing his next question: 'What exactly was Private Joe Street's contribution to all this?'

'Joe was happy to go along with the decision. Like me, he could not see an alternative - although he did point out several times that he thought it would put us in some danger.'

'Too right.' Malone seems to agree, although he would never actually say so. 'Regret it?'

'No. It was the right thing to do.'

Malone for once looks Jarvis straight in the eyes, while twisting his lower lip, signalling his doubt. Again, he takes his time to put his next question: 'And how did Private Street sustain his injuries? Exactly?'

Jarvis has been over this many times in his own mind and does not hesitate: 'The shooting must have alerted a couple of insurgents downstairs. I think they were in the garage for collection of their motor bike that Rahim had been working on. They came up to the garage roof, as we were getting ourselves ready to disappear. They carried knives and the first one slashed at Joe, who was lucky to be able to swerve away - the cut was relatively superficial across his upper arm.' Jarvis is speaking as if he is there, in the heat of the early morning, among the chaos, among the white sheets and robes hanging on their lines. 'Two insurgents hell-bent on shedding English blood, and I am reaching down to my pack, for my Glock, pulling at the leather flap, grabbing at the handle. I brought my right arm round and pumped out two shots, a bullet through each of their chests. The blood spattered the washing and they crumpled on the concrete floor. Rahim shooed us both downstairs, Joe gripping his arm. He grabbed our stuff, made sure we had it all. I tied a tee shirt as best I could around Joe's upper arm and he pressed on the wound. Rahim spoke to Ahmed about getting rid of the two bodies upstairs, when we had gone.'

Chapter 6
Wednesday November 11

A frosty first light creeps in to invade his unfamiliar room. He stirs, his body is so stiff. Fully dressed, he lies still, sore down his wounded side, listening to the distant morning sounds and willing himself back to sleep. The heating has not yet come on and the cold air Èfeels clamped around him. During the night, wondering if the Americans would come back, he listened for sounds and returned repeatedly to the window with his binoculars. He scanned the deserted crescent of Baring Street, focusing on his own front door over the road, but there had been nothing to see. At least whatever they had thrown in through the letter box had not set the house on fire.

A little later, he stirs with the clanking of the central heating pipes. He hears a few sounds of movement below. The street is slowly coming to life, a few early risers emerging from their front doors, finding their frost-covered cars or heading for the bus stop. He slips along to the bathroom still feeling dopey and gives his face a cold splash. He is not going anywhere today - he will stay out of sight, lie low and rest. Restore his strength.

Downstairs his neighbours are dawdling in the kitchen, Sam at the little fogged-up window munching his cereal, watching spikes of bright sunshine dart across his back yard; he offers toast and instant coffee, before he goes off to help his daughter at the shop. Delphie is watching an old kettle on top of the hot plate of her charred wood-burning stove. The boiling water finally blows its whistle, that reminds her of the lovely old steam trains that used to belch smoke across her bedroom window when they lived down by Limehouse Basin, back in the day.

Scuttling around, Delphie is planning to leave for some work she has lined up over in Bethnal Green. Soon, left alone, Jarvis rings through to his brother, explaining what happened yesterday at the factory. Jonathan calls him the hero of the day, saying they saw the news and that Brenda was impressed.

'I'm not going down to Factory Road today, my leg's too sore and stiff. I need to rest.'

He does not tell Jonathan about the arrival of the Americans nor that he has moved Pamela out to her mother's. 'Yeah, sure, understood.'

Under extreme darkness, in the early hours of the next morning, the mixed bunch of travellers, wounded soldiers and their accompanying carers, with a couple of duty officers to assist, tramped in a line across the rough concrete strip. There were no lamps on to show the way. A couple were pushed in wheelchairs, with drips rattling on metal stands, others limped and hobbled as best they could. Joe shuffled along in his filthy army boots, caught by the outside chill, Jarvis walking beside him, carrying both backpacks.

The Hercules was a wide-bodied four turbo-prop military transporter that had been in service for years. Parked on the forecourt waiting for its passengers it loomed up against the interminable black skyline like a huge beached whale. Joe glanced at the myriad star cover, whilst thinking of Jahinda, wondering if she was looking at the night sky and dreaming of their last evening together, which seemed a lifetime ago. He imagined himself fiddling his way somehow back to Iraq and driving up to Haditha in an open jeep, to greet her at her father's door, with laughter and open arms and a swollen heart that he had never really allowed to flourish before.

From the low terminal hut on the periphery it was a short distance to the gaping back end of the plane. They were still acting out their parts, Joe groaning with the movements and the effort, his arm strapped heavily to his side and Jarvis dressed in white overalls like the nurses wore, helping him all the way. Joe managed a yelp or two as they climbed the ramp to be swallowed up in the guts of the plane. They were hit by a pungent mixed odour of body heat, disinfectant and kerosene oil in the main cabin, not too dissimilar to the smell of fear that a battalion sweats before going into action. They settled in halfway along one side with the other dozen or so wounded and incapacitated cases, grateful to be making the trip home.

During the morning, while attempting a few feeble exercises on the hall floor and watching his house across the street, he wracks his brain over where the marines might be hanging out. They must be using a safe house, but where to look? He toys with the idea of contacting Mike Malone, but he would have to go through Army HQ and that would be difficult. Instinct tells him best not. Anyway, why would he know anything?

His aching wounds soon curtail his activity, and nothing seems to be happening outside, although he is not getting a great view of either end of the street. He has another black coffee and eats an apple.

He can hear Doris's plaintive voice over the phone last night and starts to brood about Joe once more, seeing his young face twisted with pain and anger. He hates thinking what the Americans might have done to him and tries to recall easier times, the good companionship Joe made, their time together on tour. Joe was so young, desperate to please, to fit in, to learn everything straight away, yet also keen to show his own personality and not to be a push-over. Joe was his project, Jarvis had taken him under his wing, remembering what *he* had felt like when he first joined up.

'I guess he reminded me of Ed. My way of compensating for Ed's loss to bring Joe on,' he murmurs to himself, almost out loud. He gets up to stretch and stand over by the little back window, where Sam had stood earlier contemplating his navel, looking out over the back wall at the tops of a few red double-deckers and the bright winter sunshine that's tempting him out.

Nobody had asked any awkward questions. Nobody seemed to be interested in Joe or Jarvis once on board, all the ID and paperwork had been checked at the terminal. A few names tentatively exchanged, a few cursory handshakes.

When all were strapped in, it lumbered down the airstrip and rose off the ground in an agonisingly slow manoeuvre. It seemed to hover without gaining height, before it banked sharply in a tight semi-circle, and then continued more steeply on its upward trajectory. Joe was gritting his teeth and clutching onto the seat with his eyes screwed up in a grimace of terror, praying for the bloody thing to get up there. When it suddenly flattened out after several minutes of angst, his stomach was left behind on the ground.

Thereafter with every lurch and stutter of the craft, he felt sick and empty inside. One guy was muttering prayers to himself; someone nearby was eating a banana and a dried chocolate bar. Finally, the craft settled into its rhythm with a fixed high-pitched whine, like someone scratching a blackboard with their fingernails. The noise level inside the vast cabin precluded any need for conversation and most of them drifted into sleep one way or another.

Cold beads of sweat sprung up along Joe's forehead and he had to wipe his face with his hands. There was perspiration down his back too, that felt cold later on, and as he tried to settle in the persistent humming and vibrating noise, he was shivering.

'How's the arm?' Jarvis called to him, indicating with his hand.

'Sore and itchy,' he said. 'And another thing,' Joe called back in a croaky voice, a little later as they were somewhere over the European mainland at 36,000 feet, 'as soon as we get back to Brize Norton, I'm quitting the fucking Army and I shall never don a British uniform again.'

Jarvis tried a look of sympathy. He understood that Joe was feeling cold and empty, resenting the command Jarvis had over him, for one thing. Realising he would never see Jahinda again for another. Probably convinced he had nothing worthwhile to return to England for.

It was an uncomfortable six-hour flight back to Oxfordshire. Jarvis planned to contact Pamela on landing and arrange for her to drive out to pick him up, when he was given clearance. Once down and disembarked, they were settled into local barracks for the rest of the day, with Jarvis due for a debriefing that evening with Major Robertson.

His hope that Robertson had been suitably appraised of the situation turned out to be unnecessary, as the whole thing was merely a formality, confirming name, rank, battalion and reasons for an early return to the UK. Jarvis's explanations were accepted without question.

Around lunch time, his mood gloomy, he changes his mind. Feeling morose, he needs to get out. In a black hoodie, dark trousers and trainers, he slides out of Sam's back gate, trots stiffly along to New North Road and over the canal. His casual glances reveal nothing and no one suspicious is lurking. Nearly at Old Street, he turns into the Fairbank Estate and limps up to the fourth floor of Halstead Court, a grim council block. The empty stairwell smells of urine and someone has painted a picture of an enormous erect penis with big balls on the wall next to a pair of breasts, full on with cherry nipples like targets. Along the outside balcony, past all the other front doors of peeling paint and splintered wood, to number 46. Like at his own place, the doorbell isn't working, so he knocks.

The door is pulled inwards cautiously and a sturdy darkskinned woman with black curls and a fag in her mouth appears. She looks disappointed on seeing Jarvis and walks away, leaving him to close the door after him. Charlie is slumped in a broken armchair watching the television, volume low, curtains drawn. In a singleton vest, tracky bottoms and bare feet he looks unkempt and distracted. He's grasping a half-full glass of beer. There are dark lines about his eyes and the lids are drooping. A stale body smell mixed with egg and bacon pervades the place and Jarvis has to avoid the discarded plates of food remains and loaded ashtrays scattered around the floor.

There is no sign of the girl as Charlie jumps up instantly on seeing Jarvis and welcomes his mate. 'Corporal, sir, how are we?'

They man-hug, although Charlie seems a bit wobbly. So early in the day for drinking, Jarvis worries. Charlie starts to fuss around him, does he want nothing, a beer, whatever. Sorry about the mess, that bloody girl does shit all, he needs to sort her. Sit yourself, the best chair. Anything at all? Charlie is trim, his bare shoulders built like boulders, well renowned for his supreme fitness. Just looks a little neglected, Jarvis reassures himself.

'Charlie, listen, mate, we're on. Those Yanks I told you about, they've arrived. I saw them prowling around my street last night. They knew which was my house, but I was watching from over the other side.'

Charlie is suddenly alert, sensing adventure. 'How many?'

'Three that I saw, recognised two of them from Iraq.'

'More to come?'

'Don't know.'

'Armed?'

'Probably. I think they threw a stink bomb or something in through the letter box to flush me out. They mean business.'

'Tear gas, was it?'

'Haven't investigated. Moved Pam out the night before.'

'Big muscle?'

'Yeah, big muscle, Charlie. We might need the others to help. As soon as, really.'

'Right, man, right. I will organise, something.' He is searching for his trainers, behind the couch, by the door, under a pile of cushions. He half stubs his cigarette out. 'We'll get the others, I'll see.'

'You alright, Charlie? You seem ... under the weather?'

Charlie is bouncing on his feet, leaning forwards towards the taller man, on his toes, sparring gently an imaginary opponent, with his fists and arms pumping quietly, anticipation spreading across his face. 'Just need a project, Jarvis boy, a purpose. This body needs something to do, and it will soon be back to its usual level.' He thumps his chest a couple of times. 'You see, give me a challenge and I'll be there.' He chuckles.

Jarvis points to the beer bottles on the side, mostly empties and tuts his tongue, shakes his head a few times like a disapproving teacher. He wants to apologise. Charlie nods, embarrassed, muttering no problem, no problem. They agree arrangements. Jarvis lets himself out, passes the penis and the breasts, back to ground level and a funeral collection of pigeons.

Back on Old Street, after midday. He gets a takeaway from a tiny café on the roundabout and waves down a black cab for Whitechapel and Sid's Hut. His leg is aching, but he wants to keep moving. His sandwich is consumed in a few voracious mouthfuls. He needs to relax, not panic. Telling himself to think clearly, he lists what he needs to do: a word with Sid, a plan of action. Maybe tomorrow, lure the Americans back to his house, trap them inside, where their manoeuvring will be restricted by the tight and unfamiliar space; overwhelm them, with the help of his unarmed combat team of experts. Assuming Charlie will be able to fulfil his end of the bargain. He had always had a bit of a drink habit but was able to ditch it and come good when it really mattered. Lounging about, purposeless, smoking cigarettes and the rest, that's no good for anyone. Hopefully a little bout of excitement will once again bring out the best in him.

The young talent working out at the gym impresses Jarvis and he spends a while appreciating a couple of athletic kids shadow boxing, dancing and sparring with Danny in the ring. Not for him today, although he would have liked to.

From the bar upstairs, he sits at a grimy window looking out at the pokey street below, sipping a tonic water. He chats with the barman while their attention is drawn to the flat screen television, seeing pictures of sombre crowds in Paris, lining wet streets five deep. And there is Angela Merkel solemnly laying a wreath at a huge stone memorial. Then follows Nicholas Sarkozy, and the two of them stand side by side, both short and stocky figures of much the same height, for the minute's silence. The first time in history, apparently, that a German Chancellor and a French President have shared November Remembrance Day side by side, marking their respect and memory of the fallen thousands during two past world wars and showing their growing understanding and harmony as European neighbours. Jarvis nods his approval, although he is suspicious of the little Frenchman, who seems a bit of a dodgy character and not to be trusted.

'Impressive, the size of the crowds. They can do pomp, the French, can't they,' the barman comments.

'A bit like us, really,' Jarvis smirks. He takes his drink with him along to Sid's dark panelled office, which is positioned grandly at the top of a broad oak staircase. The door is wide open and Sid, sitting ponderously behind his vast desk crowded with papers and magazines, puffing on his usual cheroots, has a clear line of sight along the corridor outside.

'Jarvis, my boy. Great. How are you?' Effusive as ever, spitting out his honeyed words, he wants to embrace his favourite hero. 'What a show down at the docks, eh? Saw you on the box. Impressive. You alright, lad?' And Jarvis is caught in his tight embrace.

Jarvis has trouble getting a word in but does eventually ask Sid directly about the American visitor he had the other day. 'What did he want exactly, was he after information?'

'He was a jolly man, wanted to admire the place, had a similar gym back home in the mid-west somewhere, just wanted to chew the fat, have a chinwag, businessman to businessman.'

'He must have wanted something, Sid?'

'He did ask about some of the members here, wanted to know if any were ex-army. Said he was looking up an old friend, worked together on a campaign or two, somebody called Collingwood, used to be a Corporal in the British Army. He was friendly, said you had worked together.'

'And you told him my address?'

'No, actually, I observed our strict rules about confidentiality. I said I knew you, of course, what a great guy you were, but that you were not here very often. I said I thought you lived up in Hoxton somewhere but not sure. That was it. Why, they bothering you?'

'Yeah, causing a bit of trouble.'

'Sorry to hear that, Jarvis, nothing you can't cope with, I'm sure. I really didn't give anything away. He seemed friendly, genuine.'

'Beefy blond guy, flat nose?'

'Yeah, with a nice tattoo on his neck, serpent and sword thing.'

Sid gushes on with his torrent of empty words, never sounding quite as honest as he hopes, while Jarvis listens with a patient smile.

As he leaves the gym, he answers a call from Pamela, sounding tremulous and not at all sure of herself. 'Jarvis, it's me. They came for me, this morning, two hefty American bullies.' She is breathing in gusty bursts and speaking fast. 'They grabbed me on the street, on my way to work, for Christ's sake, pulled me into a great black car, like a bloody bus really.'

Jarvis presses the phone to his ear, brings his hand up to cup the mouthpiece. He leans into it, whispering urgently. 'Pam, Pam, slow down. What did they want?'

'They wanted to know where you were. Said you were hiding. They hurt my arms and threatened me. One of them gave me a card with a number on it, said you must ring them by the end of the day, or they would be back to hurt me proper. Jarvis. What is happening?'

'Okay, calm down, Pam. How did they know where to find you?' He's beginning to feel frantic.

'I don't know, bloody hell,' she yells, 'how should I know? Followed the taxi from the house the other night, I should think. What are you going to do? They were fucking horrible, Jarvis, and they meant what they said. You must ring them, meet them tonight, they said or else. Here's the number, you got a pen?'

'Okay, Pam. Yes, I got it.' After a moment: 'You need to move again, sorry. Go to Stella's or another friend, it'll just be for a day. I will sort these monsters out. I don't want them threatening you again. Is your mother alright?'

'Of course, she's alright, don't worry about her, it's me that's shaking with fright. I couldn't go to work.'

'No, of course not. Ring Stella, get her to come round, pick you up. Any signs they're still there?'

'No, they drove off.'

'Don't you get nervous, the night before a mission?'

Near Times Square Mall off Dinar Street, in Basra, a bar packed with military personnel, mainly Americans, a popular spot for off-duty soldiers. A perfect trap for a suicide bomber. If he was nervous about anything, it was being in a crowded place, with no easy escape should he need one.

Joe was fiddling with a tiny brass-framed photo that he always kept in his trouser pocket. It was about two by two inches. Brought out at times that made him think most about home, times when he considered the possibility that he would not make it back. Jarvis had seen it before, a colour picture of his mother and father, sitting beside each other on a sunny day.

'Yes, course I do.' They were perched on stools, elbows on the bar toying with their icy beers at the end of another uncomfortably humid day. The air-conditioning was working for once, which was a bonus.

The autumn in southern Iraq had seen precious little rainfall anywhere for months, everything parched dry and dusty. The heat all day had been intense. And now Joe was brooding. He liked Jarvis, but recognised their different backgrounds and personalities, and worried that he was about to be put to the test, under severe conditions for an indefinite length of time. Jarvis was four years older and so much more experienced, knowledgeable and mature, so self-contained and confident in his abilities. Could they work well together, as professionals under duress, the two of them, out in the wilderness, side by side day and night? There were so many uncertainties.

Malone had briefed them yesterday, the sniper pairs, about a dozen of them. 'Need to see how it goes, see how useful the arrangements are. We may move you on after a few days or leave you in position for longer, weeks maybe. Need to study outcomes,' he intoned rather pompously. Each pair had been allocated various vantage spots around the city, and they were there to offer support to the prevailing US marines and the Iraqi army, who were trying to contain the powerful insurgent forces. The Brits had never been to Haditha, a long way north into the middle of Iraq, known for its hostile territory. Support for the networks there was a bit thin, Malone admitted, but there would be radio contact at all times provided by the Royal Signals Corps. That made Joe feel a whole lot better, but he was worried. It sounded to him like they were being thrown out into enemy territory to provoke the insurgents, to draw them out from their hiding places.

He was only nineteen, Joe was bound to feel vulnerable at this time and being close to his mother, bound to be homesick on the eve of a new mission, Jarvis appreciated all that. Would he be up to the challenge?

Joe said when he was younger he wanted to be a footballer, but he had joined the Army at the first opportunity, anything to leave home. 'Mum can be so clinging, you know, always wanting to know where I'm going, what I'm doing. She even checks my room when I am out, I know because she tidies things up. Can never find my things after she's been in there.'

Jarvis knew what he felt, a dominant mother making all the decisions was familiar territory for him. Joe was young and fresh faced; he had only just started shaving and not too regularly, with a mousy mop of hair that he parted on the left using water to hold it in place. He had a nice smile when he chose to use it and a good set of teeth.

'All my mates were getting jobs, in the trades, labouring, whatever; paid well too, some of them. Used to meet Friday nights in the Oddfellows, drank Guinness most of them. But I thought I was being left behind, had to snatch some money off me mother. So, I joined up. Nothing better to do, really.'

'And it was a good thing,' Jarvis enthused, 'you've excelled in your role. Chosen for one of these missions, that's a sign they like you. Come on, working closely with Special Forces, can't be bad, eh?'

Joe sank the remainder of his drink and offered to buy another round. 'You must miss your wife then, just married and all?'

'Two years ago, Joe. But yeah, course I do.'

'Think about her a lot, what she's doing and all that?'

'Yeah, course. What about you? Girlfriends, you must have dozens,' Jarvis toys with his younger companion.

'Oh, well, you know, one or two, no one serious. There's a club or two in Watford we go to: Canvas is quite good, disco and dance, but the drinks are ridiculous. I might take a girl there.'

In truth, Joe's experience with girls had been limited, few opportunities he would say and his inherent shyness. He had not really got off the mark, just a few fumbled hand groping sessions in the back of a cinema, or in a night club. Only a few nights before they were flown out to Iraq, he had kissed a girl outside the cinema, after they'd seen a film, by the bus stop. An old lady stood behind them and coughed, so they stopped. It was only a peck, but Joe embellished the story a bit for Jarvis's benefit, talking about her warm boobs pressed against his chest and how they had gone back to her place, for a fumble. He couldn't remember the film.

'Then there's the strip club, Beaver; me and Jake sometimes go there for a bit of a laugh. Even though he's married.'

Jarvis looked sceptical.

Jarvis is furious. Pamela must have been followed in the taxi to her mother's, the black Ford presumably, that's what it was there for. He gets a cab himself, back to Baring Street, imagining those sweaty brutes handling his wife, gripping her arms till they hurt, breathing in her face, threatening her with more hurt or worse. He grinds his teeth, flexing his fists. They tried to con him into meeting last night at his house, and when it was obvious he had not fallen for their trick, they decided to get at him through Pamela: he knew they would try. He can see Tommy standing in the feeble streetlight, legs apart, leering at the terraced housing opposite. He wants to wipe that supercilious look off his face.

Back in his hideaway bedroom in Sam's house, he is crouching safely below the windowsill, in the semi-darkness, his knees sunk into a cushion on the floor. He brings the binoculars up to his eyes. He wants to kick something, punch something, punch someone. Remaining slightly back from the draped nets so as not to cause them to flutter in any way, he observes as best he can the street up towards the pub to his right and down to his left towards the bottom end of the road.

The black Ford is back. That bloody little car, with the shadowy form of a male occupant watching from inside, is tucked into a small space at the far end of the crescent, its rear end jutting out.

John Shorter, Shorty to his buddies, is slumped in the driver's seat of the Ford, bored and stiff. He's been there since around midday, while his two compatriots went down to Streatham, where he had followed the taxi carrying Collingwood's wife two nights ago, to put the frighteners on her. Some hours ago, with hunger and boredom getting the better of him, he had gotten a distasteful bun with sausage and a takeaway coffee from the corner shop down the road. But he is still peckish and smokes Marlboros endlessly to stave it off. He's only a couple left in his last packet. The central tray is overflowing with ash and butts. He has his side window open for a while to let out the awful fug of smoke but, with the engine switched off, the inside of the car has grown so cold that he has just wound it up. He stares down the mostly empty street where nothing has happened all day, the odd vehicle or occasional resident on the move, someone crossing over to the pub or coming home from work, that's it. He knows he is looking out for Collingwood or his wife, and he knows their faces well from their frequent briefings, but he has rather lost interest as the uneventful afternoon slowly progresses.

It's early evening and dark now, the streetlamps giving off bleak patches of yellowy light and his senses far from alert. In fact, his head keeps resting back, his eyelids drooping, as he dreams of taking a quick nap, despite the cold. He's in jeans and a denim jacket and regrets not bringing his heavy coat. Back home in Helena, there would be snow on the Flathead Reservation, so he ought to be grateful for small mercies.

Out of the blue, from nowhere, an athletic figure in black darts across the road along the driver's blind spot to the side of the car. Shorty jumps at the sudden tapping on the glass. He can't see who it is, just the solid dark figure of a man. For a moment he thinks it might be Tom, come to surprise him, to check him out. He has to turn the ignition to use the electric window switch. When it's nearly fully open, a gloved hand reaches in and wrenches on the door handle. Before Shorty has a clue what's happening, Jarvis springs inside and wedges himself in the narrow space between seated driver and steering wheel, pressing a knee hard down between his legs, pinning Shorty painfully to the seat. Two thumping side blows into his kidney areas from Jarvis's fists hurt and knock the air out of him. Then Jarvis smacks his open mouth and grabs his face with his large fingers, pressing his head violently backwards. It all happens in seconds. Even if Shorty wanted to fight back, he couldn't, his arms somehow useless against the bulk of the towering Englishman, who fills the confined space around him.

Jarvis pokes his own face up close, so Shorty can be in no doubt about the seriousness of his situation. Jarvis stares eagerly into his shadowy dark eyes which are blinking rapidly and staring with surprise and pain.

'Where's Joe, Shorty?'

Shorty is beginning to struggle with breathing since Jarvis has his large hand completely covering over his mouth and flattening his nose. The whites of the American's eyes appear in a complete halo as his face suffuses red. He tries to prize the hand off with his fingers; to wriggle his body, but Jarvis's pressure is relentless. His knee jabs harder, squashing the man's testicles but not allowing him to scream. Shorty tries to choke, to burst, to swallow his own tongue. He goes limp and groans as best he can, desperate to shake his head in response.

Jarvis finally relents, easing the pressure on his mouth, then lowering his grip so Shorty can speak. 'Tell me where Joe is?' Jarvis repeats with a slow intensity.

Shorty, desperately sucking in air, has no option but to lie. 'I don't know, I was not involved in that.' The stabbing jab of Jarvis's knee and the grip on Shorty's jaw intensify horribly. His mandible is being crushed, as if Jarvis wants to rip Shorty's mouth apart.

Jarvis has narrowed eyes and a quiet but insistent voice. His spare gloved hand has carefully reached into the inside of his jacket and he pulls out a long bare-bladed hunting knife from its sheath. 'Liar, Shorty. Tell me where Joe is or I will cut your balls off and stuff them down your throat.'

He holds the blade up in front of Shorty's face. 'And then I will cut your nose off.' Even in the dull shadowy light inside the car, Shorty catches the gleaming of the razor-sharp steel. Jarvis places the tip up one of Shorty's flared nostrils. 'One more time, Shorty, and positively the last.'

Shorty's eyes are maximum wide and crossed over as he stares at the blade. He jabs his feet onto the floor, trying to find some purchase to retract his face away from the lethal weapon. 'Okay, okay,' he stutters, 'look, I had nothing to do with it, Collingwood, nothing, it was Tom, he was pretty mad. But he's ... he's dead, Joe is dead.'

There is silence between them in the car.

Jarvis is stunned, as if someone has hit him across the back of the head. With a pernicious stare and a look of uncontested venom, the terrible news that he was expecting filters through his mounting anger. Anger at being subjected to this treatment, in his own city, by some renegade foreigners, this hounding of his wife out of her home, the implicit threats to his own life, this murder of his friend. Why should he have to put up with it? And for a moment, Jarvis contemplates sinking the blade between the man's ribs to cut deep into his chest, catching his heart and then watching the life of this pathetic specimen ebb deservedly away.

Revenge is what he wants, although he knows that that won't help Joe or anybody else. It takes considerable control of his emotions and his bubbling fury to restrain himself. 'So where is he, where's the body?'

'I don't know,' Shorty pleads, 'Tom was gonna dump it somewhere out of the way. I dunno, swear to God.'

The American's breath comes hot and scared. With his knee pinning Shorty's genitals to the seat and a tight grip on his jaw with his gloved left hand, he presents the knife up in front of Shorty's face so he can inspect unmistakably the threat posed by its cutting edge. Staring all the while straight into Shorty's terrified eyes, Jarvis deliberately carves the point of the blade with his gloved right hand down the middle of his victim's chest, passing between the lapels of his jacket, along his breastbone. It takes all his strength to hold Shorty still. He wriggles so viciously, tries to scream with horror, but nothing prevents Jarvis completing his task, pressing firmly and moving downwards, with his weight leaning in, from the base of Shorty's throat all the way to his abdominal flab, cutting through the denim and the cotton beneath, down to his skin and through his skin, inch by inch. There is gritty resistance beneath, like slicing the meat along the bone of the Sunday joint. Bubbles of fresh blood well up along the line, soaking into the shirt.

His mouth fixed by terror and Jarvis's vice-like grip, Shorty is prevented from emitting the ghastly wail of agony that the moment deserves, that would undoubtedly have been heard all over Hoxton, alerting the whole bloody neighbourhood.

Still keeping the American's weeping brown eyes locked onto his, studying the two deep vertical clefts he has between the ends of his eyebrows, and noticing the pallor of his face, Jarvis stops. Shorty screws his eyes up, his face etched with pain, and then slumps flaccid as if he has fainted. With the dripping blade withdrawn, Jarvis slaps Shorty's face.

'Wake up, you dick.'

The American comes back to life, blinking tears down his cheeks, the rims of his eyes reddened horribly. He's holding himself rigid, as if movement leads to further pain. He tries to see what Jarvis has done exactly, straining his eyes down. He wants to howl hysterically. He licks his dry lips, picking up the salty taste. Jarvis speaks with contempt, flatly without emotion. 'You be brave now, Shorty, and I'll let you drive away from here. Go tell your Tommy Fucking Flynn that he best leave while he still can and not bother me or mine anymore. Do you understand? Or I will come and cut all three of you to small pieces and feed you to the ducks down by the canal.'

With that he jerks himself away, releasing the moaning Shorty, who seems to be panicking, breathing in tiny bursts, waving his hands about, not knowing what to do. The warm blood is staining through to his jacket, spreading all the while and seeping into his lap. He doesn't know whether he should touch the wound, press something onto it, it stings so. A burst of anger suddenly bubbles up and he cries: 'You son of a bitch, Collingwood.'

Jarvis wipes both sides of the knife blade across Shorty's sleeve and re-sheaths it, safely returning it to the inside of his jacket. 'Be careful what you say, dickhead.' Ducking his head under the doorframe, stepping back onto the road, he slams the door hard. 'Drive carefully,' he calls back, as he crosses to the other side, retracing his steps almost casually to the front of Baring Street, to Sam's door by the bus stop. He hesitates. His legs are shaking, his arms too, with anger, with hatred, the adrenaline still rushing around his system. He has a dark wet patch on the front of his jeans at the knee and his gloves are sticky. He darts through the gate before anyone sees him, leaps up the stairs to his room. He drops his gloves on the floor and pulls off the jeans. He washes his hands in the bathroom sink, and looks at his loveless, emotionless features in the mirror. His cool eyes for once appear troubled.

He should have slit the sod's throat and have done with it.

He is desperate for a drink. In clean trousers, he gestures at the door of the lounge for Sam to come with him and they head out the back together. Jarvis must slow himself down, make himself walk more casually up to the corner to the pub.

Inside *The Baring*, Sam insists and orders two bottles of craft Hiver, the honey beer, and they move along to the far end of the bar to take up a couple of stools. Sam can tell Jarvis is all keyed up, anxious and in need of some rest and time to think. He needs someone to talk to and Sam is more than happy to play his part.

Jarvis goes to take a leak. A wet stream of perspiration trickles down the centre of his back and he can smell the sweat from under his arms. He wonders if he has gone too far, but then he thinks of Joe, and his anger and sorrow billow up inside him and he wants to slice Shorty's head off. Flynn's as well. He inhales deeply and slowly, seeking a moment of calm, but in the mirror he sees only Joe's deathly white face.

While haphazardly conversing with Sam, filling him in with vague waffle, without detail, grateful to him for sharing these difficult moments, Jarvis is all the while contemplating what the hell happens next. How is he going to tell Joe's mother? How was he going to find him, for a decent burial? Should he get the police involved, at least they would be out looking, which might keep Tommy and his cronies at bay for a while?

A dishevelled waif comes in off the street, in shabby raincoat and dilapidated boots. Balding with flowing locks of thin grey hair down the back of his neck, he nervously speaks to Gerry at one side of the bar. He is distressed and keeps pointing out the door, saying something about the skip outside. Jarvis picks up his gestures and scuttles over to him. 'Show me,' he demands, and the old tramp turns obediently to shuffle outside, with Jarvis,

Gerry and Sam following. They walk the few yards down to the big rusty metal skip at the curb that has been taking builders' rubbish from next door these past few weeks. Jarvis glances down the crescent, assuming that Shorty has driven off long ago. To pass on to Tommy his message, he hopes. Not that that will deter him one little bit. In fact, it will probably incense him, even more. Jarvis is thinking one thing for certain: he will have to deal with these bloody Americans himself and quickly. He needs to get them, before they get him.

The old fellow is shuffling up to the side of the skip and grabbing the high edge to pull himself up on tip toes. 'Inside, there, there,' he croaks.

Something inside the skip catches Jarvis's eye, a boot sticking out at one end. He steps nervously towards it and with his height easily leans over the high metal side. He can make out a mess of rubbish and rubble, broken bricks and plaster work, copper pipes and old floorboards, dirt and stuffed plastic bags. And lying on his back spread-eagled over a pile of this stuff is Joe, as dead as a dormouse. One of his legs points up to the sky, the toe of his boot sticking out. His face is pasty yellow in the light, swollen around the eyes, almost unrecognisable. His lips are puffed out and broken, there's dried blood smears down the side of his face. A thin line of darkened blood surrounds his throat, like a necklace, like someone drew a line with a marker pen. Only, it's a deep impression and his throat is cut full circumference, garrotted, asphyxiated to death. And no doubt, placed there theatrically in the skip in the street where he lives, to be discovered in due course, as a warning to Jarvis, to put the frighteners on him.

Debriefing interview, MoD, Aldwych.
December 12, 2005.

After the two of them had been at it non-stop for over two hours, Malone stretches his long torso and leans backwards, tilting the chair with a creak. 'What sort of relationship had you established with the Americans before this happened? Any rapport?

'Not a lot.'

'Oh, what was the problem?'

'They were generally stand-offish, unhelpful. Joe got on with a few of the junior rankings, but the officers were superior and made it clear that they were in charge and that we were there at their beck and call. They hinted very obviously on many occasions how the Brits were out of their depth, not used to the heat of the desert and guerrilla warfare and that we were just not up to taking a lead role. We had a minor supportive role and should not behave as if we were their equals.'

'A bit strong. Can't have all been like that, surely?'

'Well, as I say, the officers were setting the mood. Sergeant Robert Wozniak and Corporal Thomas Flynn, for example, were bully types. They got their way by force, by shouting the loudest.'

'What attempts did you make to oil the wheels a bit? Any?'

'Impossible; they were not receptive to argument; they did not want to hear our opinions. They were louts, basically.'

Chapter 7
Thursday November 12

Despite the awful traumas of the evening before, Jarvis is up early and takes a red double decker to work.

His night has been hideously restless, images of Joe disturbing his every thought. His swollen neck, discoloured and distorted face, his eyes popping. He imagined trying to comfort Doris. After Gerry had nervously returned inside the pub to call the police, Jarvis and Sam had slipped away, leaving a small gathering of curious onlookers in the street. Jarvis was convinced the Americans were watching, from a distance; that they had set this up to see his pained reaction.

A collection of police vehicles and an ambulance crowded at the top end of Baring Street, closed and taped off, and a white plastic tent was constructed around the skip. Noises of men and women working, moving things, knocking things, calling, hushed voices, all made for a torrid experience. And then for hours bright lights intermittently flashed across his ceiling in coloured strips as he tried to grab some sleep, expecting a knock on the door as the police moved from house to house, interviewing.

Jarvis wandered through to the washrooms, a low-ceilinged shack running along the back of the US mess canteen, but a large boot was planted against the inside of the only access. The door opened an inch but was quickly slammed shut in his face. He heard the gruff voice of Thomas Flynn shouting at a young recruit who he had glimpsed lying on his back on the floor in his jockey shorts being forced to do sit-ups with his arms up, hands behind his head, while Staff Sergeant Wosniak sat astride his ankles. Every time the soldier pulled himself up by using only his aching stomach muscles, Woz slapped him in the face, which was bloodied around his nose, and he folded back down again. Flynn was shouting, 'Again. Again, you little shit.'

Jarvis leant against the door and listened. He could hear the poor lad groaning with effort and crying out each time he took another slap, while Flynn bullied him, shouting into his ears as loud as he could. 'Faster, you piece of shit, work faster, or I'll whip you around the parade ground in your birthday suit and leave you hanging on the clothes lines overnight, you hear me?'

'Stop,' shouted Wosniak's voice, with its European accent. Heavy stamping of hobbled army boots could be heard. 'What is it you must never do again, soldier?'

'Deal with the locals, Sergeant.'

'Deal with the Eyeraks, sonny. They are not worth the candle. They are shite, like the Shiites they are, you hear? You get caught dealing weed again, you're a dead soldier, goddit? And what use to me is a dead soldier, you little shit? What use?'

Another slap, and Jarvis heard the boy yelp. 'Yes, Sergeant.'

That evening, five lady singers and dancers who called themselves Angels, and had been flown in specially from Las Vegas, entertained the hard-pressed and home-sick marines with bawdy jokes and suggestive dance routines on the small stage at the far end of the barroom. The lights were down, the floor was packed with a rowdy crowd of sweaty young men in tee shirts drinking beer. Jarvis was not impressed. The girls tried their best but weren't really a bunch of talent and seemed happy enough to do a quick turn, singing Dolly Parton songs to awful pre-recorded music from a CD. During a break he saw a queue of the marines over by a makeshift curtain at one side of the stage and was told by a soldier he asked that the girls were offering their services to anyone willing to pay. 'How much they charge? Jarvis asked eagerly.

'Around thirty bucks,' was the reply.

'Not you tonight, then?' Jarvis asked with a wink.

'Naw, didn't draw the right numbers.'

God, sex by lottery. He wandered over, slipping behind a screen, and climbed over a few boxes, squeezed between stacked chairs, moving quietly closer in the shadows. By the back wall on a couple of red velvet settees, a single standard lamp gave light to a scene of four Angels lined up like human slot machines with their skirts hitched up to their waists while four lumpen men with suppressed grunting and wobbly bare clenched buttocks humped them from behind as fast as they could. Jarvis was certainly not impressed; he soon turned away in disgust.

Back at the bar, he happened to recognise the young soldier who had suffered such humiliation earlier at the hands of Wosniak and Flynn in the toilets. He was a short guy, slumped on a stool and leaning on his elbows, hiding his face behind his hands, but Jarvis could see the darker colour around his nose, the fresh scabs around his nostrils and the puffy upper lip. He had a nearly empty glass of beer in front of him.

'Hi, soldier, you want a drink?' asked Jarvis, trying to sound casual.

'Nope. I'm fine.' He wore army shirt and trousers, and his beret was tucked into his webbing at his waist. 'Thanks,' he added.

'Mind if I join you?'

'Sure,' he shrugged with indifference.

Jarvis called for a beer. Always quick to get to the point when he wanted, he said: 'You suffered a bit of a beating today, couldn't help notice. What was that about?'

The young soldier shook his head and shrugged. 'Nothing, nothing,' he murmured, looking away.

'I understand you don't want to talk about it, but I heard you were dealing weed. Is that something that happens here?'

Still no reply, a shrug, a nonchalant twist of his mouth, which made him wince with pain.

'That was abuse back there, soldier,' Jarvis persisted. 'We ought to do something about it.'

'We?' sounding surprised.

'That Wosniak fellow, he's a liability, isn't he? Needs examining, extended leave, if you ask me.'

After a pause and a sideways look, when the soldier tried to twist his gaze round to see Jarvis's face, he revealed his deeply pink marked cheek. 'He gets results.'

'Does he?'

One evening at dinner, facing each other across the canteen table, Wosniak and his cronies filling the seats along one side and Jarvis sitting with a few of his team along the other, he asked the bullying sergeant as casually as he could manage, what made him join the US Army in the first place.

Wosniak's reply was at least honest. 'What else was there to do? No jobs worth having in the Mid-West. Farming, not for me. Anyway, these A-rab countries needed a lesson.' As always, he sounded disparaging, contemptuous. 'The US of A needed to show them who's boss. I knew I could do that. I would enjoy doing that.'

'And have you?'

Wosniak looked confused.

'Shown them who's boss? Taught them a lesson?' Jarvis asked.

'I don't know, but I've sure enjoyed it, so far.' And Wosniak laughed out loud. 'I have.'

Quite a crowd are milling about along Factory Road, despite the dull damp morning. And more are turning up all the time, on foot and by buses, some obviously outsiders hired for the purpose. Jarvis is dressed for the cold, in extra layers with a beanie and scarf. He finds the demonstrators are thirty or forty strong at each of the main gates, with another fifty or so in between. At several points along the road, mobile canteens have been set up by quick-witted vendors selling hot sausage rolls and coffee out the back of their vans to queues of cold punters needing sustenance. The press corps, laden with equipment and trailing cables, are out in numbers as well, crowding around their own vans, with their home-made sandwiches in tinfoil wrapping and flasks of steaming drinks. They trot up and down the road in small groups, grabbing their best images and soundbites wherever they can. After Tuesday's coup that went down so well in the newsrooms, the editors want plenty more of the same, with as many of those personal stories they can manage.

When Jarvis walks stiffly through the mob and slips under the barrier at the car park, some fellow guards and factory workers gather round him, wanting to shake his hand, mumbling words of warmth. He tries to ignore the attention with bashful shakes of his head, pulling his beanie further down over his ears. The workers seem to be getting through alright at the car park entrance, where the security team holds back the noisy throngs. Many are being bussed in, paid for by management and which spares them the direct confrontation, so it's the drivers who take the abuse, the egg and tomato projectiles, the screams of selling out, pandering to the bosses; scabs, scum.

The same contingent of police, no different to the mix Jarvis had seen on Tuesday, are also gathered. They link arms to form lines where they can, to keep back the demonstrators when traffic arrives or lorries want to leave; otherwise they retreat to their groups out of the way. A few fearless protestors take a run at the barrier in numbers, jostling through with legitimate workers, just when it is letting a car or a bus through. Arguments break out as to who are legitimate workers and who are the protestors; and a few of the rebels get into the grounds, where they are chased around by heavy-footed police officers and guards, before being chucked out through another side gate.

All morning a container vessel from the Caribbean is moored at the wharf riverside, and raw material is being unloaded by the tonne in huge bags and craned onto the outside conveyors, whilst all the picket line trouble is going on along the factory roadside. The demonstrators cannot get access to the wharf, even if they were aware of the activity there, without breaking into the site, or taking a boat and approaching from the river, which is the sort of thing only Greenpeace attempt these days.

Jarvis stays with his team at the car park most of the morning. It's a while before he spots them, fleetingly, shielded among the pale faces of the local protestors, but when he does, the three Americans are unmistakeable. They appear to be casual bystanders, mingling at the periphery of the moving crowd, exchanging comments with some, discussing the situation with the press people, no doubt pretending they're with *Newsreel* or something. In dark belted coats, bare headed, they stand close together, free hands in their pockets. Nobody worries them or questions them. They seem untroubled, even as they look a bit out of place.

Jarvis stops in his tracks. They must have caught sight of him on the television footage, on the recent news clips and recognised the hero of the day. They could not track him down at his home, but through sheer luck had found out where he was working. They were here to intimidate him, to follow him off site when he leaves, or perhaps to invade factory territory, to trap him inside for a final confrontation. Jarvis is determined they will not get their way.

He is not sure whether they have seen him yet. He slinks back across the hundred yards of half-empty car park, blending with groups of fellow guards and workers. Slipping into the shadow of the main building, he turns to watch for a moment. He sees no sign of them. He pulls out his mobile and checks his contact list for Charlie, to alert him to a change of plan. He sends him a message with his satellite location. He warned him yesterday that considerable force may be required - Charlie understood. He would gather the others, brief them and they'd be ready, whenever. That's what he said: Charlie, drunk and affable Charlie, not entirely in control Charlie.

Jarvis can visualise his other mates, Nelson, Mat and AJ all excitedly itching for some action after all this time.

About an hour later, at the main entrance this time, when the two big battered blue metal gates have swung inwards, letting a delivery van onto the site, there is a moment when Jarvis is standing at the front and in the middle of his line of men, clearly recognisable for anyone to see, and Tom Flynn is standing in the front line of the shouting, jeering mob on the outside. He stands steady and calm, as all about him are jumping up and down; his legs apart as is his wont, both hands in pockets, a cigarette dangling from a corner of his mouth. And definitely, he has a neat trimmed goatee, which makes him look older. Tom Flynn had obviously not heeded his words of warning, conveyed through Shorty.

There is no look of surprise, just a stolid belligerence that decorates the American's flabby face. There's a persistence within this man's character; he is here with one intention only, with nothing else to occupy his mind except to get Collingwood. He catches Tom's gaze across the fifty yards of clear tarmac, for a few brief seconds while there is a gap between the gates. Thomas Flynn standing motionless, his narrowed stare fixed on Jarvis, a slow smile breaking out across the otherwise stoic visage. A smile of satisfaction, that their little problem is soon to be resolved.

Nearby is the other American from Tuesday night, whom Jarvis does not recognise. Crewcut, clean shaven, dark wool belted trench coat and hefty black leather shoes, smoking, like the others. And behind him, that idiot Shorty is standing awkwardly with a ghostly look. An expression of hardened hatred is etched across his face and even at this distance, Jarvis can make out those deep vertical clefts between his eyes. He winces as he moves, and Jarvis is a little surprised to see him at all after the cutting wound he had caused yesterday, but perhaps he is braver than Jarvis gave him credit for. A livid Tommy must have forced him to come with them. He imagines his wound getting mucky and infected, if he's not careful.

As the gates come together, blotting out his view of the threatening ex-marines, and noticing that Flynn makes no move,

Jarvis is wondering how many he might have to deal with, whether there are any more of them. Is this the time for him to consider making his escape while he can? He has three choices, as far as he can make out: find a hiding place somewhere among the myriad of factory machines and buildings on site, which would not be too difficult, although the Americans would simply wait for him outside, when eventually he would have to appear; jump aboard the vessel at the wharf which could get him to Tilbury docks, where he could return on his own; or hide in one of the buses, under the back seats, when it was leaving the site full of Tate employees seeking safe passage home.

He knows he must face them, one way or another. After a morning of dodging each other, the Americans seem in no particular hurry, biding their time. Making no attempt at approaching, happy to keep their distance, like reporters hanging back, waiting for the real action which they know will come later. Perhaps today is the day. He is confident he can lead them a dance around the factory, and then he might be able to pick them off one by one. At least until the seventh cavalry arrives.

Another hour of grafting, the crowds outside as persistent as ever, Jarvis and his troops as efficient as ever, controlling the movement at the entrances without further untoward incident. A delivery lorry with plane dirty white plastic sides and canvas straps threads its way along Factory Road, among the wandering demonstrators. Crawling along behind is a slinky black Mercedes, the perfect emblem of privilege that the top brass persists in using, and the two vehicles are moving forward carefully in line, both planning to pass through the main entrance. Blocking the way across the blue gates is a thick throng of angry men and women who have reached close to a tipping point, intent on causing maximum disruption this time, determined to induce a proper reaction from management. Violence not ruled out. The numbers amassed are excessive for ordinary picketing and both the police and the security team recognise this. Everyone is out in force. The media people are crowded around the periphery, driven by instinct.

The driver of the truck turns in towards the gates, which are making their usual preliminary cranking noises as they start slowly to open inwards. A barrage of rotten fruit and vegetables are hurled at the truck's windscreen. The driver comes to a halt, protestors shouting obscenities at him through the glass and banging the cab and the sides of the truck. The limousine also stops a little way behind, surrounded by more angry protestors, bending down to gesticulate with repulsive expressions through the darkened glass at the anonymous occupants.

With no apparent chance of getting inside the factory here, the driver of the truck decides to try for the other entrance further up the road, and so puts his vehicle into reverse. Accompanied by the sound of high-pitched beepers, the truck edges backwards, turning through ninety degrees and then begins to move forward up Factory Road. Half of the rowdy mob follow him, away from the gates, some men clambering over the outside of the cab, grabbing at the windscreen wipers, trying to pull up the tarpaulin covers, hanging onto the sides or pulling at the driver's doors. Roars of approval go up from all the bystanders who cheer their comrades' every move. They crowd around the outside, waving their fists and giving him the middle finger. The driver carelessly winds his window down to return a bit of the verbals, as good as he gets. Someone jumps onto his running board, holding on while wrestling the driver.

Sensing some fun, the other half of the crowd stay with the chauffeur-driven limousine, which is turning towards the blue entrance. Surrounded by a noisy sea of aggressive yobs, threatening, gesticulating, rattling and bumping the sides of the car, placards bashing its roof, the chauffeur, like the lorry driver before him, panics. Although the gates appear to be slowly parting and a gap opening up for their pathway into the factory, he decides that he would be better off out of it altogether. He slips the gear into reverse and slowly, using his wing mirrors, manoeuvres the car back the way it has come, intending to drive backwards all the way along Factory Road down to where he had seen lots of police vans hanging out, sure that the forces of law and order would come to his rescue.

The mob follow the Mercedes, still bouncing it from side to side, smearing horrible stuff over the windows, hounding the driver.

The luckless driver of the lorry is hauled down from his cab, landing on the roadway with a horrible thud on his shoulder and hip, and is set upon. The rush of mobsters and their growling rage attracts the security men and the police, both outside and inside. Half of them rush over towards the truck.

At the same time, there is the sound of broken glass as one side-window of the black limousine is smashed, and a crescendo of cheers go up. Those guards and police that remain at the gate rush over towards the car and set about preventing a chaotic brawl.

The full mob of demonstrators that were at the main gates is thus split cleanly in two, one bunch heading eastwards up Factory Road with the lorry, the other westwards down Factory Road with the limo, each followed by half of the security guards and police. The media circus is immediately drawn into a split as they rush like groupies towards the different action sites, relishing the chance as always to get footage of police bashing and street brawling. Leaving a glaring void in the middle, directly outside and in line with the widening entrance.

And so, as the gates reach their fully open position, Jarvis is left standing, stranded and feeling slightly foolish in the middle of the open concreted space, inside the main entrance that is now completely exposed to the open road outside.

Except there is one man standing alone in the middle of the cleared roadway, fifty yards away, bulky, threatening.

Tom Flynn, broad figure, legs apart, coat belted and hands in pockets. Standing still, looking ahead, straight at Jarvis. Any time, mate, he seems to be saying. We're ready. Are you?

And then the other two Americans amble across and take up statuesque positions at arm's length, either side of Flynn. Shorter on his left, and the third one on his right, who Jarvis suddenly recognises, recalling the Haditha chariot race. Mortarson. The leading rider with his whip was Ralph Mortarson.

All three stand still, for a few seconds, staring directly across the bare yards of void concrete that separates them, with smirky menace in their expressions, directed at him.

For a fraction of a second, Jarvis freezes, not knowing what to do, questioning why he had not organised for himself a proper escape route.

He wants to turn away and disappear inside the buildings without being noticed, but that's no longer possible. As if a starting gun has been fired for the race to begin, two of the ex-US marines spring into action. They lean forward, their legs push at the ground, their arms start to pump. They want to get through the gates before they close, to catch Jarvis in a sprint before he disappears through the security doors twenty-five yards away. Only Shorty is a bit slow, on account of the searing pain in the front of his chest every time he moves, and so he hobbles along at the back, grimacing, and he's the last to skip through the gap, hearing the gates clang together a few moments later behind him.

At last Jarvis reacts and turns, his long stride taking him swiftly to the heavy steel doors into the primary processing plant. He swipes his electronic pass card and after hearing the clunk, pushes through the door, immediately dashing right along a corridor. All the time listening out for the reassuring return clunk of the security door, before the Americans have time to reach it. But he does not hear it, making the assumption that one of the big men has managed to stick his foot in the door in time.

He does not turn to check, but dashes deep within the processing shed. All he can think of is to lead his adversaries in and around the jungle of heavy apparatus to create confusion and to gain an advantage, so long as he can remember the details of the layout himself. He moves into the centre, a vast poorly lit space like an aircraft hangar that relies on some daylight from skylights way above and a few overhead lamps. It's a noisy steamy atmosphere and the factory seems to be in full action. The various milling and refining processes are spinning, pumping, heaving and vibrating, apparently all on their own, with steam hissing from here, gurgling coming from there. There are conveyor belts and rail tracks, and miles of piping of all sizes passing between machines and tanks. A maze of wrought iron walkways links multiple platforms at different levels, with staircases and ramps going up or down like a giant layout of three-dimensional snakes and ladders. There are engineers in white overalls and rubber boots studying banks of glass-fronted recording and measuring devices, some on the ground floor while others are up under the roof one hundred and fifty feet above. Most staff operating the machines wear earmuffs and face masks, and as further reminders of the potential dangers that lurk around every corner, visitors are encouraged to read the many yellow signposts written in emphatic black lettering.

It's like being in a huge kitchen, with massive pots and cylinders and pans, some chopping, some whizzing and whirring, some heating up. Jarvis dashes into the thick of it, ducking under gangways, hopping over treadways, twisting around hefty metal tanks. He scampers towards the furthest section, where he catches a glimpse of the river and a grey sky outside. Raw cane deliveries are being trundled across from the outside wharf on rails and continuously tipped into a massive conveyor system. The first part is a metal grill eight feet wide that rolls steadily on clinking cogs towards the next conveyor in line, a wider rubbery track. This one has serrated teeth to hold the loose material, as it tilts upwards at an angle of thirty degrees, to the top, fifty feet up, where the contents are tipped into a giant shredding machine.

John Shorter emerges from the corridor onto the factory floor, alone and bemused. His two fighting comrades have spread out the other way. Shorter is a small figure moving hesitantly towards the giant machines in the vast space, surprised by the noise level and suddenly aware of the earthy sweet smell and sticky taste in the atmosphere. He brings his hand up to his mouth and sniffs uncomfortably. The machines are old, a hundred years or more in some cases, and they look it: hand-built in chunky iron and dull copper, tanks and piping sitting on monstrous girders, with heavy legged supports, all painted in thick creams and blues. Past remnants of an earlier age, nothing of the modern era that Shorter might have expected: no shiny gleaming steel, brushed aluminium or sheets of glass. He wonders what the hell he has let himself in for but catches sight of Jarvis away over by a giant sliding doorway through which several yellow diggers with enormous rubbery wheels are passing in and out with loaded buckets of sandy powder, dripping piles of excess over the sides as they trundle about.

He watches Jarvis scrambling onto a moving conveyor, among a ragged heaped pile of canes, shells and leafy bark, and then sees him jumping down onto the next one. Determined to show Tom how useful he can be, by blocking Jarvis's retreat, he follows as swiftly as his stinging chest wound allows. It's his turn to have a knife ready, drawn from a sheath he keeps strapped and hidden on the inside of his shin.

A yellow sign stands within a metal fence placed around the low start of the conveyor, warning of the dangers of getting too close to the moving belt. An experienced operator, ready to hit the red 'off' button on his console, stands nearby and in Shorter's way. With one neat clean punch across the jaw, the poor fellow is taken out, dropping like a stone with a wide-eyed look of surprise. Shorter stumbles over him wincing and clambers up onto the slow-moving belt, catching his shin on the metal edge. He thinks that anything Jarvis can do he can do as well. So, he ploughs on regardless, and is soon preparing himself for the jump with all the canes and roughage together, down onto the next level, just as he saw Collingwood do.

It's a couple of feet down, but he loses his balance and hits his knees on the rubber bottom among a heap of loose canes, sharp and rough-cut. The steepness of the belt catches him unawares, and he must lean forwards, scrabbling for a foothold among all the scratchy and pungent stalks and canes, fearful of tumbling backwards as he tries to find something solid to hold onto. He cannot see properly where he is going but catches glimpses though the leafy branches of Jarvis up ahead of him. For a moment, he worries that he has made the wrong decision, following Jarvis on this route. These conveyors are definitely not made for humans. Gripping the knife firmly in his right fist, for courage, he finds himself longing to be back in Montana walking over the forested mountainsides with his dogs, instead of dealing with this idiot Englishman in this God-forsaken country. He gathers himself for the leap he needs to make off the moving belt. He stares fixedly at the crouching figure up ahead, instructing himself to follow exactly what Collingwood does. Gritting his teeth in a moment of wild hatred for his adversary, he reminds himself that this is the nasty turd that not only cut him down the front of his chest, but also shot Wosniak through the neck. He delights at the idea that he might be the one to stick Jarvis with his blade.

For the final approach with less than twenty feet to go, the incline drops off to about five degrees. Jarvis places a tough boot on the chain-metal edge of the belt, shifts his weight over it and readies himself. At the right moment he springs up and across onto a steel mesh platform, that is fixed at a slightly lower level than the conveyor, where he lands like a feral cat, softly, with bent knees and in comfortable balance. He swivels quickly around, watching for the American to come leaping up after him.

Shorter continues his unpleasant ride upwards, watching with an excruciating look of uncertainty. He fails to understand how precisely Collingwood had pushed himself off the conveyor, which he assumes correctly is not going to stop for him at the top. Unless the operator he knocked out with a right hook at the ground level was to press his red button? He thinks he can follow suit and has about six seconds to prepare himself for the sort of leap that Collingwood made, seeing no reason why he cannot manage it.

Unfortunately, he does not get his balance right, his foothold uncertain on the shifting spiky husks and canes with their leaf and flaking bark offering nothing firm in the way of support, from which he can push up and make his jump. By the time he realises he needs an alternative plan, with one leg cocked awkwardly over the side, reaching out with a hand in desperation for a solid metal railing that he sees approaching, it is too late and the momentum of the moving conveyor is taking him past the platform. His six seconds are up.

The conveyor hangs over the rim of an open steel plated cylindrical tank about eight feet across that contains dozens of razor-sharp blades at several levels that whiz relentlessly around a central axis at roughly a thousand revolutions a minute. Crudely, it shreds everything within the tank into tiny bits very quickly. John Shorter desperately thrashes his arms about trying to grab onto something that might save his fall, but there is nothing, and he simply tips helplessly headfirst together with the full load of raw sugar cane over the advancing edge, still gripping his army knife, into the swirling spinning maelstrom below.

The resulting product of this process, described for obvious reasons as shreds, drops down into a container six feet below, where a shovel-like arm automatically and constantly empties the floor into another funnel, ready for the crushing process that follows. Jarvis is trying not to think too seriously about what he has just witnessed, even as he hears several thuds and a dull grinding, cogs jamming if only momentarily, before resuming their usual swirling high-pitched whine. Several splashes of something slimy and indescribable, stained a reddish colour, have landed on his woolly beanie and across his cheeks, which he wipes, flicking the sticky stuff off his hands.

Jarvis is ready to move on.

Despite his fatigue and the stiffness of his wounds, Jarvis has gained a little more confidence. No one seems to have witnessed what happened. He is on a platform that is part of the walkway encircling the shredding tank. He takes a narrow, fixed ladder down to the level below and crosses over an open space thirty feet above ground level, where he sees a couple of figures in white crossing the floor below him with their iPads. From another platform, this one, wooden slats, he passes behind a triple collection of solid iron tanks like the bulkheads on a ship, painted thickly in gloss cream about a hundred years ago and discoloured with age and repeated indiscriminate leakages ever since. There is no one about. He can take his time, hidden among the machinery, while he tries to discern where the other two Americans have got to.

He assumes they are both armed, so he keeps close to the solid machines that gently whir and hum. He spots a couple of engineers at a console some way away, fiddling with their switches and flickering needles. Steam is hissing from an outlet above their heads as they concentrate behind their masks on jotting down notes and they pay him little attention. He scrambles over some pipework and slips into a tight space between two of the tanks. Moving through and towards the other side, he gains a reasonable view of the inside of the rest of the factory. He scans the gangways and walkways close by, the ladders and various platforms around him, and much of the floor space below.

And then two bare-headed figures in dark coats emerge from the shadows on the far side of the floor. They stand back to back, scouring the strange machinery all about them, seemingly at a loss. A few battery-operated buggies pass quietly by, others walk past, no one taking any notice of them; everybody going about their own business with quiet efficiency. Tom Flynn has his right hand deep in his raincoat pocket gripping something and Jarvis is offering no prizes for guessing what that might be. Mortarson has something tucked inside his coat. Suddenly Tom points up among the pipes and tanks with his free hand, towards Jarvis, and Mortarson follows his direction. They exchange words and decide to split, Tom heading out of sight to another section, Mortarson more direct, moving at a trot straight towards Jarvis and a collection of sturdy ladders that will bring him up to the same level. When he glances up from the bottom of the ladders to where they had seen Jarvis, he is no longer there.

Mortarson climbs to the next level and is drawn along a path into the dim recesses of the working machines, where everything is bigger, the spaces tighter and darker, the gangways labyrinthine. After several minutes of deliberate approach, with a baseball bat held out in front of him, he catches a glimpse of Jarvis's retreating figure, climbing another ladder to reach the very top of the three huge tanks, where he can walk around the gangways peering over the rims into their contents.

Mortarson finds another route up, another ladder to climb and eventually reaches the top level, under the huge vaulted roof of the factory. He does not like the height he is at, and is confused by all the walkways, like a maze, but on several levels, some of the interconnecting gangways crossing over voids in mid-air. They are mostly of meshed steel, noisy to walk on but easy to see through, with minimal safety protection or barrier, sometimes just a pair of wires strung from one post to the next. A skylight nearby allows a glimpse of London's dull clouded sky.

Under dirty steel girders, with artificial lighting from neon bulbs hanging bare on chains from above amid a criss-cross of suction pipes in aluminium foil, three monster open cylinders, each containing fifteen tons of slowly churning syrup, cluster together on a steel erected floor. Amid the constant sound of humming motors, Jarvis listens to the gurgling and slurping sounds within. He can feel a gentle vibration on leaning over the rim of one of the tanks, at his waist height. From a ten-metre tower outside the building, sulphur dioxide is fed into the bottom to syphon through the mix while lime powder is funnelled from small provider tanks above. Churning away under the perpetual agitation of rotating blades is the clarified sugary substance bleached and decolourised, curdling away in the warmth. The mix thickens into a thick slurry that looks like clotted yoghurt, a dirty cream colour, and sloppy suds like detergent foam collect over the surface. At times sulphates give off a sickly odour of rotten eggs that catches in his throat.

Jarvis has been up here before, mesmerised by the process, the changing shapes like egg whites and sugar aerated to achieve peaks for a giant meringue. This off-white sugary curd that smells a bit sour must be scraped off by rotating paddles that skim over the surface at intervals from a slowly rotating beam, shovelling the gooey mush over to the sides. Like baby snot, it slides down the outer surface of the tanks, to be collected in gutters that surround the outside like an apron, with a couple of wide drainage downpipes taking the stuff away to be fed into a recovery and waste cycle. Which leaves the syrup mix settling underneath during a six to eight-hour session of churning, to be forced away later through filters as it proceeds to the next stage.

Cautiously watching for the American to appear around a corner at the far end of his platform, Jarvis eyes a collection of sampling ladles that hang in a row from a rack, like musical chimes, in increasing size and length. They are all made of steel, and he selects the thickest and longest one from the end.

Mortarson appears at the top of a ladder on his level, twenty-five yards away and advances eagerly with his baseball bat out in front. He is about the same height as Jarvis, with the same long stride, but he is a bit heavier, a bit chunkier and lacks the leanness that makes Jarvis so agile.

'Hey, Collingwood,' he shouts, 'you maniac, now we've got you.'

Jarvis interprets this as meaning that Mortarson is hoping that Flynn will burst onto the scene from somewhere behind him, thus trapping him between the two of them, so he must face them together, no escape. He turns quickly to make sure he is not missing anything and sees there is no sign of the other threatening American for the moment – he needs to take Mortarson down quickly before Flynn does turn up.

They eye each other, Mortarson and Jarvis at opposite sides of the same tank. At this close range, Jarvis can see better the clean-shaven square jaw and deeply set black eyes of the American. He watches him discarding his coat, throwing it over an outer railing, moving his bat from hand to hand. He looks slightly out of breath with his rapid climbing of all those ladders. He has a thick mop of hair and a good physique. He looks ready for business, in a navy woollen top and slacks. He advances and Jarvis retreats, two steps forwards, two steps back. They can both see that it's going to be a game of cat and mouse, one chasing the other round and round the big tanks in circles, like schoolboys in a yard, until the cows come home or one of them collapses from exhaustion. Or till Flynn appears at one side to alter the balance. Jarvis reckons he could outlast Mortarson in an endurance race but might struggle to overpower him in close hand-to-hand combat.

Mortarson is already trying to figure out how to surprise Jarvis, maybe by going over the top. He advances around one side of the circular tank, his attention distracted by the churning of thick creamy-white stuff swirling and folding over itself at the syrupy surface, something he has never seen before and he's not at all sure what it is.

'Tom, get your ass up here,' he calls out, 'I've got Collingwood cornered.'

Which is quite difficult to do when you are going around a circular structure. The general noise level is high, so he cannot be sure that Flynn heard him. 'Come on, Jarvis, you're trapped, admit it. Come to me, son. Let us get this over with.'

Jarvis sneers back at him and says nothing. He happens to be doubting at that moment that his team of supporters are ever going to get to him in his hour of need.

Mortarson tries the direct approach again. He rounds the tank crouching slightly with his bat held up and Jarvis backs away. When Mortarson picks up the pace, he retreats faster, never letting him closer than half a turn. They circulate, one way then the other, sometimes stepping slowly, then Mortarson sprints and Jarvis likewise dashes away. Their relative positions remain the same. Mortarson is getting a little tired and is puffing heavily after one such sprint, when he dashes one way and suddenly turns the other way, to try and catch Jarvis out. School boys in the yard, without a doubt.

On the next occasion, Jarvis allows the American chasing him, to come closer, merely a couple of yards, before suddenly stopping and turning to aggressively aim his long ladle at Mortarson's head. The ex-marine is not so easily fooled and defends himself with the baseball bat, parrying and then attacking with a few heavy swings towards Jarvis's head. Jarvis ducks and swerves, the bat hitting the side of the tank twice, sending judders up Mortarson's arm each time. Jarvis hits him hard across the hips and then pokes the ladle at his face, catching his nose. Wounded and angry, drawn into attack as Jarvis turns to run away, Mortarson charges forwards a couple of paces behind.

Jarvis suddenly turns around when they are close, swinging his ladle as aggressively as he can, clashing with the heavier wooden bat of Mortarson, and neither taking advantage. They bundle themselves into an angry grapple at close quarters, where there is no space for wielding bats and ladles.

'It's Ralph Mortarson, isn't it?' Jarvis asks.

'Bricks,' Mortarson replies.

'Just checking.'

Bricks's strength might have come more into play, but Jarvis's superiority lies in his nimble footwork, learned from the boxing ring, combined with his long reach with his fists. He catches Bricks more than once across his jaw and then his nose, full on. Bricks backs away, tasting his own blood and retrieves his baseball bat, regretting he did not bring along a proper weapon with him, like Tom.

Where the hell is Tom anyway?

Jarvis's bare knuckles are beginning to hurt. Bricks is swinging his bat again without finding its target, but twice bashing the end against solid metal. Jarvis retreats through a gap between tanks and draws Bricks after him. As before they start to circulate around a different tank, Bricks dashing forward a few steps, Jarvis retreating as fast. They go around a complete circuit before Bricks has another go, dashing forward, swinging his bat for all its worth, accompanied by wild shouting and animal grunts. But Jarvis sidesteps and parries expertly with his steel ladle and engages briefly with a direct shove into Bricks's chest, which unbalances him. Jarvis gets a whiff of his sweat before aiming another blow to Bricks's head with his ladle. Bricks side-steps this time. He elbows Jarvis in the face and then delivers a body blow, thumping him in the midriff with the butt of his bat.

They are forced to grapple once again. Bricks is angry and frustrated; he tries headbutting Jarvis in the jaw. They crash back onto the outer gutter of the tank, and Jarvis loses his footing. Bricks senses a break and presses hard, punching him across his face, and trying to deadleg him with his knee. Jarvis topples over the low rim of the gutter, crashing in on his back. As wide as a big human, swirling with creamy scum from the main tank, it's slippery on the steel inner surface. Bricks is desperate to press his advantage, leaning over with the baseball bat raised for what he hopes will be the decisive blow. More by luck than anything, it misses its target, as Jarvis slips around, but it strikes him with a heavy thud across his shoulder. He manages to grab at the bat and Bricks's arm at the same time, pulling him hard with all his might and toppling him over into the gutter as well.

Smeared in grimy curdles of slimy sticky goo, they both struggle to get any sort of grip. They roll over each other, grunting, Jarvis twisting and kicking. He pokes Bricks in the eyes. Somehow Bricks gets up onto a knee, as Jarvis slides away out of reach along the gutter in the slippery sludge, with the baseball bat surprisingly under him. He grips the side and manages to get to his feet, retrieving the bat with his other hand, which he then uses on Bricks with a blow that glances off the side of his skull. But the slippery bat slides out of his hands and sails away into the distance with a clatter.

Bricks is stunned and Jarvis grabs him by his collar from behind, trying to get his big hands clamped around his neck to throttle him. At the same time, he purchases his feet against the outer wall of the gutter and forces Bricks back over the rim of the tank. Bricks twists himself around but is still bent backwards, struggling with his breath, losing his footing, with the edge of the tank pressing into his lower back. Jarvis holds him in that position, forcing him as far back as he can manage with his arms fully stretched, squeezing across his airway as tight as he can. Bricks is thrashing with his arms but keeps losing his footing.

The frothy foam that forms above the syrup surface in each tank is swept away by rubber paddles, angled in a way that pushes the scum outwards over the rim of the tank, and which are fixed under a horizontally rotating steel beam, like a solid girder. Turned by an old motor that uses bicycle chains and pulleys to chug relentlessly above the centre, the beam reaches across the full twenty-foot diameter of the circular tank and swings round with about six inches of clearance above the rim. About seven seconds separates each half sweep.

With Bricks' resistance waning as he is forced backwards, his head twisted over the tank and the heavy beam approaching around its circuit, it is easy enough for Jarvis to hold him there, although Bricks is thrashing with his arms and trying to kick his way out of Jarvis's grip. Bricks does not see it coming. Jarvis jerks the man's head into the path of the moving steel girder and his skull is cracked with a crunch. Bricks's head is knocked like a cricket ball to one side, his body suddenly hanging limp and heavy in Jarvis's hands, wedged against him and the outside of the tank. The beam passes on its way steadily without a pause.

Jarvis heaves the man up against the rim of the tank until his hips are on the top edge and then it is a simple matter of letting him topple over into the scummy white froth that bubbles all around. Bricks Mortarson disappears under the gooey surface without trace, without a splash or ripple, into the caustic substance that readily burns bare skin. The soles of his boots are the last thing that Jarvis sees.

Exhausted with his efforts, he carefully climbs out of the slippery gutter back onto dry walkway. He discards his sticky wet uniform jacket, and walks away to the end of the platform where there is a tap for running water to wash the gruesome suds off his hands and the outside of his trousers before they can start to burn. He sits for a moment, uncomfortable and wet, to catch his breath and his thoughts. He looks around, checking who might have watched the action and whether Tom Flynn is anywhere nearby. But it seems he is alone.

He knows now that he only has Flynn to deal with.

Joe was resting on his pile of sacks in a corner, in the warehouse basement; Jarvis had settled on a rug against a cardboard box, after pacing around for a while like a caged tiger. They had only been down there an hour, no more, when Mustafa came to the door at the top of the stairs again and quietly signalled for Jarvis to come up for something. Behind him looking distraught was Ahmed, the young lad from next door who helped Rahim in his garage. Mustafa said Ahmed had come down in a hurry on a motorbike from Rahim's and wanted to talk with Jarvis. Important and private.

The three of them found a storeroom along a corridor filled like the whole warehouse seemed to be with assorted boxes. Mustafa had found a can of fizzy drink for Ahmed who was out of breath and sweating, his tee shirt wet down his spine. His black curly hair was wildly dishevelled. He carried his bike helmet, wearing filthy jeans and open flip-flops with bare feet.

Ahmed swallowed several sips of drink and looked tearful. He spoke a little English. 'Oh, Mr Jarvis, sir, I cannot tell. I don't know what.' He struggled and quickly stumbled into Arabic, rattling off a long passage in which Jarvis recognised the names of Rahim and Jahinda. Ahmed kept wiping at his eyes, with oil-stained long fingers, dirt under his fingernails. He looked older than eighteen.

Mustafa played catch up: 'He says the Americans came to the garage and found the place on the roof. They knew the soldiers had been there. They were nasty.' Mustafa tried to reassure Ahmed with an arm around his shoulders, a hand patting his chest and words of encouragement. Ahmed rattled off another nervous passage, and once again Jarvis picked up the name of Rahim.

Mustafa continued: 'They roughed up Rahim, punched him in the face. They were shouting at him, but he said nothing, he told them nothing.' Ahmed continued after a pause and Mustafa translated: 'He says he ran next door when he could, he was scared. He hid upstairs in the roof space, where he could look over into Rahim's bedroom, behind the pipes and water tanks. He says one of them attacked Jahinda, very very angry, screaming at her, had a knife; on the big bed, took his trousers down. She screamed and he hit her across her mouth again and again until he had finished.'

Ahmed dropped his face, covered his trembling lips with his hand, there were tears in both eyes. Mustafa was looking rattled, wanting to know more. Further Arabic conversation was exchanged in rising tones, Mustafa almost shouting. Jarvis has tensed, his teeth have clenched and a cold sensation was rippling through his guts. He put a firm hand on Ahmed's shoulder and then lifted his face up. He asked what the soldier looked like, could he describe *him. Mustafa helped with the questions and then Ahmed responded in a faltering voice.*

Mustafa spoke: 'He was big man in army fatigues, with guns and his radio in his chest. He was blond hair, clean-shaven.' Ahmed added something and Mustafa said: 'He had tattoo on his neck, like a snake and a dagger.'

Ahmed spoke some more. Mustafa said: 'The soldier left Jahinda and then they grabbed Rahim and dragged him outside, out to their truck, shouting that he would show them where he taken the soldiers. Ahmed had dashed downstairs and out in the road, saw the big American truck drive out of town towards Guadalahasha valley, an area out west of Haditha. Rahim must have made up the story to get them away from his house. Ahmed went back to Jahinda, found her grandmother. He wanted to tell you so you could do something.'

'Rahim not come back, will he?' Ahmed asked.

'The vermin. They're sheer vermin, Ahmed.' Jarvis leant forward, he was still gripping the boy's shoulder. 'You did well, son; I'm so sorry.'

Resting for a moment on his haunches, leaning against metal infrastructure, he is able to observe some of the factory from his tucked-away position. He has no weapon at hand and has no idea where Flynn might be at that moment. The three Americans had obviously started out trying to cover some of Jarvis's options, by separating in three different directions. If they had stayed at strategic places on the floor, they would have had a better chance of catching him when he eventually would have had to come down to ground level, but the first two guys had not been able to restrain themselves and had made fatal errors. Tommy Flynn would probably be more subtle and careful in his approach.

Jarvis can sense that the moment for him to take his revenge, after four waiting years, is close.

Jarvis can't stop thinking of Joe and Jahinda. He always knew nothing good could come of it. They are sitting cross-legged in the grass in the shadows of the hidden wall behind Rahim's garage, talking, teasing sweetly. They are walking in the woods at night, their shoulders touching, their hands holding on in the moonlight. Smiling Joe is invigorated, a sense of purpose in his work. So innocent, so naïve. And so young. Poor Joe. Poor Jahinda.

There are a few workers moving about with purpose unaware of the battle happening above them, the surrounding hubbub enough to disguise the noise. He sees a movement away to his right, sixty feet below him, a shadowy figure in a dark coat. It must be Flynn, among the big centrifuge tanks, slipping from the shadow of one machine to the next, cautiously peeking around corners. He has a gun in his right hand, held loosely out in front of him. He has to duck under steel structures and step over insulated pipes.

Tilting his head back for a moment, Flynn catches sight of Collingwood moving forwards in a crouch along a mesh steel gangway over to one side and far above him: he slowly points his Beretta M9 semiautomatic, with a look of relief creeping across his face. Unaware of what has happened to his colleagues, content to think that they will be behind Collingwood somewhere, blocking his retreat, he gleams at the idea of blowing a hole through the Englishman. Once he has him in a closer range with a clearer shot, Flynn will have the advantage he needs. He takes a few short steps up to another gangway that runs in a curve behind a couple of massive shiny tanks like giant cans of baked beans without the labels. He creeps ahead, gun cocked, steeling himself around the first one, peeping round towards the second tank.

Jarvis is thinking to head nearer the river exit, close by the packaging section, from where he might be able to get across to the wharf. Suddenly there's a cracking sound, a gunshot with a ricochet off the metal bulkhead next to him. He ducks involuntarily and retreats, getting himself behind solid metal. He takes a detour on the trot around another monster pot, then lies full length on his stomach along a mesh gangway, aware of the wetness of his clothes and watching for activity below. He sees a shifting shadow and someone moving between the centrifuge tanks. Then Flynn emerges cautiously, twenty feet below him, dark and bulky in his coat. He's holding onto a railing with one hand and his pistol in his other.

There are some fresh drops of water on the gangway ahead of him. Several more drops splash from above his head, and Flynn bends down, about to reach forward with bare fingers to touch them, test them, when from nowhere, someone lands across his back, like a monkey dropping from a tree in the woods. It's Mat and they tumble to the floor below. Mat swings a fist and bundles Flynn over, kicking and stamping on his outstretched arm. The gun flips away from them and Mat turns to swipe Flynn again with his fist across his face. Charlie and Nelson miraculously appear as well and the three of them move to surround the American. But he is a ferocious fighter with an instinct for survival. Almost without hesitation, Flynn scrambles to his feet and takes a charging run at Mat, hitting him hard in the midriff with his bullet head. Mat's head jerks violently with the impact and he drops heavily to the floor, stunned. Tommy makes a grab for his fallen Beretta and runs hard away from them, leapfrogging clear of a low brick wall that is arranged in a sort of horseshoe, with the three ex-paras slow to pursue.

Unknown to Flynn, he could not possibly know, he vaults feet first into the factory's main overflow drainage system, a brick-lined deep-sided bowl as wide as a tennis court, that funnels all the excess waste of the entire factory process into huge drains like sewers. It's dry at the moment and Flynn has jarred his ankles painfully on landing. He is rolling on his side and moaning, beneath a vast rectangular collecting tank that acts as a conduit, suspended above the bowl.

The brick surface is slippery with discoloured syrupy collections from previous wash-throughs. Strands of drying sticky sludge hang blackened in thin streaks from around the closed sump at the bottom of the fluted tank. The three soldiers watch from the safety of the wall as Flynn looks around confused, unsure of his footing, waiving his Beretta around. He fires off a couple of shots to show who's boss, that ricochet off the brickwork.

On seeing his friends at last, Jarvis drops down from his position and hurries over to the action. At the waste tank he carefully steps along a gangway that bridges over to the operating platform by the funnel, where a large steel wheel painted red, worn down to bare metal in several places, manually operates the opening of the sump. On applying all his strength, it moves with a judder and a squeak.

Flynn looks up and waives his gun around, but can't see who it is above him, from his grounded position. Glutinous sludge like liquid cow manure starts to dribble from the sump and splash onto the mucky floor a few feet below. Flynn urgently struggles to his feet. The smell is appalling, and everything is quickly covered in the sticky brown muck. The wheel turns some more and the dribble turns to a rush, pouring down around Flynn like a hose, slapping up the front of his trousers onto his coat. He tries to step out to the side, to lift his feet clear. But it just keeps coming, the level rising in sloppy waves, thick glutinous sludge clinging to his clothes. He slips and drops onto his knee and the ghastly stuff splashes his face. He struggles to stand, tries to wipe his eyes. Jarvis keeps turning the wheel, and a torrent of the stuff cascades into the bowl.

Flynn has lost his gun and looks defenceless. He struggles to wade ashore, losing his footing, his ankle pain still bugging him. He sees Jarvis, leaning over the wall. 'Collingwood,' he shouts, 'you shouldna done what you done, yer know that, right?'

Jarvis is leaning over with an outstretched hand, for Flynn to grab. The American wades through the sludge, making huge efforts to get closer to the wall where Jarvis is crouching. After a while he stretches out his arm to reach for the helping hand. Their eyes meet, Flynn's fearful, Jarvis's arctic and venomous.

'You killed Rahim. You raped Jahinda. You shouldna done what you done, Flynn. And you know that.' Jarvis withdraws his hand, coils himself, balances on one foot as he kicks out the other with brutal force and accuracy, catching Flynn full in the face, with the sole of his booted foot. The blow crunches into Flynn's nose.

A hurt expression erupts across the American's face, his eyes screwed up in pain, a spot of blood at his nostrils. Within seconds the level of fill is up to his chest. He is swept along in the fast-flowing river of sludge, with nothing to cling on to, for a moment submerged. When he resurfaces, his head desperately poking above the surface to reach air, he looks for Collingwood and screams across at him: 'Get me out of here, you murdering bastard.'

'Not possible, Flynn, I'm afraid. I did warn you.'

And with that, Flynn disappears, for all his strength and determination, sucked under by the relentless tide of molasses that flows over his head, carrying him rapidly towards the exit, into its vortex, spinning anticlockwise. The massive runoff drains out to storage vessels on the River Thames. Only, with the tide being out at that time, there are no vessels waiting for the deluge, which gushes freely from the overhanging gutter that throws it beyond the sides of the key into open space. Which means that Tommy Flynn falls a goodly distance down onto the hard, sandy shingle shore of the riverbed, scattered with stones and rocks. If the fall does not break his neck, the landing certainly will have broken a few other bones, making crawling somewhere to safety impossible. The incoming tide over the next few hours will drown him thoroughly. His body will very likely be carried eventually downstream to some far-flung corner of the estuary, beyond Tilbury, you would imagine.

Jarvis closes off the wheel as fast as he can. The foul sickly smell of the molasses is almost overwhelming, and he is sure he will never want to taste sugar again.

Charlie, Mat and Nelson are waiting for him on the safe factory floor, explaining to a few men in laboratory coats and white plastic overalls that the molasses will be closed off, there's nothing to worry about. They gather to congratulate each other on the afternoon's work. Without any explanation to anyone, or objection from anyone, they amble out of the factory side-by-side, Jarvis leaving wet footprints across the floor. Through the car park, off the site, they are quite happy to be leaving the protestors protesting and the boys in blue doing their duty.

Debriefing interview, MoD, Aldwych.
December 12, 2005.
There appears to be no official record of events, there are no files to consult. Was the small tape cassette going to be the only record of Jarvis's actions? Malone is sure to be keeping that to himself. Will he even be making up a file after the interview?

Jarvis takes a breather, standing up and drifting away towards the floor space under the window. Feeling the guilt of Rahim's fate and Jahinda's injuries heavy on his conscience, Joe's death weighing on his shoulders, knowing there will never be a day in the future when he does not feel sorry for what he did. Of course he regrets what happened, nobody condones what happens when countries go to war. But he did what he had to do, under difficult circumstances: Wosniak was a criminal, a murderer, out of control. Whereas he, Corporal Jarvis Collingwood, was a dedicated, allegiant soldier, ardent and blessed, a wilful assassin.

Malone stares for a while at the recording device, watching the little spools rotating silently. 'Any military inquiry into the Haditha shooting, if the US are forced to hold one, would be based in Washington. What will we say when the shooting of Wozniak gets out, I'm not too sure, Collingwood.' With that he stabs the top of his fountain pen back over the nib, tucks it away in an inside jacket pocket and reaches for the tape-recorder. 'Interview suspended at 12.32 hours.'

After a moment of silence. 'That will obviously suffice, for now at least. May want to come back to you with further questions in due course, Corporal.'

'Thank you, sir.'

Malone retrieves his coat and marches across the carpet to the door.

Jarvis realises that Malone does not have the authority or the wherewithal to proceed any further, that he is probably out of his depth and pay-grade as it is. Jarvis is being dismissed. With relief creeping across his face, he walks past the statuesque captain without a sideways glance.

Epilogue
London,
January 13, 2012

Friday January 13

Major Mike Malone, First Battalion Special Forces, Parachute Regiment, wants to end his career on a high note. He knows his record is good, his performance more than adequate in Northern Ireland, Cyprus, Iraq, Afghanistan and elsewhere, even if not particularly outstanding. So where is the credit? He has few commendations. He craves more recognition for his services, which he is proud to tell you, were exemplary. He envies some others, like that devilish young corporal, Jarvis Collingwood. *He* has at least three bravery medals, a handful of commendations and a personal mention from his battalion commander on more than one occasion. He was surprised to hear that Collingwood had retired from the British Army, so early. He could have gone onto so much more, achieving senior rank, better pay and pension and all that. If he had hung on a few more years. Still, Malone supposes that the incident with the Iraqi shooting in Haditha had been testing enough, more disturbing than he cared to admit. He probably decided he had had enough, especially if it transpired that he was at risk of wiping out all the preceding good work with just one mistake.

Malone is clear in his own mind: it had been a mistake, a serious error of judgement. You don't take out an officer of an Allied partner on your own account, on the basis of not liking what you saw. Especially not in the heat of battle. And certainly not a serving marine in a respected company of the army of the US of fucking A. Poor Jarvis, the moral dilemma had been too intricate for him. Did he honestly think Malone was going to believe his cock and bull story about being attacked by al-Qaeda insurgents and that Private Joe Street was injured with a knife wound?

Of course, there was no way he was going to allow such a controversial action as Collingwood's assassination of an American officer on foreign soil to come out, in all its gory detail, under his watch. Oh no, he had to corroborate Collingwood's made-up story. He was not going to disclose all the details and risk his own reputation. He knew Jarvis would keep quiet about it, and so long as Street did too, then he, Mike Malone was sure to cover over the issue and let the whole thing drop. The fact that the US authorities had been persuaded largely through media attention to pursue what appeared to be legitimate legal proceedings against individual Kilo Company marines and that the presence of a British witness at the scene was to become known, would not have made any difference to his chosen course of action. He would stick to the simple story, rely on confusion and unreliable reporting and a lack of other eye witnesses for the courts to believe that Wozniak had been shot by an insurgent (even though everyone knew they did not have the skills or equipment required and used a different calibre bullet than the British).

When the opportunity arose, and Malone saw it as an opportunity and not an unwelcome chore, for *him* to testify in Washington on behalf of her Majesty's British Army, let nobody say that he flunked it, that he backed off, lost his nerve. Far from it, he relished the chance to take centre stage and to testify his plan to deploy some of the British Army's finest snipers around the city to assist their US partners in the hazardous role of suppressing the insurgent activity, especially tricky in such a lawless place as Haditha. And that how during this particular incident, it proved vital in preventing further bloodshed of innocent Iraqis, which Kilo Company seemed hellbent on creating, under the command of Sergeant Robert Wosniak. Malone *would* reveal that one of his British snipers had taken out Sergeant Wosniak as the only way to prevent further slaughter and that he, Malone had been part of the decision. The soldier in question would remain unnamed and under personal protection for his own security, and Major Malone would not be at liberty to reveal his identity. He would finish by reminding the court that the atrocity at Haditha was just one more in a long list of war crimes committed by US forces against the occupied Iraqi population.

Humph - see how that would have gone down. Would that have appeared in the American popular press? As it was, he need not have worried, as he was never called upon to testify to anything. The US military originally charged eight marines with unpremeditated murder. Several Iraqi witnesses who were due to be brought over to the Appeals Court promptly withdrew and could not be traced. There followed numerous examples of official marine corps intransigence, senior army officials dragging their feet, nobody in authority wanting the truth to get out to be added to the relentless list of US atrocities that Malone and others would have alluded to. It had taken six years and countless wasted tribunals, appeals and other court appearances, and goodness knows how much in legal fees, to arrive at that position.

And then Collingwood decides to answer the call of duty and is ready to take himself off to Washington to give evidence out of a conscience or guilt or something. Which would have placed him, Major Exemplary Malone in the shit. That was not right. Definitely not right.

It's early evening, in the middle of a cold January. A light afternoon fall of snow has turned the City streets wet and slippery. Every time the black doors of *The Samuel Pepys* swing open, as people come and go, Jarvis catches sight of the chilly slush outside in Stew Lane. He is enjoying the comforts within, where a log fire burns bright and the comradeship of friends is better than anything he knows. It's his birthday and Pamela even now, he imagines, will be clattering in the kitchen with bubbling pots preparing a hearty meal in her distinctive chaotic manner. He remembers vaguely her telling him about some other guests coming round later, which only makes him crave more for the male company present and to stay precisely where he feels safe. A few mates are sitting close, others milling about, enjoying the atmosphere, a couple of guys slumped close to the fire, all relishing being reunited. They had not seen each other for a while, they all had some catching up to do. There were stories to tell, experiences to share, some from home, some abroad; some victory tales, some funny incidences, and some too sad to retell, about mates lost but not forgotten.

Strength in numbers, although the danger has passed, Malone said so. The three American killers were quietly dispensed with, no fanfare. What possible repercussions could there be, it was in the past. Happily. Malone had said so. He was here earlier, Jarvis told them, wanted to talk about the good times. Looking smart in a city suit.

Malone had called Jarvis, wanted to have a private word, before all his friends turned up.

Jarvis had never seen Mike Malone in anything but impeccable Army uniform, with its emblems and colours and pips, and so has a double take when this confident man with neat moustache and straight posture strides through the swing doors into the middle of the public bar looking about him with an air of confidence. He has a newspaper tucked under his arm, a rolled umbrella in hand. He discards his camel hair coat and leather gloves, revealing a bespoke double-breasted grey suit and black shoes. Jarvis hesitantly steps up from the bar to face him and Malone greets him with a soft handshake. There's an expensive gold watch loose at his wrist.

They settle on red velvet covered stools, order their drinks. Jarvis has to remind himself that he is in the presence of a major now. Malone picks up with the small talk, how are you, busy I expect, all quiet back at camp, although we are still deploying our battalion in Basra. 'And the lovely wife? How is Pamela?' Malone was good with names. He lives alone, had never had a woman, as far as any of the boys knew, so Jarvis finds idle domestic chatter with him awkward.

'She's fine, yeah, we're getting along.' Although Jarvis is not quite sure what he means by that. Malone prattles on, Jarvis still wondering exactly why he was so keen to meet with him, surely not to celebrate his birthday.

'Actually, glad I caught you, like this. Before the others arrive. It is all over, at last. The Navy-Marine Criminal Appeals Court wound up the case two days ago. Official. Summary findings available in print; all investigations shut down, witnesses released from obligations, counsels dismissed. Case closed, period.'

'But not forgotten, sir,' Jarvis ventures.

'Oh, well, no. Such an impact. I mean, you retired early, for one. A little premature, in my opinion.' Malone with a quizzical look, nods with satisfaction, pleased that he is keeping up with all the news. Was he fishing for compliments? 'The NCIS investigation ran to 35,000 pages.'

After a moment while both men sip quietly at their beers, Jarvis asks: 'Why, has it all ended, with no justice?'

'Well, after a couple of years, the charges against the marines were dropped, they were granted immunity. Including Wosniak's commander, Lieutenant Callaghan, who argued that the marines were strictly correct in their conduct, within the law and rules. The surviving marines claimed they had been fired on after the roadside explosion, that they were convinced there were insurgents attacking them from those houses. They proceeded according to their rules of engagement.'

'There was never any evidence on the ground that any insurgent bullets had been fired at the marines, from those houses or elsewhere.'

'The defence lawyers argued well. Another year or more of muddle and appeal and counter-appeal - at one point two marines who were thought to be involved confessed, to something, was not clear exactly to what. There was a plea bargain in there somewhere. Anyway, it all combined to bring a halt to the whole process with virtually no compensation for the Iraqi families and no prosecution of a single marine responsible. Seven years after the event, on January 11, 2012, Sergeant Robert Wosniak was posthumously convicted of a single count of negligent dereliction of duty, with a rank reduction.'

'And a pay cut, obviously.'

Malone chuckles to himself. 'So, it's over, that's the main thing.' There is relief in his mellifluous tones. A few more customers have arrived, hanging around the bar and the general noise level has increased. Malone wants some space. 'Let's go outside.'

They take their glasses with them onto the balcony to catch the last of the day's wintery light. 'Actually, a total of $38,000 was offered by US military to the families of killed Iraqis in Haditha. A pittance, really.'

'That's about $2500 to each family,' Jarvis comments.

'Look, there is an article in today's *Times* about it, actually. Their War Correspondent, Nicholas Sommerton, has written a leader, page 15.' He leaves the paper on the banister top in front of them, folded open. He gulps a mouthful of beer, scanning his vision across the chilly waters of the Thames. The skyline opposite is grey and familiar, although new building sites and skyscrapers are going up all the time. They can make out the newly constructed tower, known as the Shard, pointing up into the bleak sky over to their left, beyond Southwark Bridge. It had not quite been topped out yet but was due to open soon.

'Owned by a Qatari real estate group, sign of the times, eh?' Malone comments.

'Has eleven thousand glass panels on the outside, I read somewhere. Tallest building in Western Europe, 790 feet high.'

'Extraordinary.' Malone sounds wistful. After a while he says, 'Anyway, wanted you to be the first with the news. You did a fine job out there, Collingwood, you know that, much admired.' Malone had seemed certain of himself, at first, but now Jarvis senses a feeling of regret.

'Thank you, sir.'

'Mike, please,' Malone murmurs, trying to sound friendly.

'So why did you betray me, to the Americans?' Jarvis's voice is cold, distant, untroubled, not angry. 'Didn't want the true story to come out, I suppose?' he says. 'Make the paras look bad, sour relations with the Yanks?' Jarvis stares across the water, his eyes unfocused, cool and pale, not giving anything away. 'Upset the Malone bandwagon, tarnish the reputation?'

'Something like that, Collingwood.' Malone is frowning into his drink, studying the slowly fading patterns of the froth on the top. 'It was the only way to get Shawcross to agree, to fly you two out. What you did was a mistake, a bloody foolish act of ..., what, I don't know? What were you trying to prove?'

'Moral disgust, trying to stop a terrible wrong becoming even worse. Nothing personal, sir.'

There is a further silence between them for a while.

'How did you know?'

'Instinct,' Jarvis says. 'My address, not available to anyone without clearance. You were the only one who could have shared it with the Americans.'

'Well, you obviously coped pretty well, with the disturbance. Saw them off, no doubt? In your own unique way.' A sarcastic sneer plays across Malone's thin lips, his moustache twitching with disdain. He, of course, had no idea what had happened when the three American killers arrived in London three years ago in search of their prey. It is not clear to Jarvis that he even wants to know.

'Disturbance might be one way to describe it.'

'Well, you can understand. No hard feelings. Turned out alright in the end, eh?'

'Not for Joe Street, it didn't.' And he cannot keep a hint of bitterness out of the tone, his lips slightly pursed.

Malone downs the last of his drink, dumps the glass on the side and picks up his things. 'Yes, I am sorry about Street. Tragic.' He clicks his heels and nods emphatically. 'Collingwood,' he says, like it is goodbye. And with that, he turns and strides calmly out, straight-backed as ever, retrieving his coat from the hooks by the door.

Jarvis slowly walks after him. Once, he was seriously considering whether to dispatch Malone, to bump him off. For Joe. Nobody would miss him. Instead he remains as an irritating sore in Jarvis's mind, festering.

Outside, the sky is darkening rapidly and the temperature is dropping. Gloomy buildings encroach on either side of the narrow way down towards the river, and with the tide well out, a small strip of wet sand reflects shiny sparkles of the lowering daylight. A few black-headed gulls and cormorants are scavenging along the edge of the rippling dirty brown surf, their long beaks stabbing deep into the shingle as they bob along. Outside the doors, a stray dog is sniffing along the old walls.

Jarvis settles by the fire, trying to relax. He picks up yesterday's folded *Times* and reads Sommerton's article, under the headline: NO JUSTICE FOR HADITHA FAMILIES. *"It appears that justice for Iraqi victims of US War Crimes will never be found in American Military Courts. The NCIS has concluded that no one is to blame for the killing of twenty-four innocent civilians by Kilo Company in Haditha in November 2005. Justice for Iraq will only be found in the eventual, and inevitable, military defeat and expulsion of the US occupation through a guerrilla war of attrition by the Iraqi Resistance, and by a War Crimes Tribunal to hold the US government and its military accountable for crimes against humanity.*

"The atrocity at Haditha is just one in a long list of war crimes committed by US forces against the occupied Iraqi population, crimes that include the well-known torture chambers of Abu Ghraib; the gang-rape of Iraqi teenager Abeer Qassim al-Janabi, by US soldiers who then shot her in the head, burned her body with kerosene and shot her parents and sister to cover up the crime; the murder of captured Iraqi Air Force Major General, Abed Hamed Mowhoush, who was unceremoniously beaten and stuffed head-first into a sleeping bag, tied in the bag with electric cord and then sat on and smothered to death by US Interrogators who didn't like his answers;

the forcing at gunpoint by US Army personnel of 19 year old Zaidoun Hassoun, to jump to his death off a Bridge into the Tigris river; and of course, the destruction of the City of Fallujah and killing of thousands of its inhabitants as revenge for the hanging from a bridge of the corpses of four members of the Blackwater mercenary force."

He pauses to see whether there any signs of his friends arriving. He needs a break from the compelling, disturbing narrative. He goes over to the bar for a tonic water and ice. Back by the fire, he continues with his reading: *"In a number of these cases the US government has paid 'blood money' reparations to the victims' relatives; however, there has been little if any actual punishment for the many individuals and military units who carried out the crimes, and none should be expected, as these 'trials' appear to have been mostly just for show and public consumption."*

'Friday the thirteenth, Jarvis. Your birthday. Thirty years young and still so handsome. Something special will come of this day, I'm sure.'

'Thanks, Billy, hope you're right, but I can't see anything on the horizon just yet.'

'Don't go looking. Let these things happen, when they're good and ready. I believe in it.'

'What, fate?' Mat asks, placing a heavy tray of beers onto their table.

'Well, yes. Jarvis deserves it, with all he's achieved.'

'Yes, but quite often it's not the deserving that get their reward.'

'Alright, Charlie, enough of your cynical views. Let's be positive.' And Jarvis drinks to that, happy to be with his friends, all respected and unwavering servants of the organisation to which he devoted eight years of his life.

'You should never have left the regiment, not so soon. In my opinion.'

Jarvis is drinking Samuel Adams, something of a specialty

at the *Pepys*. 'Tommy Flynn told me once he was from Boston,' Jarvis says, with a broad grin, 'so this is sweetly appropriate, don't you think?'

They all snigger.

'To the dead Americans, sons of bitches all,' Charlie calls, raising his glass and several of the men tip theirs together. 'Amen.'

'Yes, whatever happened to Tommy The Tank?'

'Well, Charlie will tell you. Lost in the intricate workings of the Tate & Lyle sugar refinery. I think John Shorter will continue to turn up in millions of tiny bits in our country's white sugar for many years to come.' There is both sniggering laughter and disgust at the thought.

'You had many years and postings left in you, Jarvis, and so many others would have benefitted.'

'Thank you for that, but the time had come, you know. Better to leave a bit early than outstay your welcome, I always say.'

In his black cab a little later, on his way home to Pamela, he reads the final paragraph of Sommerton's article: "*Unfortunately, the US were not the only Army to commit to this sort of behaviour. The Black Watch (of the British Army) had its own distasteful prison at Stephen Town, where prisoners were regularly tortured and sometimes 'accidently' killed, with no admission and no compensation. No personnel have been found guilty or dismissed from the Army for any of these crimes.*"

'War is a terrible thing,' Jarvis mutters to himself.

reviews

Authors do benefit from having reviews of their books.
So if you liked this book or have read any of the others,
I would be so grateful if you would post a review on
Amazon and any of the other digital platforms.

And go to my website for more information:
www.danielpascoeauthor.com

Try these other books by Daniel Pascoe

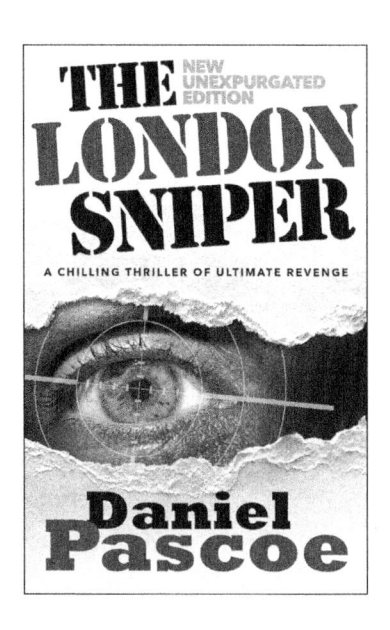

THE LONDON SNIPER

A CHILLING THRILLER OF ULTIMATE REVENGE

Jarvis Collingwood and Leon Deshpande are incarnate warriors of the modern age, cool, calculating and determined to win, professional in all that they do, heroes both in many ways.

Jarvis is an expert sniper paid by an old man desperate for revenge on those he holds responsible for a son beheaded in Iraq. Leon is an expert security man and maverick alpha-male with some points to prove, who always gets his man especially if the price is right. Jarvis uses a young naïve Naomi as part of his cover while Leon hunts him down, reaching their final shoot-out in a remote forest hideaway.

"a gripping novel with twists and turns."

DEAD END

*A BRILLIANT MIX OF HUMOUR AND INSIGHT,
A TRAGIC ROMANCE, ULTIMATELY THRILLING.*

A past secret revealed. A search for a long-lost child. Murder and mayhem on the south coast of Spain. Wouldn't you want to rescue your daughter if she was in trouble?

Dead End is really two stories: one romantic and sad, of a young man's coming of age and first love, an unseen child and the obsession to find her; the other fast-moving and tragic, thrilling episodes of avarice and theft, of kidnap and torture among menacing drug dealers and ruthless politicians. The link is the foppish courageous Matthew Crawford, who first reveals his secret at his daughter's wedding and then walks into Sophie's chaotic and dangerous life in Marbella.

DEADLINE

AN EVERYDAY TALE OF CONSPIRACY AND POLICE COCK-UP, SPRINKLED WITH TRAGEDY, MISHAP AND JUST A LITTLE ROMANCE.

What could more effectively turn a girl's head, but an artist with magic in his fingertips and mystery in his brush strokes?

Olivia wants to be a writer and plans a biography of the charismatic Hugo, but their previous experience as lovers haunts them. Olivia is liaising with the mysterious Louise, while Hugo still hankers after his long-suffering muse, Samantha. A police shooting, a kidnapping, and a desperate search leads to a breathless finale, while the lurking Edward threatens in the background with his own deadline.

"The plot was so good I couldn't work out the ending, so it kept me gripped."

FAIR GAME, FOUL PLAY

WHO KNOWS WHAT GOES ON BEHIND CLOSED DOORS?

Sometimes you never know what goes on within a marriage, even your own, until some catastrophe happens.

Arnold Westlake is a decent, likeable bloke who plays golf. Helpful, reliable. Unsettled, bored, pent-up. Tamara is a lovely lady who bakes cakes and plays bridge. Thoughtful, kind. Frustrated, directionless. They avoid, they circle, they both keep secrets. And with Ben, the rich and outrageous show-off, the complete alpha male, they play a dangerous game. After an unexpected burst of anger, who will emerge a winner when tragedy strikes?

"A cosy crime novel, a great read, intelligent, explosive…"

Visit Daniel's WEBSITE for more INFORMATION and a chance to join his READERS' CLUB for regular bulletins, background information and insights, both informative and entertaining.

danielpascoeauthor.com

Printed in Great Britain
by Amazon